The Sea
Shall
Ever Be

A novel by Frank Linter

Published by

MELROSE BOOKS

An Imprint of Melrose Press Limited
St Thomas Place, Ely
Cambridgeshire
CB7 4GG, UK
www.melrosebooks.co.uk

FIRST EDITION

ISBN 978-1-909757-47-9

Printed and bound in Great Britain by:
4edge Limited
7a Eldon Way, Eldon Way Industrial Estate
Hockley, Essex
SS5 4AD

FSC
www.fsc.org
MIX
Paper from
responsible sources
FSC® C020822

Chapter One

The weather was typically English as the Royal Navy ratings arrived at the dockyard gates, some sad because their leave had finished. Others, having imbibed in what alcohol was available in wartime, were quite happy and oblivious of all their surroundings: Able seamen, signalmen, stokers, nurses and chefs, all drafted to a ship together, marching in the rain to the Customs House steps in Portsmouth.

On arrival at the dockside, the new ship's company viewed their ship, which looked as though she was 'doing thirty knots alongside the wall', their eyes seeing a Dido class cruiser lengthened by forty feet to accommodate her extra weapons. That was HMS *Hecla*, squat, powerful and armoured. She looked like a recruiting poster for the RN receiving her men up her gangway, ready to turn them into a fighting machine like herself. On the upper deck, the new ship's company were allocated their messes and given station cards before picking up their hammocks and kit bags, then going in all compass points to find their messes, while the captain and his No.1 Commander Colin Davis watched through a porthole.

Captain Alec Hamilton felt so proud at this moment, feeling the ship beneath his feet trembling like a pedigree racehorse, as the turbine generators screamed away, pushing out power, to give life to the woman that is in every ship.

Gradually as the men settled in, Alec saw one or two names he had already served with.

"Poor devils," he thought, as he saw the list of home addresses destroyed by bombing. Thank goodness his Sally and their two daughters were safe with Sally's parents in Somerset.

Calling Colin Davis to his cabin, Alec told him he wanted the lower deck cleared the next day at 0900, to give a pep talk and read his commission to the ship's company. Then offering Colin a drink, they both sat down for four hours discussing the working up trials at Portland, and learning from each other, thoughts and methods that each of them preferred, both wondering how *Hecla* would handle in the heavy sea, and how the men would handle *Hecla*. Finally, they both agreed that their bunks were calling loudly, and staggered off, wondering why the ship was moving while she was alongside the jetty.

As Colin left the captain's cabin, a sudden, very well known noise split their ears, a high-pitched whistle, and then crump! The huge dockyard was under air attack, and Hecla stood, with very few experienced gunners on board, and expected to fight off an air attack with the rest of the fleet. Action station gongs sounded urgently, their clamour deafening, sending all to what could be their action stations, manning the anti-aircraft guns while others went down to the magazines preparing to keep the guns supplied with ammunition at all costs.

The bombs landed in sticks of eight, nearly destroying the submarine base at HMS *Dolphin* and hitting with success the workshops along the dry-dock area, making the repair of ships impossible, at least for a while.

The raid went on through the night, some destroyers and

other smaller ships setting sail, to get away from the slaughter, before they too were hit by a German bomb. An old destroyer while sailing past Old Portsmouth caught a thousand pounder direct on the bridge. She exploded, seeming to jump out of the water before returning to the sea, in pieces with no survivors, her magazine having caught the main explosion.

Hecla got her guns into action at last, her stag mountings, which consisted of eight heavy cannons firing in unison, started their hammering, the flashes lighting up the gun-crews' faces as they toiled to keep the weapons firing, some noting that the bombs were landing closer and closer to the ship causing big geysers of seawater as they exploded underwater.

While the action continued above decks, the stokers and Petty Officers were slaving, trying to flash up the huge boilers of the cruiser, so enabling her to put to sea, where she stood a better chance of surviving the battering. Soon, black smoke issued from the funnel and the big forced draft fans started to do their work, building up air pressure in the boiler rooms.

Bunker Hill looked at his mate Snake Eyes, and said, 'I dunno what they see in staying up there Snaky, it's alright if you like firework shows, but nah, I'll stay 'ere eh? What about you then?'

'Too bloody noisy for me up there mate, if the ABs like it, they can have my share an' all,' and carried on checking the evaporator before disconnecting it from the shore side supply of steam.

The stoker PO heard this exchange, and wondered if Hitler knew what he was taking on with men like this. It might have been bravery, it may have been stupidity, but he would never mention it to Bunker. To call a man like Bunker stupid was a very silly thing to do.

"Thank Gawd he's on our side, an' all like 'im an' all," PO Brown thought, though wishing the Luftwaffe were not quite as accurate as he heard the bombs landing so close to the ship. Suddenly the ship lurched instantly letting everyone know she'd been hit. Damage control parties were piped for, to muster on the foc'sle where the German bomb had hit her, and minutes later, the small fires were put out, and the capstan made secure, with the anchor chains being double locked. All this carried on while all the guns in Portsmouth continued with their horrific symphony of noise, hiding the screams and the horror of the city.

Three more ships were hit by bombs before peace returned, and Portsmouth waited, waited for the next wave of bombers to mass over her, trying to destroy her homes, her citizens, her soul.

The uneasy quiet lasted for an hour before the siren went off, signalling the raid was over. Sighs and cries of relief sounded throughout the whole city, with curses being shouted at anything German, and the quiet grief, as people found dead relations or friends. Grief too for the houses, hit by fire and gutted, leaving them with nowhere to sleep, and no belongings left; just what they stood up in.

Then suddenly, a little voice began to sing a song, about Hitler only having odd bits of his body, and Himmler the same when slowly but surely, the rude song echoed around the streets, thousands of voices meaning every word they were saying.

Royal Navy personnel were being marched into the city to give help, and as they neared the damaged area, they heard the sound. The sound of love and hate, love for their country and hate for their enemies. Woe betide anybody that resisted.

The bomb damage was serious, and all the sailors worked to clear the roads and support the people grieving. Feeding the crowds was hectic, with a lot of people giving their food to their children or older relations, before they went out to help the Navy boys, some so young it was a crime that they were experiencing this sort of life at so young an age. But they did, and grew up fast.

Nobby Hall was helping an old lady who had lost her leg, and she complained that she wouldn't be able to support Portsmouth football team now. Then as he laid her down gently in the makeshift hospital in the Town Hall, she looked up at Nobby and said, 'Give them lousy Germans some stick for me?' then her head sagged to the side, a smile on her face in death, as in life.

Nobby looked at her, tears welling up and running down his face as he stroked her old face before covering it with the old lady's coat. Looking up into the sky, he vowed that he would die getting his revenge for Ada, for that was her name.

A rough hand grabbed his shoulder and dragged him to his feet. 'Come on you lazy sod, we ain't finished yet, go over...' then he saw Ada lying on the floor, and realised what had happened. 'I'm sorry Jack, I know how you feel, but there is more out there needing you, and men like you, not to fight, but to help them survive the rest of tonight, so give us an hand will ya?'

'Yeh course I will, she was such a nice ol' lady too, just like my gran in London. She got killed in an air raid, wiv all me family an' all. Who can make war on people that already beat them German bastards in the First War? What a shit world this is,' and followed the air raid warden to help more people.

The air raid warden looked at the tall youngster beside him as they walked, wondering how somebody so young, could ask a complex question like that.

They soon found a double decker bus on its side, with people inside, and a few standing around looking for help, not knowing what to do.

Getting them organised, Nobby crawled inside the bus to see what could be done to help while waiting for the Fire Service to arrive to get the passengers out and into ambulances.

The bus yielded its injured, with no dead, but a lot of broken bones, which was to be expected, but everyone was singing. Singing about Hitler only having one something or other, and Nobby smiled thinking of Ada, and knowing she would have sung too, joined in singing a sweet descant too sometimes!

Chapter Two

Eventually, the streets were passable for transport, and the bomb-damaged buildings had been made safe enough to walk past. The sailors returned to their various ships in the dockyard, to get into their hammocks, and have a good sleep, before the next round in the struggle for life with freedom instead of shackles.

Onboard *Hecla*, the experienced hands were giving instructions to the newly joined men about everything to do with working in a big team. From the chefs, who supplied good food to them all, to the gunners, who protected the ship, until at the end of the day, the new men were a bit wiser than they were and were looking forward to the next piece of action, all of them thinking how easy it all was, to go helping people ashore in an air raid.

Nobby heard them talking eagerly to each other, and calling them back, sat them down and told them the story of Ada. After explaining the final outcome, he looked up, only to find them all with tears in their eyes, and saying to themselves, "what would I have done?"

'Never forget, all those old ladies are a gran to someone, it could be yours, his or mine next to you. But they fought in a war before you were born an' they deserve our respect, so remember that," and walked off before they could see the emotion showing on his face.

The rest of the day was a make and mend, giving the ship's company the whole day off to catch up on their sleep. Also, they may be called on for their help tonight and a rest would be good for them, and Portsmouth.

Nobody went ashore that night, Alec thinking, he'd rather have them close to hand in case the Germans visited again, "but I hope not," was his last thought before dropping off to sleep.

All RN ships wake up every morning with a Royal Marine blowing reveille out of a contorted piece of tin called a bugle. Alec's eyes opened, he looked around wildly for a second, then he realised where he was and relaxed for two minutes, then getting out carefully, he showered and dressed. Fifteen minutes later he was having his breakfast, namely toast and a cup of tea brought to him by his steward, Carter. Writing a pep talk was not his favourite hobby, so he kept to the same usual theme, hoping he would stop his nerves from showing themselves to the ship's company. All too soon, he heard the Spithead Nightingales piping clear lower deck for the captain, so rising slowly, Alec walked through the bulkhead doors, and on to the boat deck by the two funnels.

'To all officers and men of HMS *Hecla*, I'm giving notice that I have been commissioned by the Admiralty to take command of *Hecla*. We will go for working up trials at Portland Bill. Now we have three weeks of hard backbreaking work, but I've noticed we have a lot of experienced ratings, mixed with some men fresh from finishing training. I expect all the new recruits to be helped in every way possible by you old hands, the same way you were helped when you joined. Don't forget when someone is saving your life, you don't ask them how long they've been in the service, so dig in and square them up. If at any time, any of you have problems, your Divisional Officers are available, and all you have to do is knock at their doors. Incidentally, thank you for the work you all did ashore last night, I've had good reports about you,' looking at Bunker Hill, 'all of you, so we'll splice the main brace. Thank you,' and walked away to his cabin amid a thunderous cheer as the men realised what they could look forward to.

Colin Davis followed him to his cabin, where he invited the captain to the wardroom for a drink with the rest of the officers.

On entering the wardroom, all the officers were present and he was introduced to them all, including the "snotty", who was seventeen-years-old, and looked as though he would make a good rugby prop. Alec had a good feeling about this crew, ninety percent of the officers being battle-experienced, while five of the officers including Colin Davis had served on cruisers. Destroyer men were abundant below decks, owing to the heavy losses of the "Greyhounds of the seas", as destroyers were called, but they would be replaced, Alec hoped, with the new submarine hunter type destroyer.

The U-boat war was seriously damaging the RN. surface fleet and the Merchant Navy. Ships could be replaced, but there would be no more qualified seamen; that was the crux of the matter.

As up spirits was piped, and all below decks received a double tot of rum, which was what splicing the main brace meant, Alec bought all in the wardroom a double, wishing them all the best, and good "hunting" in the world's oceans, then left for his cabin, to read his newly arrived orders.

"Well, this working up at Portland should do nothing but

good," thought Alec, remembering the hard work involved in "Rendezvous At Sea", for refuelling, refilling magazines, action stations and damage control.

The engineer officer assured Alec that the ship was fuelled to the brim. He knew the engineer was busy, familiarising the new stokers with all the engineering spaces.

The two Walrus aircraft were not on board yet, so that meant there were eight "airy-fairies" to join the *Hecla*. Alec looked at his diary, finding out that the magazines of the 6' inch main armament, the second armament of 4', and all others, including torpedoes and anti- aircraft guns, were all replenished.

"At least the ship was ready for war," Alec thought.

He was jolted out of his reverie by the sound of an air raid siren ashore in Portsmouth, so slamming his hand on the ship's action stations gong, he ran to the bridge, to make ready to protect themselves and the other ships in the dockyard.

He was made aware that the anti-aircraft weapons were all manned and armed, then thanking the gunnery officer, he said those dreaded words, 'open sights', meaning to fire at will as soon as the Luftwaffe came into range.

The German bombers were spotted, and veered away when the AA weapons opened fire, a dull sky parting to allow the shells' passage to their target. The number of shells fired from the ships in the dockyard was far too accurate for the slow moving bombers, so after dropping their bomb loads in the surrounding countryside, the bombers returned to their base, concocting several stories about the aborted mission, including the number of Spitfires and the accuracy of gunfire from the Royal Navy.

The all-clear sounded, and the ships returned to normal,

the repairs being resumed, and the *Hecla* loaded.

Getting everything done was a relief. Food and slops, the Navy expression for clothing supplies, were already being issued to the galley and issue officer and so far, the chef had produced very good quality meals. The rum was stowed away in the spirits locker, and all was in place, or going to be. The slight damage on the fo'c'sle was quickly repaired and painted, so Alec relaxed in his cabin before making a tour round the ship, knowing that dockyard workers were extremely touchy with the mountain of work they had to undertake including corvettes, severely damaged, with frigates that would have sunk, but for the shoring up with hammocks and steel plates, to enable the pumps to gain on the water. Destroyers being the mainstay in the defence of the convoys were in desperately short supply, and what was left needed refits and boiler cleans, but Alec had a feeling Hecla was going to bolster up the morale of the service and civilians. He knew the inspections had to be done regardless, although the ship looked tiddly, (RN slang for smart), with her upper looking in pristine condition, untouched even. After the shakedown at Portland, he wondered what would be learnt, lost and forgotten.

Alec progressed from for'ard to aft, chatting to the ship's company and urging the recruits to ask anybody all the questions they needed to know the answers to. Going down to the boiler rooms A and B was his worst nightmare; the unimaginable heat while he was in his thick blue uniform. He looked at the watchkeepers and noted them looking at gauges and turning sprayer control valves on the boiler front. They looked so cool and professional, but theirs was a dreadful part of the ship to be in. Torpedoes hit here or the engine rooms first.

"Alright, the *Hecla* was armoured with eight inches of steel, but what a terrible fate," Alec thought, as he scurried up the steel ladder. The engine rooms were cool in comparison to the boiler rooms, so he lingered a while under the forced draught fan outlet, blowing in cold air from the inlets on the upper deck.

"This ship is a beauty," Alec thought, as he saw the polished brass and copper, thanking the "tiffy" (artificer) before going topsides. Being so impressed by the cleanliness and tidiness everywhere, he would mention it in daily orders tomorrow. Feeling refreshed after a shower, he put a clean uniform on, which had been laid out for him by his steward.

After dinner, the air raid siren sounded, causing every ship in the dockyard to close down to action stations again. Bofors guns and stag mountings were manned and sweeping the skies, together with the countless batteries on Southsea Common. Thirty minutes later, everybody realised it was a Moaning Minnie flying, that was sent over to make all and sundry jittery, so the all-clear was sounded. As soon as everything was secured, the ship's company relaxed, washed or showered and turned in, with just the old hands telling the new ones that they would get better at the job one day. Old hands told of all the ships they'd served on, places they'd been to, and "ladies" they had become acquainted with. The phrase "swinging the lamp" sprang to Alec's mind, as he carried out another inspection, and smiled to himself when, as a midshipman, he was told to go to the stores for a bucket of steam, or a left handed screwdriver. "The RN has its own humour," he thought, even crossing the Equator, when someone dressed as King Neptune, boarded the ship, and ruled for a day. He laughed aloud as he passed a seaman, who gave him a sick smile and a funny look and hurried off on his errand.

"So to bed," Alec thought, and he wasn't long climbing into his bunk. The humming of the auxiliary machine, generators, pumps and ventilation fans didn't stop him from falling asleep very quickly.

Chapter Three

The following morning, a refuelling barge was secured alongside, and oil was soon pumping through the pulsing hoses, on a last top up, causing stokers some anxiety, with the fear of flooding the spotless decks with filthy fuel oil. The scorn that would be poured on the stokers' heads would be cruel, but they were alert, and the refuelling passed by without incident, apart from the stink, that was inevitable anyway.

Shortly afterwards, while the stokers were getting cleaned up, Alec once more inspected the ship. He found nothing out of place, then met "Guns", the gunnery officer, to hear any moans about anything. "Guns" was the "Old Navy", and these new guns were things of beauty, so easy, and too complicated, but he had read his books and he had experienced men in the gun crews, so knowledge cut both ways in learning.

Alec strode along the upper deck, walking aft to the quarterdeck, on whose hallowed ground, long-handled scrubbers, squeegees and sanding blocks, coupled with water, had rendered the oak deck white and gleaming. Alec imagined a cocktail party here on the quarterdeck, and his Sally whirling around and smiling up at him as they danced.

'My word I love you Sally,' he whispered, as his memories appeared, as they often did, ready to be taken out, dusted off, and used again.

Looking over the ship's side to the jetty, he noticed a despatch rider propping his motorbike on its stand. Knowing it was his expected orders from the Admiralty, he walked to the gangway, ready to receive the package from the despatch rider. After entering his cabin and ordering tea, he opened the package and read the Admiralty orders to sail for Portland tomorrow at the first tide, if the *Hecla* was fit and ready. Alec was elated as he lifted the phone and dialled the coded message, accepting his responsibility.

Informing the officers was done by the simple method of telling Colin Davis, who quickly passed it around, telling all heads of department to check, and then re-check their parts of ship. The ship's company and the ship were too valuable to put either of them into jeopardy.

No shore leave was given, to ensure Hecla would have a full complement when she sailed. They all needed the work-up, to work together and find out what limitations if any there was. The new men in particular were vulnerable at this stage, moving over the line from trainee, to professional, but Alec knew it would happen eventually. The crossing of the line happened slowly, but suddenly, by not asking as many questions, and not wondering why.

Standing on the bridge, Alec saw No.1 checking the foc'sle party were present, while "Guns" checked the quarterdeck. The ship's company manned the side as the ship glided through the boom defence at Old Portsmouth, and Alec wondered what thoughts were going through the heads of the people massed there, waving sad goodbyes to their sons, husbands and fathers, wondering when they would see them again.

After they passed The Needles, the revs on the turbines

were increased, pushing the ship faster, until she settled at twenty knots, when the first seagoing action stations were piped on HMS *Hecla*. Slow reactions and a few hands didn't know where to go, which was normal the first time. The guns were manned, but remained unloaded, which made Alec worry how the newly recruited men would react, at the first broadside. He remembered his first and had a secret smile, when he recalled how he had jumped. He noticed as more action stations were piped, each time was a slight improvement. By the time the ship had secured from its fourth action station, they were nearly at their berth at Portland.

As the buoy jumpers secured the ship to the buoy, Alec finished with the main engines for the day, and Hecla was swinging on a buoy for the night. Shore leave was given until midnight, after Alec came to the conclusion that it would make a good ship, a happy ship.

There was nobody adrift so *Hecla* sailed at 0800, practising action stations, swapping experienced men here and there, trying different combinations until a balanced, quick response was natural, and immediate. Day after day for a week, the whole ship's company worked continuously, and when they tied up alongside, they were better. They were really working at it, but as far as Alec was concerned, they needed more, and then a lot more practice.

Shore leave was given, and a few pints of Scrumpy went home that weekend and came back the Monday morning. Alec was invited to the wardroom, and offered free gangway, i.e. using the wardroom at any time, as there is no rank in the wardroom, consequently, caps are not worn. It is considered bad etiquette to wear your headgear below decks, on somebody else's Mess deck.

On Saturday morning, it was found that a liberty man was adrift. Regulating staff and Royal Marines went to Weymouth searching for him, as he was a new man. His divisional officer was worried, in case he had gone home to Coventry after the blitz on that city. His family lived there, so it was natural that he was worried, or petrified is a better word. Junior Seaman A Kerr was posted as Absent Without Leave on Saturday evening, under extenuating circumstances. Alec was worried, pacing the upper deck until the early hours. He wondered what his own response would be, if he thought his own family were threatened. He couldn't bear thinking about it, so he turned in, shedding a secret tear, as he thought of what could be going through Kerr's mind.

The following morning a civilian policeman come on board, and asked to see the captain. A body had been found in the water, just off Chesil Beach, in RN uniform. The name in the paybook was A Kerr. Alec was shocked, as the policeman said that apparently, Kerr had missed the last bus back to Portland, and had attempted the old sailor's story of swimming back to Portland from Weymouth. Kerr had been told that the swim back to Portland was simple by a person in a pub, and believing it word for word, tried and died.

'It's not possible,' Alec said softly, then thanked the policeman, and offered him a cup of tea, which the policeman gladly accepted.

The policeman, who had discovered the pub Kerr was drinking in, said Kerr was frightened of getting punished, so he ran out, and tried to swim to Portland.

"I'll have to give some thought to the dreadful letter to be written to the Kerr family, if they had survived. How many more of these would he write?" Alec thought. He later found out that Kerr's family didn't live through the terrible air raids on Coventry, so Alec made arrangements for the burial in Portsmouth, that being the best answer to the problem.

After refuelling and receiving supplies, Hecla sailed on Monday for the last fortnight at sea, always shadowed by two corvettes, one of which towed a splash target for gunners to shoot at, all out chasing that one statement to be sent to the Admiralty, "Very Capable", a signal every captain wanted to receive. The RAS's started off, much the same as the gun crews, but finished the work-up, with the words, very capable.

When the ship returned to Portsmouth, she was an efficient fighting unit of the Royal Navy, and the whole ship's company manned the ship's side as she entered harbour, all feeling as proud as Alec, who stood on the bridge, knowing that both civvies and Navy, were looking at his *Hecla*. Alec surveyed the work as the ship's company scrubbed, and painted the *Hecla* back to her original condition, and shore leave was available to all, every night. There were few air raids, and when there was, the Luftwaffe kept clear of the dockyard. The weapons of the ships in harbour had an awesome firepower and made them feel unwelcome.

Alec noted the sailings and the damaged returns throughout the week, and sadly, saw the majority were convoy escorts that were taking the punishment. The U-boats were the curse of the Navy, even though the boffins had cracked the German Enigma Code; these U-boats were continuing to hurt us badly.

Portsmouth suffered another air raid, with ships getting hit, and people on board getting killed or maimed. But the damage to Portsmouth was dreadful. The German crews dropped the bombs on the city rather than the dockyard, because of the blistering defence the various ships put up.

'Yellow bastards,' Nobby said, his heart full of hatred, and aching for revenge. Somehow he'd get it, he vowed to Ada and his gran.

All the sailors on board ships, and in the barracks were ashore, dragging people out of buildings and cars, and some ratings, while walking past an air raid shelter, saw that it had suffered a direct hit, and on crawling through to the space under the rubble, found nobody alive, so carefully, the sailors, faces streaming with tears, managed to pass the bodies out to more people waiting for relatives or friends. The task was a brief vision of hell, with the living helping the dead out of their would-be tomb, and being allowed to rest in a place of peace.

A lot of young men grew up and aged that night, all, without exception, vowing revenge on the cowardly killers inspired by Hitler and wondering why they should take prisoners-of-war when to shoot them was much neater, quicker and cheaper to the country. Then they remembered, that would make them as bad as the enemy, so let's get on with the war!

Chapter Four

Sally's letters cheered Alec up no end, and in her last one, she told him she'd be in Portsmouth on Saturday. He was ecstatic until Saturday came, so slowly, agonisingly so, until there, on the railway platform at Southsea Harbour was Sally. Linking his arm through hers, they walked along the seafront to their hotel Alec had booked, where they had a few drinks, then indulged in as good a meal as was available with their ration coupons. Lingering for a while in the bar, Alec and Sally talked about the two girls and their grandparents.

'They're really enjoying themselves Alec, and Dad takes them out walking as much as he can, to tire them out, so they sleep well!'

'Thank God your parents have a large house Sally, poor old Portsmouth is taking a beating, easing off now admittedly, but it still isn't as safe as Somerset.'

'Have you missed me then? Oh good, well you can show me this ship of yours tomorrow then, but first, we have to get through the night, so what do you suggest?'

Walking up to their room, Alec's hand touched hers, as their lips touched oh so gently, like a butterfly landing on a rose. Entering the room and locking the door, they stood in the dark, rescuing each other with the love they had. Clothes began to fall to the floor as the two of them walked towards the bed, Alec finally steering her gently on to it. As Alec cupped her breast with his hand, Sally gasped, and drew Alec into her, showering him with kisses and sighs.

In the morning Alec woke up, to find Sally fully dressed and watching him in bed. They smiled at each other. Alec had a wash, with Sally pestering him, then as she chased him through the bedroom, they caught each other, and kissed like there was no tomorrow.

Everybody's eyes were watching as they approached their table, wondering what a Royal Navy officer was doing ashore, but the pair handled it like politicians, smiling to them, then ordered their breakfast.

'Well darling, we'll see if the dockyard workers have done any work on your ship, they've had enough time, don't they know there's a war on?'

'Yes, Sally they do, but they must get their priorities right, cruisers come second to convoy escorts, because there's more of them to repair.'

After saying "good morning" to the guests, Alec and Sally took a walk to the dockyard, to look at *Hecla*, waiting for her final bit of spit and polish, to look tiddly. Sally's eyes opened wide, as she tried to take in the ship that was home to over a thousand men and officers.

'Are you really in command of such a big ship? The admiral must think you're very special. I know you are to me, will you show me your cabin please sir,' said Sally in a little girl's voice.

'Well Sally, I'm not sure if I should, people might talk, and we wouldn't like that,' then dragged her into the aforesaid cabin, to show her the inside, and forgetting to, as her kissed her mouth and shoulders sweetly.

Going to HMS *Victory*, they met Colin Davis and "Guns", who were giving themselves a treat, and having lunch ashore. They were very quickly bedazzled by Sally, her beauty, and sense of fun so refreshing, at a disruptive time like now, when food, ammunition, men and ships were the most important, even more so now, with the convoys to America always in so much danger from the U-boats, and the threat of surface raiders.

'What do you think of *Hecla*, Mrs. Hamilton?' inquired Colin. Sally looked around, then whispered her thoughts to Colin.

'I'll call you Colin, if you call me Sally, and that goes for you too Guns, although it's a funny thing to be called, but if you don't mind, I'm sure I don't.'

Guns smiled, surprised that the captain's wife wasn't intimidated in any way.

'I've been called it for years now Sally, and may I say it's an absolute pleasure to meet you, Captain Hami …'

'Alec in private please, Guns,' said a smiling Alec.

'Where was I? Oh yes, Alec has mentioned you to us a few times, quite a few times in fact, and he wasn't exaggerating either,' finished Guns, standing, and toasting Sally with a glass of beer.

The four friends went for a stroll after lunch, all thankfully to be in such nice company, but secretly, in their minds, returning to, the war and when will it end. On arriving at Old Portsmouth, at the entrance to the harbour, the public house where Lord Nelson stayed is still there, the tiny window panes looking out over Spithead, the scene of so many departures, but a lot less returns, throughout the years. Eventually, Colin and Guns decided to return to the ship, both to see if all was well, and secondly, to give the Hamiltons time together. They felt like gooseberries really when they saw Alec and Sally holding hands and looking at each other.

'See you two in the morning, our sailing orders might arrive tomorrow. I wonder what surprise we've got coming?" said Alec.

Colin and Guns wished Alec and Sally a good and safe night, and walked off in the dusk, towards Portsmouth dockyard, wondering if there had been any crises on board *Hecla*.

'What an amazing woman Sally is, I didn't realise there was anybody around like that anymore. She's an absolute stunner,' was Colin's decision, as the two officers walked through the gates, leaving civilian normality, and entering the regime of the Royal Navy.

The following day being a working day, Alec kissed Sally a fond goodbye, and took a brisk walk to the dockyard, remembering with pleasure, yesterday, and his Sally, and how so very proud he was of her. On getting back on board, Alec went to his cabin, to wait impatiently for his sailing orders, if any. He didn't want the ship to become part of the jetty. Sure enough, promptly at 1000, a despatch rider stopped his motorbike at the gangway, and walked on to the quarterdeck, to ask for the captain personally. Alec signed for the package, called for No.1, and went below to his harbour cabin.

As Alec and Colin sat at the table with tea, they opened the package, and placed it on the table. Reading quickly, they came to the lines they wanted to read. Atlantic convoy CC41 was desperate for protection, being a large convoy, and it might cut *Hecla's* teeth, as well as the ship's company, so he looked for the sailing date from Portsmouth, praying for the action, and hoping his newly forged crew didn't lack the "get up and go" department.

On finding the date, 23rd of May 1941, his No.1 Colin Davis relayed the news to the ship's company, via the tannoy, to be met with jeers and groans.

'Don't worry Colin, all Jacks will moan, whatever the news is,' finished Alec.

Chapter Five

Sally and Alec kept the room at the hotel until Thursday, when they would part, but they enjoyed each other as though there was no tomorrow. The clock was ticking on remorselessly, never slowing, until Thursday burst upon them, making them realise it was here, ready to break them apart, without a second's thought or tear.

'Let go forward, slow ahead main engines, starboard rudder, let go aft, three points to port, increase revs to seventy per minute...'

The orders rolling off Alec's tongue came naturally, and quietly to the coxswain.

Calling No.1 over to take charge, he went to stand on the port flying bridge as the cruiser was drawing up to Old Portsmouth. He looked, and saw Sally waving a scarf to her beloved man standing on the flying bridge, waving. He couldn't see her face, but he knew she was crying as he whispered her name to his fingers, and waved his hand to her. Alec hoped she knew how much he loved her before going about his duties, checking the ship's course with the navigator and the coxswain.

HMS *Hecla* went on through the Atlantic's grey, stormy sea, always unfriendly, always sinister, ready to catch the unwary, with Alec fully aware all the time of the threat of U-boat attacks, as was the whole ship's company. Then one day, on the 29th May, they received a signal informing all, that the *Bismarck* had been sunk. Yes, on the 27th May, the British cruiser Dorsetshire sank the 35,000-ton battleship, after a British fleet, consisting of HMS *Renown*, HMS *Rodney* and HMS *Ramillies*, accompanied by two battle cruisers, two aircraft carriers, and a number of destroyers led by HMS *Cossack*, had crippled it.

"Prinz Eugen," the *Bismarck's* consort, "got away very quickly, but her day would come," Alec thought, and clearing lower deck, he told the ship's company the good news, but also the bad news about the famous HMS *Hood*, sunk by the *Bismarck* by a single shell. So in the middle of the Atlantic, a ship's company mourned for one, and cheered for another ship, that would never be seen again, attacking British convoys. The news of the German warship's demise was small compensation for losing the *Hood,* but the ship's company were cheered by the fact that the enemy raider hadn't got away with it. All the action stations they had practised, and cursed at, stood the ship and ship's company in good stead, but they got better. Better at everything, including boat stations, action stations, anti-aircraft stations and U-boat stations, all the way to New York, but before berthing, seamen poured over the upper deck and painted *Hecla's* rust-streaked hull, into a brand new, unmarked warship. As she was manoeuvred into her berth, the American pilot kindly commented to Alec: 'Gee captain, you gotta swell ship, an' a good group o' guys here.'

Alec appeared calm and collected, but underneath, he was bursting with pride.

'At least the Yanks recognise a bit o' class when they see it dun they,' an AB said, on the starboard side.

Alec and No.1 looked at each other, then roared with laughter, holding each other up. The AB watched innocently, thinking, "bloody officers, they gotta be barmy," not knowing he had broken the tension, and the final metamorphosis had occurred. *Hecla* was whole, the AB one of hundreds. He was eighteen and on his first ship, and had come to the same opinion as most ratings in the Royal Navy.

After two days enjoying New York, *Hecla* was ordered to sea, escorting an important convoy of oil tankers and grain carriers. Alec kept the ship's speed down to the slowest ship, twelve knots. The experimental radar set was working well because of the mild weather, but Alec knew it would blow bad halfway across the Atlantic, both weather wise and with U- boat alerts, but until then, practice makes perfect, and with all guns functioning, and gun crews working hard, they were good, they were really good, the best gunners Alec had seen, but they still moaned. Alec expected it, but the accuracy and speed would do some damage to the enemy.

On the seventh night, in the Stygian darkness, an oil tanker erupted in a blinding flash, throwing aviation fuel blazing into the air, lighting up for a short while the merchant seamen trying to abandon ship, even though all the lifeboats were all burnt, and didn't exist anymore. "Damned aviation fuel," Alec thought, as he moved Hecla to port, while the radar-man shouted contacts. Only the convoy showed at first, then a slight contact came on the screen, showing a U-boat further round to the port side of the convoy. Increasing speed, Hecla was fortunate enough to catch the U-boat with its conning tower above the sea so Alec fired a pair of torpedoes. The U-boat was submerging when a torpedo hit it, tearing it in half.

'Cease-fire! Cease-fire! If lookouts see any survivors, yell out at once, no messing!' ordered Captain Hamilton.

The lookouts, both fo'rard and aft, kept their eyes peeled all the more, praying that they would spot survivors, but it was not to be. "Sixty men died, either burnt, or drowned, all for some aircraft fuel," Alec thought "But we wouldn't survive without it. How sad!"

Up forward of the convoy, a grain ship was hit with two torpedoes and soon her stern reared above the surface of the sea, with oh so few lifeboats bobbing around, with men in them. A corvette hurried round with depth charges having the fuses inserted, when the torpedo hit her midships. *Hecla* picked up what survivors there was from the grain ship, before going to the tiny corvette's side, as near as Alec dared. Throwing scrambling nets over the side, able bodied helped the wounded, but all were covered in oil from ruptured tanks. Lurching suddenly, the corvette vanished, still flying her white ensign and taking thirty-one crew, including her captain.

The *Hecla* moved off as the last three men were clambering up the nets. Alec was nervous about being a sitting duck for so long, and with the escorts down to two corvettes and *Hecla*, the odds were that *Hecla* had every chance of being attacked, as she was the most powerful ship.

For the rest of the night, Alec was peering through the windows. The North Atlantic was in surly mood, and until daybreak, would be in favour of the U-boats. Sally and the girls were uppermost in Alec's mind, praying for them and pinning his colours to the mast in support of the ship, and the ship's company. The only chance for the ships on the convoy was the cruiser and two corvettes. The convoy was scattered to all four points of the compass by now, so at daybreak the corvettes started chasing them up together in some sort of order.

For the next few days, things were uneventful, apart from lookouts seeing non-existent U-boats quite often, until one day, one of the corvettes moved on to a course, tracking a U-boat on the Asdic. The sea was suddenly churned with propellers and depth charges, but if it was a U-boat, it escaped its fate, much to the disgust of all. Alec kept his flock together, zigzagging, the times of each, varying all the time.

Then *Hecla* was hit with two torpedoes, one hitting the paint locker up fo'rard, the other, hitting the thick armour plating, covering the engine room. The two explosions rocked the ship, followed by plumes of water and smoke. The hole up fo'rard was easily dealt with, by simply closing the bulkhead doors, while the midships' strike sprung a few rivets and smashed a few gauges in the engine room. The fire and bilge pumps worked perfectly, and kept the flooding down to a minimum, though the stokers were taking seawater showers, to save fresh water. Alec was very concerned about the damage up fo'rard, the twisted metal, and plating causing a loss of speed, and bringing into play again, the sitting duck syndrome.

'I'm proud to serve with the team this ship has, you've proved to me, yourselves, and your country, that you are more than able to combat any problems you meet, even if it is only getting a shower on the engine room! Thank you, I salute you, and No.1, splice the main-brace.'

A huge trio of hurrahs followed, then the deck was empty, as the ship's company made their way quickly to their messes, to get their "bubbly".

Liverpool appeared on the horizon four days later, so the

escorts weren't required, as the RAF could cover the convoy adequately, with Sunderland flying boats. Ships' sirens sounded, as the escorts made course for Pompey, the five-day trip keeping all occupied, tidying up and painting for the return of their home port, looking very bent up fo'rard, but the two corvettes looked nice and tiddly.

HMS *Hecla* finally got alongside, where, as soon as power cables, and a water supply was established, with a donkey boiler for supplying steam for heating and operating pumps, she was shut down for boiler cleaning, and maintenance to the machinery spaces.

Chapter Six

Alec walked ashore over the gangway with Colin to survey the two places damaged by the torpedoes.

'I feel robbed Colin, only sinking one U-boat, after the loss of both ships, and men. This is not going the way I would have liked it to go. But this damage to us, well, I would think there is at least two month's work here, after we get time in a dry dock, and with the work the poor old dockyard workers have to do, and the work they've got waiting, that will be between now and never.'

'I don't think the damage up fo'rard will take long Alec, we did manage to get the bulkhead door shut, before it got too much to handle.'

Alec looked around him, agreeing with Colin, by nodding his head, but a damaged ship was a very sad thing to look at, *Hecla's* bow jutting out at a peculiar angle, which had caused such a loss of speed. A car pulled up sharply, and Alec leaned forward to rebuke the driver, when the door opened. Sitting there was Sally! Crying with joy, she climbed out of the car and threw her arms around Alec, causing him a huge amount of embarrassment in front of Colin, but spinning round, found Colin had vanished back on board.

'My word darling, a big hairy-arsed sailor being shy!' Sally shrieked, reducing Alec to an uncontrollable jelly on the jetty. Minutes later, they walked up the gangway to Alec's cabin where he ordered tea and cakes or biscuits from Carter.

While explaining his worries about the repairs, docking, and time to do the work, Alec noticed his wicked wife smiling, and he accused her of having an evil sense of humour, but Alec would be treated better in harbour, while waiting for *Hecla* to be repaired. He learnt it from Sally, when she suddenly sat on his lap, smothered him in kisses, that told Alec he wouldn't miss going to sea in a very convincing way.

'What are you doing, Sally?' he murmured.

'What on earth do you think I'm doing? I thought naval officers were supposed to be intelligent,' laughed Sally.

She looked out of the porthole, and saw a row of buses and ambulances waiting to take the injured men to hospitals in the town.

'So why didn't you tell me about these poor men Alec?' she said as she went on to the upper deck.

Soon, she was helping wherever she could, the walking wounded, helping with a stretcher, and giving men a cigarette if they wanted one, being thanked in several ways, a saucy wink, a grin or a gentle nod of the head as they were carried past her. Some men with fuel oil burns, or blinded with fuel oil, had their faces gently stroked by her hand, while she knew they wouldn't last through the night.

All the men were eventually moved off the ship, to hospital, sent home, leaving Sally mentally and physically exhausted, and on reaching her husband's cabin, broke down, and sobbed uncontrollably. Alec cuddled her, trying to soothe her, but it was only after a shower and clean clothes from the car, that she reverted back to being calm and collected.

'If anybody ever belittles the Merchant Navy in front of me, I think I'll tell them to see if they'd like to do the job,' looking into Alec's face, adoring him, as much as he adored her.

Sally went ashore to book the room at the hotel, while Alec, with the Admiral of the dockyard, inspected the damage and estimated the time to be allocated for repairs. Alec had an idea to speed things up.

'Well sir, would it be possible to put a cofferdam over the damage, using underwater welding gear? The coffer dam would be ending up above water, enabling all the water to be pumped out, and after preparation, riveting the replacement steel plates behind the dam, doing the job without using a dry dock.'

Alec was excited about his proposal saying to the admiral that a simple flame cutter would get rid of the cofferdam afterwards, then we could paint ship, and concentrate on the damage inboard.

The admiral looked at Alec, not letting him know what was going on behind those grey eyes, which were slightly smiling at him.

'I'll think about that if you don't mind captain, a most ingenious idea I must say. I'll see the dock yard manager, to see what he thinks.'

Saluting the quarterdeck he strode off to his car, with a naval rating as his driver.

Alec gave fourteen days' leave to the port watch, as from tomorrow, which had the starboard watch upset, but they understood why half the ship's company had to stay on board, what with the maintenance and repairs to be done, but their fourteen days would come, don't you worry about that! Later that day, at 1800, Alec went ashore to meet Sally at the hotel. They went out together, for a show in Southsea Theatre

Royal, then for a dinner afterwards, before returning back to the hotel.

'Where did we get up to on the ship? I'm afraid you'll have to remind me Sally, I would appreciate it if you would.'

Sally dutifully reminded him so nicely.

Waking up with Sally beside him was heavenly, her arms reaching for him as he got out of bed, and winning, in the small token struggle that ensued. Kissing her lips, he gently pulled away, knowing the work onboard ship was preying on his mind, but it was there to be done. Sally understood as he explained, cocking her pretty face to one side, just like an elf wearing a sweet smile, and nothing else.

HMS *Hecla* appeared the same when he arrived on the jetty, except for an RN lorry pulled up at the bows of the ship. On saluting the quarterdeck, as the quartermaster saluted him, he saw some ratings, and two lieutenants looking over the side, by the damaged midships.

The two officers walked over to where Alec was standing, and explained they were the dividing team of the shore base, HMS *Vernon,* and they would like to study the problems they might be working on.

'Well sir, your idea of welding a cofferdam over the fo'rard damage is a method that we could use throughout the fleet, but we are here to see if it's feasible. At present, we are surveying the size that the cofferdam would have to be, and how deep it would have to go down, below the water line. So far we think it would need to be twelve feet deep, by eighteen feet long. Now, to give the riveters room to work, they would need space three feet wide, is that what you envisage?'

Alec looked at the two officers, knowing they could accept, or refuse the scheme he had devised.

'If it's reasonable, and economical, saving waiting for the dry docking, it means other ships would be spending less time disabled. I think it would save time, but you'll have to see if it's workable,' Alec replied.

He showed the two lieutenants his drawings of what he imagined the construction would look like, and the work involved in bringing it about.

'Obviously the riveters would need plenty of room, in fact, I was assuming more than three feet, but otherwise, Yes it is what I imagined, but you and your men are here to weld the cofferdam. What do you think of it personally?'

'We think it's a perfectly sound idea, and if you don't mind my saying so, very simple, and very clever. This idea could get ships out of harbour, and working again, much quicker, if the damage wasn't too bad, and this damage sir, is not very bad at all, in fact, if the Navy adopt this idea, we'll call it the "Hamilton plan", if that's alright with you. Now sir, we must go and chase up some steel for the job, and that's not going to be easy,' Lieutenant Proctor said, rising from his chair, followed by his companion, who left the cabin after shaking Alec's hand, and thanking him for his hospitality.

On reaching the jetty, Proctor whispered to Kelly: 'Such a simple idea, why didn't we think of that? It takes a seagoing captain to do that, as if he hasn't got enough to do, while we sit around studying our navels.'

With that, the two friends found a pub and went in for a couple of wets.

Chapter Seven

As Alec walked along the jetty the following morning, he saw the diving team, sorting out their equipment and looking as though they had been there very early; "They must be keen on the job anyway," Alec thought, and asked them if they would give him a day by day account of the progress. They agreed, surprised that a captain would be interested in work on his ship in harbour, while living in a hotel, with a popsy for a wife. But then, that's sailors for you.

The week went by swiftly, All that could be heard was the noise of the dockyard workers with the 'windy' hammers and 'windy' chisels, (tools powered by air), while up fo'rard, the bumping and scraping of the steel hitting the hull, as it was measured and cut, was terrible. The starboard watch of the ship's company were hard at work as well, maintenance on the weapons always paramount, for the security of the ship and its company. Stokers were climbing in and out of the bilges and boilers, whitewashing steam pipes, and polishing brasswork. Cooks were replenishing their pantries and freezers, while the 'chippies' ordered wood from the stores for all sorts, from the coffee tables, to nine inch by nine inch, by fifteen feet shoring lengths, in case they had to shore up any more holes in the hull, unprotected by a bulkhead door.

So Alec continued, working all day, deafened, and with the liberty men, a hangover occurring most mornings:

self-inflicted injuries. Alec and Sally were staying at the hotel and had peace and quiet most evenings, except for a few air raids, or 'moaning Minnies', flying about, and keeping everybody awake.

Then one day, Proctor and Kelly, giving their daily report, finally noted the "Hamilton Plan' was fixed and welded to the ship, with a big tarpaulin draped over it, so it wasn't too noticeable from the Gosport side. Elated, Alec hurried down to the focs'le, to see his baby, the cofferdam. There on the ship's side was a huge steel box, rising above the water by three feet, and looking like a hideous carbuncle on a baby's bum. "How long would it be there?" he wondered, but as he walked back to the bridge, he noticed sheets of steel turning up by the lorryload on the jetty.

Alec invited Proctor and Kelly to his cabin for a hot drink as the weather wasn't as good as it could be, to see if there was anything he could learn, or help them with. But no, they assured him, everything was under control, what with riveters setting up an air compressor, to power the rivet guns, also the small furnace they used, to get the rivets red hot before being hammered into the holes, with the man on the other side of the hull, hammering it as it came through the holes. Soon, the riveters inspected the inside of the cofferdam for water, finding it dry, but very cold, so acquiring a small electric fire, they used it to warm the compartment, and make toast. They'd be there, in the space for heaven knows how long, and with the dockyard workers, comfort was of the essence.

Two hours later, the cacophony started, the noise of a thousand aircraft engines, on full throttle, would not have been heard above the noise. It was so bad, forcing Alec up to the upper deck, where it was just as bad. Clearing the lower deck during a lull, the whole starboard watch formed three ranks, and were marched off to barracks, the noise being totally unbearable. Alec knew there would be noise, but noise wasn't the word. An AB went to the sick bay when he started bleeding from the ears.

Half the ship's company were put to work in barracks, and reserve fleet the following day, while Alec continued to go to the *Hecla,* but only when the rivet guns where silent. Looking down over the ship's side every evening before going to meet Sally was a habit that became a ritual, seeing the twisted black metal inboard of the hole, slowly being taken out and replaced, or simply bent back with heat, into shape. The ship's side looked terrible, with welding burns and paintwork burnt away, but Alec was so pleased his idea was working so far, and being able to relieve the queue for dry-docking, which was a good contribution to the war effort.

Then Alec realised how happy he was, seeing Sally every single night, which was like being in a normal marriage. The children were sorely missed, but they were safer with Sally's parents, than being subjected to the air raids that were plaguing Portsmouth in recent weeks, trying to slow the RN with repairs, maintenance, and storing up ships with the necessities of war. It hadn't worked so far; in fact the massive anti-aircraft gun build up caused the Luftwaffe more harm than good.

Alec saw the work progress, until from inside of the paint locker, it was all gleaming white paint, and the ship's side was a smart shipside grey. Finally, to everyone's relief, the "carbuncle" up for'rard and midships was lanced so to speak, and the bows and ship's side of HMS *Hecla* was unblemished, and up to the RN standard. The starboard watch came back off leave, and the ship had her full complement, there were three AWOL, but after two days' grace, then they would be deserters in the strictest sense of the word.

But slowly, the ship came to life again, and all shorelines were disconnected and decks were tidy again, while stokers used enough Bluebell metal polish and paint to sink her. Sirens on the fo'rard funnel were tested and polished, causing men to look up, cursing. Turbine generators screamed again, dropping two thousand revolutions temporarily while the load was put on the switchboard. Three days later, when Alec and heads of departments were satisfied that everything was as it should be, Alec radioed the Admiralty, informing them HMS *Hecla* was seaworthy, while thinking of all the days and nights spent with his darling Sally. That would all come to an end.

The work of victualling the ship, refuelling and filling magazines started eventually; also unseen by most some plates of armoured steel, with a door cut into one plate, was assembled in an empty magazine. The lower deck were oblivious of it, thinking it was further armour protection for the ship. Officers were curious about it, knowing it reduced considerably, the duration of firepower. The empty magazine was the secondary armament, the four-inch armament in fact, so the *Hecla* would still have the full use of her main armament. It cut *Hecla's* secondary by twenty five per cent, which was making Alec unhappy, but "never mind" he thought, hoping it was true that God works in mysterious ways sometimes.

Sally still waited for Alec every night in the hotel knowing that sailing orders were not very far away, and when it came she knew she would be hurt by the parting, as she knew Alec would be, "Although," she thought, "he'll come bounding into the room, with that cheeky mischievous look in his eyes when he had news," but they'd had a brief time of normality, only the war would end it temporarily. She cried quietly in the hotel room sometimes, seeing the pain and death in the faces of the survivors, coming ashore from *Hecla* and all the other ships that had rescued merchant seamen, and times when men went home on leave, to find a pile of rubble, and notices pinned to a post stating who was under it. Air raids were over Portsmouth every night now, with Alec and Sally sometimes spending most of the night in the hotel shelter, and knowing everybody who used it. It was like a social gathering, someone playing the piano sometimes, or all having a singsong. But the veneer was very thin, some people asking about their son or husband, brother or uncle, praying, hoping, wishing and crying... Some people didn't appear in the shelter, sometimes they wept alone, like Sally.

Alec burst through the door as Sally was thinking, and he brightened the room, an altogether better hue than it was before, for Sally. Throwing herself at him, she called his name several times, knowing what was going to come from his lips, but she would make full use of their time together, while she could. Alec gently sat her down on the bed, and explained that his orders were through, and the ship would sail in four days, the destination to be revealed after sailing, in sealed orders. Sally looked up at him, her eyes drowning in tears, as he held her hand. Her face finally collapsed in a huge sob of grief and despair, as Alec caressed her face and hair, gently kissing her beautiful tear-streaked face. Spending a quiet evening at home together was their need, and luckily, the Germans stayed at home, making it very special for them, especially when they got out of their shared bath, and dried each other.

Alas, the morning arrived, and Sally looked at her sleeping man lovingly. As she looked away, wondering, just wondering as wives do, she caught him opening one eye, then quickly shutting it again, in the reflection of the mirror. Sally waited silently, and then suddenly stripping the bedclothes off him, she leapt on him screaming he was an old fraud, and she loved him so. They received some funny looks and smiles in the breakfast room, causing Sally to blush a deep crimson.

The last days went so quickly, Alec could not believe it when departure time arrived. Too soon, the time came, when he was waving to Sally at Old Portsmouth, as she waved her scarf, and blew kisses to him. Closing his eyes, Alec locked away the vision of Sally waving, and weeping for him. Clearing his throat, he strode over to the captain's chair, and jammed his binoculars to his eyes, before anyone saw the tracery of tears running down his face.

'God, give me the strength to stop the bloody war, there surely must be a superior being somewhere, to end this torment and agony of millions of people, everywhere,' Alec whispered to himself, then went below to his cabin, to read his orders, calling Colin to his cabin on the way.

As Colin entered, Alec looked up at him, and said one word, 'Murmansk'.

'I suppose we should have expected something like this Alec, we've had it cushy for a while, and its catching up with us now, so let's do the job,' and drank the whiskey that Alec had poured for him.

Alec wrote a note to the navigator, giving the course as laid out in the Admiralty sailing orders for the Russian port that all sailors hated, then drank his rum, murmuring, 'Of all the places to be sent to, they pick that godforsaken hole,' and quickly poured another two drinks.

A week passed uneventfully, the North Sea behaving itself for a change and giving the cooks an easy time preparing and cooking meals for the ship's company. *Hecla* was able to make good use of the mild weather and covered a lot of miles very quickly, the ship's company secretly giving thanks in prayer when they were able, without being noticed.

On reaching the estuary leading to Murmansk, a Russian pilot boat came alongside, and up climbed a burly person, swinging on to the deck from the rope ladder, then walking to the bridge. The foul weather clothing was removed, and much to Alec's and Colin's amazement, revealed a woman!

'Ha, I see you are surprised at a woman doing this job! Well we are not soft in Mother Russia, like the capitalist Westerners; the men fight, we women work and fight. Now captain, you can follow my orders, or I will do the job for you, it's up to you. Which do you prefer?'

'Oh please madam, you are fully experienced in the job, so I'll leave it to you completely. But would you care for a drink first to warm the cockles of your heart?' Alec finished.

'You will explain to me what these cockle things are if you please captain, and do not try to make me drunk. A lot of men have tried, but none have succeeded yet. I was a tug skipper before the war started, a very hard teacher, but thorough.'

Escorting the woman to his sea cabin adjoining the bridge, he asked the steward for a variety of drinks, but mainly vodka if possible. The steward winked at Alec and left to do his duties. Returning with a tray full of a variety of spirits, he gave the Russian woman a half-pint glass, causing Alec to glare at him for his gaffe.

Picking up the glass, she said to Alec, 'I'm glad you have

good sized glasses captain, it saves getting up to get refills,' and a roar of laughter burst forth, causing Alec to jump as she slapped him on the back. Filling the glass, Valentina looked at the contents fondly before throwing it down her throat in one, making her gasp a little, but saying, 'It is not as strong as the real Russian vodka, but very nice for parties.'

Three bottles later, she decided to take *Hecla* in to her berth, which had been cleared for the warship, between Merchant ships. The skill she showed at manoeuvring the heavy cruiser into position, earned her a round of applause from all on the bridge.

Valentina smiled, thinking to herself, "That captain, I could make a man of him if I wanted to. Yes, I would like to, but these Westerners, they are all degenerates, most unnatural to look like that captain, he is very beautiful, I wonder if he …" she was interrupted by the captain holding out her heavy coat out, to help her on with it.

'Thank you captain, will you be going ashore tonight? I know all the places of interest in Murmansk,' thinking at the same time, "oh yes, my bed if I'm lucky, captain."

'No, I'm afraid not madam, work never stops for the wicked does it?' smiling inwardly at the way he had avoided going ashore.

'Goodbye then captain, when you come to Murmansk again, ask for me, Valentina, the best pilot in the port.'

Alec held her hand, and kissed it lightly, making Valentina simper and blush. She'd never been treated like that before! 'Please be assured that I certainly will ask for you, and only you on my next visit to your lovely city,' mentally wiping all memory of her from his mind.

Chapter Eight

Nobody went ashore that night, Murmansk not having any creature comforts or decent beer, so Alec showed two films in the ship's company dining room, which went down very well, mainly because it was warm.

The following day, under a stormy sky, Alec read the second part of his orders, and when he finished, he was amazed, calling for Colin. The steward made tea, and served it as Colin entered.

'Tell me what we're here for then, Colin. You'll never guess, never! Nine tons of Russian gold, that's what! It'll be on the jetty at eleven o'clock this morning, then as soon as it's loaded, we sail on the two fifteen tide. I wonder if we'll have the same pilot? I hope not Colin, oh I pray we don't. We haven't got any vodka, she drank it all. I won't buy local rotgut, it's bad for your socks, so she'll have to do without. What do you think?'

Colin looked at his captain, a twisted smile on his face as he said, 'Yes, she was making course for you wasn't she? She must weigh twenty stone if not more. Ye gods, Russian women don't appeal to me Alec, ever. I'll get the upper deck parties to load the stuff, the secondary magazine will be ok, I don't want to clutter up the main armament magazine up with gold. Is that alright Alec?'

'Certainly Colin, you know how I like things by now, and that's the best we can do I think. Our cargo is due shortly, we'd better get up to meet the Russian team. Get the men organised, will you? There's a good chap,' and followed Colin out of the cabin.

The wait wasn't very long, and a Bedford truck pulled up by the gangway, and a lot of men armed to the teeth got out from the back, and formed two lines from the truck to the gangway. Another truck pulled up behind the first, and disgorged a dozen men, obviously to unload the gold and carry it on to the ship. Colin issued some orders to the effect that he wanted twenty men ashore to help with the loading of the cargo, but as soon as the men walked between the two rows, all weapons were loaded and aimed at them making them very uncomfortable, so turning, they returned to the ship, a look of amazement on all their faces.

'Well if that's their altitude, they can stay up there' AB Ward said, 'Let's watch'em instead then, and leaning on the guard rail, he proceeded to do just that, to the amusement of his pals, until the petty officer gunnery instructor saw him, and a scream, similar to a sailor receiving a short pint from a landlord in Portsmouth, echoed round, frightening the gulls and putting them up into the air.

The loading didn't take long, the Russians taking directions to the magazine, and stowing the gold carefully until it was on board. Alec signed for the gold, and thanked the Russian crew for their speed and doing the job well. He prepared the ship for leaving harbour, and hoped that Valentina didn't come to take the ship out of the harbour.

Promptly at the turn of the tide, who should drive up in a dilapidated van, but Valentina herself!

Groaning inwardly, Alec And Colin went to the gangway to welcome her on board, then standing on the quarterdeck, she placed a big box in front of Alec, then her fractured English said, 'Just a little gift for you, hoping you like it," then marched off to Alec's cabin.

Alec and Colin looked amazed at the audacity of the woman, smiled, and then followed her, where they found her sitting in an armchair, with Alec's steward already serving her.

'Good, we are together again captain, it might become a habit, 'and gave a bellow of laughter, but missing Alec's back this time.

'Open your gift, captain, they will suit you I'm thinking,' she said mysteriously with a smile and a toast in whiskey.

Alec wondered what the hell was in this box that this huge woman had given him.

Suddenly the contents were revealed.

A pair of pure silk pyjamas, accompanied with several bottles of Russian vodka, "The genuine stuff, that blew your brains out no doubt," thought Alec, as he thanked her so very much for her kindness.

Picking a bottle from the pack, Valentina opened it and poured out three full glasses opening another to do this. Then she offered it to the two RN officers and shouted, 'Cheers', and put the glass down. She emptied it so quickly that Alec wondered if she had drunk it. But she had, and filled her second glass too. Soon, there were three dead bottles on the table for the steward to throw out and Valentina was on her way to the bridge, to pilot the ship through the river.

As they slowed down for the motorboat to pick up Valentina from the *Hecla*, she whispered to Alec, 'I've enjoyed our two dates captain, hurry back and I'll give you a good time, you naughty man,' and waving her ham-like hand at him, she pursed her lips making him cringe but he was wearing a smile thankfully, so she didn't look upset. He watched her swing herself down on to the small motorboat, went down into the cabin, and re-emerged with a bottle in her hand, waving it in a toast to the next time they would meet. Alec dodged back into the bridge, and sighed with relief as the boat tore off, transporting Valentina back ashore. Looking at Colin, he saw that he was rocking with laughter and as soon as Alec saw this, he burst out laughing himself.

'Good lord, Colin, what did the crew think, seeing that thing making cow eyes at me? I'm never coming here again,' he said finally, which sent Colin off in a fit again.

Alec looked at the coxswain at the wheel, who was trying very hard not to laugh, and said, 'You dare, that's all coxswain, you just dare!'

The coxswain lost his deep booming laugh filling the bridge, followed by spluttering as he tried to control it. Then he waited for the course from the navigator.

The *Hecla* soon pointed her elegant bow towards England, and her screws churned the sea to creamy foam as the revolutions increased on the engines, the decks vibrating under the tremendous power. Then she started gently to dip her bow into the water, cutting a bow-wave into the surface, like a surgeon's scalpel, dividing the sea for the hull to pass through it.

Handing the bridge over to the duty officer, Alec and Colin went down for a meal, confident the ship was in safe hands, and all was well.

Sitting in the officers' mess afterwards, Alec decided that

the gold was payment for the weapons, planes and ammunition the Russians had needed, to fight the German foe, and were doing it very well.

'I feel sorry for any German coming up against a battalion of soldiers like Valentina,' remarked Colin, causing Alec to put his drink down before he spilt it.

'Colin, if you come out with anything like that again, I'll... let's have another one eh?'

The weather was mild and the trip home was like going on the Isle of Wight ferry, then on the third day, the wind came to life very suddenly, sending the waves higher, the spume seeming to defy gravity as it returned to the sea, so slowly. Having lifelines rigged on the upper deck, to save losing anybody over the side, was paramount in everybody's mind, the ship still had to be worked and a call for action stations could come at any time. If a seaman fell in the seething cauldron, they wouldn't survive, even if the deck crew managed to launch a boat, which they couldn't anyway.

So it went on, the ship being buffeted about like a child's toy in the bath. The cooks couldn't cook the meals, so they served up ship's biscuits, and dog's micks, (corned beef sandwiches), with never ending cups of tea. The lower deck's smell was a mixture of men's bodies, vomit and fuel oil, which is unequalled on this earth.

The sixth day saw the sea quietening slightly, and normal duties came back into force, but it was still bitterly cold, so cold in fact that the stokers rigged some steam hoses to the upper deck, to make sure the gun turrets, gun mountings, and torpedo tubes didn't ice up, which would be fatal if they were needed urgently. The ship's boats were made more secure but one of the whalers was stove in, so some seamen dropped it over the side with No.1's blessing, then carried on tidying up the decks, and trying not to look over the side. Alec prayed for their final tying up alongside the jetty at Murmansk to arrive. Nobody in the RN liked the Russian convoys, if not for the unfriendliness of the Russians, then it was definitely the ghastly weather.

On being told the radar scanner was damaged, Alec sent up the radar artificer to repair it. On returning to the bridge, the artificer, shaking his head, informed Alec, 'Beyond repair sir, the drive has completely shattered.' Alec contacted the Admiralty straight away making them aware of the lack of radar, whereupon the Admiralty told him to proceed to his original map reference. Cursing under his breath, he went to his cabin with this bad news preying on his mind, but falling into the arms of Orpheus very quickly.

His sleep was greatly disturbed, the worst not being *Hecla's* movement with the sea, but of Sally and the girls, cowering in terror from the sea, and Alec for some reason, not being able to move to rescue them. Ingots of gold showered on them, causing the female Hamiltons, more injuries, and distress. Very suddenly, silence reigned, and Sally and the girls settled down to sleep, so calmly and timidly. Alec woke up, his eyes flicking open and all his senses alerted. Then realising it was a nightmare, he tried to get off to sleep again, but failing dismally, he got up and dressed, to see if he could cadge some strong kai, the Navy's second drink, then walked up to the bridge for a nose around and hear what the new

Chapter Nine

Oberleutnant Carl Vogel wasn't pleased when he looked at the state of the U-boat. . It had been caught in a cross current, and rolled it about like a cork, even though she was submerged during the day.. It surfaced at night to start the main diesel engines, to rest and recharge the batteries that powered the electric motors to use when the boat was submerged.

U169 had been on patrol for nearly six weeks, in the forbidding grey hell that was the North Sea, and had seen nothing at all for eight days, then since the weather had worsened, he thought there would be less hope of sinking any British shipping. His periodical rising to periscope depth, and sweeping the surface, was more a cry of desperation than hope, but he kept vigil, always hoping. As he swept the scope south westerly, he noticed a smudge of smoke, which disappeared with the wind, but having his curiosity aroused, used the telegraph, to signal full ahead both. The hum of the motors started, and the boat moved off towards the south west horizon. On correcting his course every half hour, Vogel came across a British cruiser making hard work of the conditions.

Looking at his ship identification book, he learned it was HMS *Hecla* from Portsmouth, recently refitted, and fitted with the deadly radar that was beginning to account for the U-boats and their crews. Changing to the high intensity periscope, he noticed a funny thing, the radar scanner was not turning as it would normally, and checking for another scanner didn't find one. Not believing his luck, he called for action stations, and loaded the six fo'rard torpedo tubes.

These new design torpedoes were working well, and were one hundred per cent accurate, so come on my beauties, he thought, let's see what you can do. His plan was to fire the torpedoes in a fan, spreading the courses of the six weapons, thus damaging the enemy as much as possible. The night was drawing in now. So Vogel blew his tanks, so that his conning tower was breaking the water.

This was the critical time when a submarine was at its most vulnerable, but as yet there was no response from his quarry, so he settled on a course that would enable him to use his main armament properly.

His course was correct, he was in range, so, 'Fire one,' ten seconds, 'Fire two,' ten seconds, 'Fire three,' ten seconds, 'Fire four,' ten seconds 'Fire five,' ten seconds, Fire six.'

The lookout in the main mast saw the wake of the incoming torpedoes and phoned the bridge. Alec ordered action stations, and ordering open sights on the difficult-to-see U-boat.

'Range one and a half miles, fire, fire, fire.'

The six-inch opened up, bracketing the U-boat.

'Down fifty, fire, fire,'

Two six inch shells ripped the U-boat in half, just after the first torpedo tore into *Hecla,* five more torpedoes hit at regular intervals, the last one hitting the tiller flat, where the twin rudder controls were housed. The ship was mortally injured, her armour plating unable to deny entrance to the torpedoes, or water.

"Abandon ship, boat stations to be manned now," Alec shouted, as he watched the two halves of the U-boat sinking. Throwing the lead-lined ship's log over the side; he pulled his "Mae West" on over his thick watch coat. Dashing towards the boat deck, he heard some men screaming in the boiler room air lock, and looking through the small window he forced the locking bar over. The hatch cover popped open, seven men climbed out, fear etched on their faces so deeply, Alec would never forget it as long as he lived, and that wasn't a good bet at the moment, he thought.

He went down several hatches, helping men out, and up to the upper deck, where he saw a young seaman who needed help; he watched the light of life die in the young sailor's eyes, his poor body torn into shreds. Then he looked for a position where the wounded would receive treatment and the fit could help with the loading of the boats. Calling to anybody who was in the compartments, he assisted, pulled and cajoled men from the sinking *Hecla*, all the while, hoping the magazines wouldn't blow up, as they did on the *Hood*.

Reaching the boat deck, he found that No.1 and the other officers had organised the boats and the wounded, everybody pulling together, and loading the boats, wounded first. *Hecla*, thank the Lord, seemed to be waiting for everyone to get off, so Alec went to the radio shack, where he found a signalman badly injured. He carried him signalman out of the shack and went back, to make sure the continuous remote SOS button was down. Leaving the radio shack, the ship lurched, slamming the heavy armoured door shut, straight on to Alec's leg. The pain was terrible, and screaming in his mind, he crawled, with the unconscious man on his back, to the boat deck. His leg was a mass of pain, as he looked at it, and saw bones sticking out at odd angles, and blood pouring out of a wound on the knee.

On seeing him, three stokers ran forward to help him, and lifting him as gently as they could, carried him to the sea boat.

Alec regained consciousness in the boat, which was quite lively in the heavy swell of the North Sea.

Daylight forced him to screw up his eyes to protect them, my God that sun is bright, thought Alec, then slowly, as he looked around him, he saw some anxious faces, all looking at him.

'What are you monkeys looking at?' he joked, before the sheer agony hit him.

'Sir, we were sunk three days ago, but the RAF have found us, and a destroyer is coming for us. A Wellington came over, to parachute some grub and water, as well as morphine to us, but we haven't got much left sir, and your leg is looking very poorly,' said a Petty Officer, whose head was bandaged, as well as his shoulder. He went on to explain how, when Alec saw wounded men in the water, he would jump in to save them, 'But I'm afraid your leg injuries let you down sir, and we had to restrain you.'

The pain was still with Alec, when the destroyer, HMS *Ulysses*, carefully pulled alongside the sea boat, and unloaded its human misery.

Ulysses searched around the area, looking for survivors, and found boats, but sadly, nobody living, only the dead, floating over quite a wide area. The lookouts were in tears, as they saw the pitiful little bundles brought on board. Alec was sad to see the signalman among the dead, as he lay on the bunk in the sickbay, which was soon full, so the wardroom was made into a makeshift hospital.

Alec had begun to wander in his mind, His feet were still planted firmly on his beloved *Hecla's* bridge, then torpedoes hit, and he was hurt even more, falling out of the bunk. The pain was so intense, that the nurse had to tie him to his bunk, and inject him with tranquillisers, while the little destroyer glided through the ocean, leaving a creamy wake behind her, attempting to save Alec's leg, and perhaps his life.

All nineteen survivors of *Hecla* were busy thanking the ships of the company of *Ulysses*, who told the cruiser men they just happened to be that way, so thought they might want a lift.

The ship hove to for a burial-at-sea ceremony. The whole ship's company of Ulysses, was standing to attention, swaying to the rhythm of the sea, as the canvas wrapped bundles were slid into their last resting place. Then away the destroyer went continuing her mission to Portsmouth.

"Portsmouth harbour never looked more welcome than it did now," Commander Preston of *Ulysses* thought, and on being assigned a berth alongside, noted the ambulance on the jetty, ready for their charges to get in. Alec was still in a coma, so he had a short boat trip across the harbour, to the Royal Naval Hospital at Haslar in Gosport, where he was wheeled away for surgery on his leg.

Meanwhile, a lot of talk and signals were bandied about, regarding Alec, of which he was completely unaware.

Chapter Ten

When Sally received the telegram from the Admiralty, she begged and borrowed petrol coupons, then sped off on the road to Gosport straight away. Arriving at Haslar, the RN Hospital, at three o'clock that afternoon, she made arrangements to stay at a hotel. Getting in touch with a counsellor, she asked, 'How is he? Will he live? When can he come home? How long will he be in here?'

Holding up his hands up and with a slight smile on his face, sub-lieutenant Wall said, 'Mrs. Hamilton, your husband has had his right leg removed because of gas gangrene. He is in a coma at present, but the surgeon has the highest of hopes for him.' Taking Sally's hand, he continued, 'You already know of your husband's courage Mrs. Hamilton, well, because of his insistence to try and save lives as *Hecla* went down, he's been put up for a medal.'

'Nonsense, he wouldn't want that,' Sally sobbed, thinking how strong her husband's legs were.

Leading Sally to a small anteroom, he brought her a cup of tea, and pointed to a bell push, in case she needed him for anything.

Alec woke up four days later, asking, 'Could I have a cup of tea? I'm spitting feathers,' and looked around the ward.

'Damned leg, it's still hurting like hell,' and put his hand towards it to rub it. Not feeling anything, he sat bolt upright, causing a scream of pain in his head, then looking down, he saw a left leg present and correct, and a bandaged stump. Stump? No! Panicking, he called for a nurse, who wiped the sweat and tears from his forehead, and face, then explained what the surgeon had had to do, to save his life, then said, 'Your wife has been here all the time, do you feel you would like to see her?' Nodding his head, he looked around for Sally, very frightened, that she wouldn't want him any more. Sally came running in, and gave a cry as she fell into Alec's arm, her body heaving with sobs as she whispered, 'I love you, I love you, I love you, I love you,' over and over until she fell, exhausted, body and soul. Alec looked into her mascara-streaked face, kissed her nose, and said, 'Hello funny face, where have you been?' His mind forced himself not to cry for his wife and daughters, or for himself.

'Do you really love me, now I'm only half of what I was Sally?'

'How could you? How could you say such a hurtful thing? I love you for our daughters, I love you because you love me, also, I love you, because we are expecting another baby, I love you, because you are you, nobody else, just you.'

Her smudged face made Alec adore her more; he couldn't ignore the pricking of tears in his eyes, demanding the sunlight. They made each other's cheeks wet. 'When and how?' he asked, causing Sally to laugh. 'Oh the usual way I imagine, can you remember?'

The days went by, leading into weeks, seven in all, when Alec was measured for an artificial leg, his stump being nicely healed, and with a good blood circulation. The tin leg arrived two weeks later, accompanied by an expert fitter, who stayed in Gosport for a week, altering padding and adjusting straps, until it felt comfortable on the stump. One day, two nurses moved him to parallel bars, to see if he could take his weight on the leg.

He fell several times, once crying out, 'Christ, I'll never manage this thing, why didn't you let me die?'

A nurse brought a wheelchair, and helped Alec into it, to take him to the specialist. To remove the leg, and put a slightly thicker sock on the stump. Replacing the leg, Mr. Boyd asked Alec to flick it, rather like a whip. Trying this, Alec at last succeeded in flicking the knee straight.

Having learnt the secret, Alec wanted to carry on trying, all day and night, but the nurses saw he was exhausted, and tried to stop him.

'Nurse Blundell, I'm going to walk in a fortnight. If Group Captain Bader can do it, then I can as well,' he said resolutely.

The next fortnight went by with Alec falling less and gaining confidence, until at long last, he was capable of walking with two walking sticks. Two days after he started using the sticks he was summoned to Buckingham Palace, for a ceremony to take place in three weeks time, namely, HM the King would present him with the Victoria Cross, for his bravery on HMS *Hecla*.

Reading it several times with Sally, Alec said, 'How damned silly this is,' and was dumbfounded every time he read it, not believing it, but looking at Sally. She nodded her head at him and cried with happiness. Alec had to order a new doeskin uniform and kit, so a civilian tailor took his measurements and told Alec, he would receive everything in ten days.

Alec walked everywhere with his sticks, in fact, so much, his stump needed padding and dressing several times, when it started bleeding. He was managing to put his tin leg on easier by now, so when his kit arrived, he was able to try on his new No 1 uniform. Perfect! "Fit for a king," he thought, looking into a full-length mirror. Shame about the sticks though, he thought he would try with one to see how that went. A trifle wobbly, but he mastered it in the end, although it made him sweat a bit.

Eventually, the day before the great day arrived, and Sally's parents brought the girl to Pompey. They gave Alec a rapturous welcome. The Hamilton family hardly slept that night, the excitement was like a huge electric charge, but the morning came at last, as they always do, and found Alec, Sally and the two imps, all dressed up in their best clothes. Swiftly dispatching their breakfast, a RN staff car whisked them off to London. Alec was surprised when two police motor bikes, serving as outriders, cleared the way to London, chiselling a lot of time off the otherwise boring journey. They arrived at Admiralty House in plenty of time to have a cup of tea, and gather their nerves together, surrounding the turmoil inside, with serenity outside.

The ceremony didn't last long surprisingly, although all the people present knew the King and Queen visited all the bombed areas daily, to keep up morale, and the two royals felt they had to do something, after all, their eldest daughter drove an ambulance in London, and was hailed a heroine.

Walking to the car, the Hamiltons were besieged by photographers from the papers, but after two minutes, they reached the car, with the aid of some Royal Marines, who were on their way back to Pompey, after a medal presentation at the Palace. Alec, Sally and the girls, without exception, fell asleep on the way home to Pompey, Sally and the girls staying one night in the hotel, before Sally returned the girls to Somerset the following day.

RNH Haslar was eventually reached; Alec fell exhausted on his bed, the VC in its box on the bedside cabinet for all to see.

Chapter Eleven

The weather was dull, but Alec strapped on his tin leg to wash and get shaved, looking forward to seeing his wife and children, before they left for Somerset.

'Ah, good morning nurse, I'm very hungry, so I'll eat my breakfast before I go,' Alec cheerily said to the nurse, as she came in with his meal.

'My word, captain, you'll catch any girl's eye with that ribbon on your chest,' as she made sure he took his pills, then left him to eat his meal.

After he walked to the jetty at HMS *Dolphin*, to wait for a liberty boat to take him to Portsmouth dockyard, idly, he looked up the harbour, at all the power of the RN looking so peaceful at nine 'clock in the morning. But looking at the turrets of all the ships, he realised again, what awesome power these ships carried.

Slowly and gently, the boat pulled alongside the jetty, the seamen swiftly seeing the ribbon and saluting, but Alec wasn't affected, he wanted to see his three girls so much, and he knew they wanted to see him. He caught a bus to Elm Grove, noting the bomb damage from the night before, where there was a fire crew, with some air raid wardens writing in their notepads.

Alighting from the bus, he strolled round the corner, to enter the hotel. The remains of the hotel were surrounded with smoke, and people crying, or calling out names. People were carrying bodies wrapped in blankets, into the school hall. Something was wrong, very wrong as he hurried to the hotel, and his girls.

'No! No! No!' he gasped, as he burst into the school hall, seeing rows of bodies lying neatly in rows, the final hopelessness and despair of men and women alike, identifying loved ones, and others, forcing themselves to look under the blankets, then to shrink back, with a howl of pain, sorrow and anguish, and a lot of hate.

Alec knew the feeling, his gut squeezing up enough, to cause him to throw up his breakfast, then falling over his tin leg as he tried to hurry, being helped up by somebody but feeling no hurt, just a terrible pain inside, freezing out all others, but revealing itself in one prolonged scream in his mind. At long last, he found his Sally and girls, lying under a sheet, together in death, as in life, forever. Darkness enveloped him, like a womb, protecting him from all pain.

The RN ambulance took him to RNH Haslar, broken arm, ruined tin leg, and in a coma, that wouldn't last long, but protection to his mind, in place, and his body slightly damaged.

His coming round was painful, the memories of the four of them, playing pirates in a meadow behind the Glastonbury Tor. Everything flooded back, then he put the memories away, as the scenes in the school hall flashed through his mind. Absolute, and complete pain crossed his face, as he sobbed until he was exhausted, until the mind protection came to the rescue, giving him a brief respite..

His in-laws visited him, not wishing to wake him, but to give him something, not strength, they didn't have it, but they were there if needed. He needed them. He needed them more than they could ever know, just to sit there. Two days later, Sally's parents returned to the home that they all loved, in Somerset with the bodies of their daughter and grand daughters.

Alec slowly repaired himself after the funerals, which was like ending the final chapter of a favourite book, but he at last accepted what had been dealt to him, it did him good, he was a widower, but there would be a lot more before this war was over.

His new tin pin seemed to be better than the first, and his arm healed, enabling him to walk a little, gradually lengthening it until he could manage to reach a pub.

Things were nearly normal, when he received a letter from the Admiralty, asking him to make himself available at Admiralty House, the next day at 0800 hours.. A car would call for him.

His new job was with an office with the dubious title, Hazardous Missions, where he proceeded to throw himself into his work with great gusto. He loathed desk work, but his job of finding RN officers and men, and slotting them into a variety of difficult and dangerous assignments, made it very interesting for him,and kept him going. He managed to walk a short way without sticks, then he admitted to himself, that he must use one of them, but at least he was on equal footing so to speak, meeting other officers in the wardroom, and trying not to hurt as much.

Sitting at his desk, reading reports from France, he realised that this war was hurting everybody in Europe, and the way these Nazi bastards were gobbling up countries and lives, the outcome of the war, if Germany won, would be unbearable.

Returning to his reports, thinking of Sally and the girls, he read about the French resistance movement, and their numerous pinpricks, that were beginning to irritate the enemy, proved by the way French civilians were thrown down in a fusillade of bullets from SS execution units, many dying with the words "Vive la France" on their lips.

Chapter Twelve

Pierre offered no resistance when the German troops seized him. They gave him a chance to run, on condition that he would understand why they shot him, He knew they disliked taking prisoners, because it took up time and food. He didn't run, so shrugging their shoulders, they threw him into a cell for the night.

Thinking carefully, he reviewed what happened before his capture; "It was a pure fluke I'm afraid," he thought, knowing that Claude and Henri had seen the event, and escaped, possibly following them to the village, he hoped.

His situation worsened the following morning, when he was chained up, and thrown into the back of the decrepit SS truck, used for conveying prisoners to the Gestapo or the SS. headquarters. Luckily, his newly set up resistance unit was self sufficient; he just hoped he had high pain tolerances, He smiled ruefully to himself, as his guard climbed in the back, and he received a stubbed boot in his ribs, just for a welcome,

'My name is Feldwebel Mueller, and I am God as far as you are concerned, so stay there and shut up if you want to live,' the German growled, 'I want to study these wines you frogs make.'

With a booming laugh, he took his first bottle to task, and seriously lowered the level. The cab doors slammed, the engine was started, and the truck lurched off through the village.

The heavy truck climbed the hill steadily, leaving the town and harbour, as the mist rolled and swirled in from the sea. The engine started to protest at being worked so hard, and the driver started muttering to himself, cursing the useless wartime headlights he'd been afflicted with. Eventually, to Otto's relief, they reached the top and he pulled in to stop. Shouts ensued, and Feldwebel Mueller, banging on the driver's door noisily, demanded to know what Otto was playing at. With a twist of his lips, vaguely resembling a smile, Otto Braun tapped the temperature gauge, and replied, 'It's as cold as ice in here, but the engine's a good substitute for hell right now,' then jumped from the cab, and picked up the water container from the rack behind the front wheel,

His pal, Willi Schmidt, was in the back of the SS painted truck, and after filling the empty radiator, strolled back, and asked Willi if he was alright.

Willi replied in a harsh whisper, 'The schnapps is my favourite heating anytime,' while offering Otto some in the bottle, then he let out a bellow of laughter, and kicked the manacled prisoner on the floor, very hard to the ribs, making him groan again.

Otto could never understand the SS being so evil, even his pal wasn't like he used to be in his youth, He wondered what the hell had gone wrong with this world, as he glanced at the wretch lying in his blood and vomit, with pity and shame.

Pierre saw the look of the driver, and decided there was one German human being on the truck, as it lurched away again, nearly throwing his guard out of the truck, reducing him to a screaming vicious drunk. "Very, very dangerous," thought Pierre, as he waited for a boot to find its way into his ribs again thinking he would be glad when all this was finished and he wouldn't have to pretend to be so badly hurt. He looked at the road behind the truck, thinking he knew where they were, so he tried to ease himself into a more comfortable position, noticing his guard was in a drunken daze now, and very close to falling asleep.

'Sleep well, and when it comes, I'll wake you up before you die,' Pierre muttered.

The truck followed the dark grey ribbon of road for twenty-seven kilometres, the two occupants in the cab cursing the weather, and the instigators of their discomfort and misery. To his surprise, Otto had a wine bottle jammed in his hand by the normally nasty Feldwebel Heinz Mueller, as he invited him to drink up, to get warmer. This he did receiving in return, a slightly warmer feeling in his bones. Otto couldn't stop thinking of the Frenchman in the back, and wondered if he was alive or dead by now, in Willi's tender care. "Willi's changed to what he used to be," he thought, "full of the drug called the SS," and then wondered how long Willi would last at being a bastard.

Easing off the throttle, the truck slowed down before going down the hill. He knew the dangerous bend, and the narrow river bridge at the bottom and kept his eye on the speed and the road. He saw the bridge lift in a flash, turning the dull morning, into day, and a second later, the sobbing roar as the sound wave hit the truck like Thor's hammer, sending it careering off the road, into a gully, where it came to rest on its side. Then the silence, awful in its entirety, blanketing the scene, with nothing moving. Several minutes later, after the dust settled sown, and the debris returned to the abused earth, two figures ran from the other side of the bridge that was, and took a look in the back, immediately shooting the uniformed thug dead.

'Pierre's alive, quick, lift him out with me Claude, we'll be smothered with Germans in a minute,' said Henri.

As they lifted him out from the wreckage a shot from a Luger rang out and Claude fell without a sound. A second later, another shot echoed the first and Feldwebel Mueller with a victorious shout still in his throat, fell dead at the feet of Otto, who ran forward and helped Henri with Pierre, who was coming round.

'Let's get the key for his chains,' said Henri, levelling his pistol at Otto.

'No, no,' shouted Pierre, and tripped Henri with his legs, 'he helped us Henri, quick get me free.'

Otto ran to Mueller's crumpled body, and got the key out of the hated man's tunic. As the chains fell off, Henri gave Pierre a bottle of wine, which was gratefully received.

'It's lucky the SS used the same truck as usual,' laughed Henri, 'otherwise we would be in mourning, that pig was after your life I think,' he said, as he cleaned Pierre's cuts and grazes.

'It's a good job you are fit, you have three busted ribs Pierre. Are you sure it wasn't a wild bull in the back with you?' Henri remarked, as he strapped up Pierre's chest.

'I feel like an Egyptian mummy now,' said Pierre, as he was helped into the van that Henri and Claude had arrived in. Looking up, he noticed Otto's face, and thanked him for both the look while in the back of the truck and killing the hated Mueller.

Shaking his hand, he said his farewells, and they wished one another good luck, after one last swallow of wine. They went their different ways, one wishing, and one hoping.

Carefully hiding the van, Henri and Pierre searched around for anything out of the ordinary, before they entered the shed, hidden in the copse halfway up the hill, and being aware that they couldn't light a fire, they ate what Henri had brought with him.

'These sheds are well used, but keeping food in them is getting harder, with the new German camp, and patrols always poking their nose in,' said Henri. 'The sooner the Allies give them the order of the jackboot, the better.'

Pierre was thoughtful; his friend's outburst had perturbed him. Obviously, the Germans were up to something or other. He'd studied the electrified fence with its guards, and high wall, he couldn't work out why they wanted to protect a dangerous piece of land, jutting out into the sea, and ending in a sheer drop on to ugly grey rocks, sticking out of the sea, like giant discoloured and broken teeth, that all the ferocity of the North Sea had failed to destroy for century after century. Why? The puzzle was intriguing, and with the aid of Henri's binoculars, and a few cautious reconnoitres, so far, much to his annoyance, he'd discovered nothing. The traffic into the site was endless, going in carefully with shrouded tarpaulins and leaving empty, as clean as a new pin. Trucks of all sizes were on the road, causing the village to get very dirty and dusty, but nobody daring to complain. Yesterday, Pierre had seen gangs of men laying railway tracks, working a shift system, to get twenty-four hours work, continually forging ahead to their destination. What was going on here? Pierre wondered as the noise from the site carried on.

'Dear, oh dear, we must find the answer Henri, for my own peace of mind. Our enemies are methodical, so they have reason for this manifestation, I must know,' Pierre muttered, 'we must see it from the seaboard. We're missing something. I will not rest till we find it.'

'I know an old fisherman in the village. It's only seven kilometres, so perhaps he would take us fishing,' answered Henri, 'We will see him tomorrow.'

He was talking to himself. Pierre was sound asleep, sitting at the table.

'Come along,' Henri whispered, half lifting Pierre on to a crude bed.

'These two weeks have been tough on us, we must get fresh food and fruit, and do you like fish?' Henri asked, his eyes telling Pierre he loved fish, he also had a liking for good French cooking, and French wine, of which there was an acute shortage, all the production going to the German camp, as most of the food did. Pierre was making the last dregs of yesterday's coffee.

'Waking up in the morning is very depressing,' said Henri, 'especially when your breakfast is air sandwiches, with the last two pieces of black ersatz bread, as hard as a witch's heart.'

'After drinking this er…um…hot water, we must go to the village, and get provisions, also, we will call on Francois, we must see him today, otherwise we won't get fish, or fishing until tomorrow, and you're worried about what our enemies are up to. Well, there are enemies in the village, but they meet the SS man in charge of the village, so let's move,' said Pierre, pouring out the liquid to no avail. Both of them left it on the table, and cautiously, left the shed, staying in the shadows of the trees as long as they could.

Reaching the country lane, the two Frenchmen carefully

circled the cottages on the way to the village, Henri sometimes invading Pierre's thoughts.

'You'll get a ploughed field on your forehead if you don't
stop frowning,' laughed Henri. 'Your face is like an old
prune.' His infectious laugh eventually affected Pierre, when
his face cracked, and fell in half with laughter. Arriving on
the outskirts of the village was dangerous for, them with the
unknown number of German troops in the streets.

Then on finally reaching the fishing boat jetty, they were
disappointed to see a German fast gunboat tied up, ready to
go out on patrol.

'It's lunchtime, so let's look for Francois and visit the bar,
we may learn something, there again, we may not,' Henri
said, 'but we must try, especially in the bar,' Henri said with
a grin. They glanced through the window, they saw no troops,
so the two sidled in.

On seeing Francois, Henri motioned Pierre into the corner
table, and idled towards the fisherman, who was trying to
drown himself in wine.

'Francois, you old villain, your boat should have sunk
by now with your blubber, you're catching me up,' shouted
Henri, and then slumped on to the chair next to Francois, who
promptly poured a glass of wine.

Henri waved to Pierre, saying, 'This rogue is Pierre, and
this,' nodding his head to Francois, 'is Francois, where cruelty
to fishing boats originated.'

Pierre smiled and held out his hand, and having it seized
instantly by a rat trap, disguised by a bunch of sausages.

'Henri and me go back a long way, so a pal of his, is a pal
of mine,' Francois said between swallows from his glass. 'Do
you need any help?'

Henri and Pierre explained what they must do, but the more they went into it, the more Francois looked worried, until he put his finger to his lips, and explained, 'The German patrol boat makes fishing very difficult, if they stop your boat, they take your fish, if you haven't got much of a catch, they make sure they get their feelings known to you. So let me think about it, but in the meantime, here is some money to buy some food, but try to stay at Marie's tonight, she'll make you welcome,' winking a big bloodshot eye, and nudging Pierre and Henri at the same time.

Keeping clear of the troops was easier in the afternoon, so they spent a while, shopping for food and wine, with tobacco coming from another pal of Henri.

They stopped in the three other bars of course, making sure there were only locals in them, but Henri knew so many people, and the wine was getting better as they drank that in the end, two burly fishermen each took one of them and carried them to Marie's house, where luckily, she didn't have any visitors.

The following morning was awful for Pierre, not only did he have a ninety per cent hangover, he had Henri's singing to endure, as Marie noted, "would do justice to a ship's siren."

But having a breakfast soon had Pierre on his feet, and the two pals went for a stroll down to the quay, wondering when they would see Francois.

Suddenly, two German officers strode towards them, talking between themselves avidly, animatedly talking with their arms. Looking as nondescript as they could, Henri and Pierre read a paper in the shop they were close to, and listened.

'When the guns are fitted my friend, they will control the North Sea, in liaison with the other gun emplacements, the

Allies won't have any idea how we are able to accurately sink their shipping,' said the senior of the two. 'The invasion of England will quickly follow the heavy destruction wreaked on them by the glorious bomber crews of the Third Reich. The range of the guns is phenomenal, boosted by the new propulsion unit built into the shell, we could and will fire on England.'

Henri and Pierre looked at each other as the two Germans swept past, full of anticipation of victory.

Chapter Thirteen

Waiting for the dark was nerve-racking, so the three went for a meal at Francois's, making Louise happy. 'Please eat well, you've given my big Gorilla something to think about, and do, if I'm not mistaken.'

At four o'clock, three shadows moved slowly down the street to the quay, thankful for the thick socks covering their shoes, and the Luger pistols, mysteriously given by a resistance friend of Pierre's, who frequently wondered how these people managed to get hold of these strictly banned weapons. But he recognised the German Army issue Lugers and stopped wondering.

As they climbed into the boat, they heard coughs coming from the E boat, and froze for a minute; sound carried a long way over still water, and it worked both ways.

Sitting silently on the decking, Francois started lashing the pipe to the main trawling line, at the deck level, and two feet below water. Now, if the E-boat approached them, Henri or Pierre could slide over the side, putting the underwater end of the pipe into their mouths, and support their bodies on the ropes attached to the nets, God willing! Francois busied himself, sorting out lobster pots, ropes and fish boxes. Checking the engine, winch and lights. Henri and Pierre work in the same kind of clothes, to that one would be below deck, while the other was "helping" Francois on the deck, with ropes and nets.

'The Germans use the patrol boat at irregular hours,' said Francois, 'so we must expect them at any time.'

The fishing boat nosed carefully out of the harbour, gently rolling in the slight swell, the engine murmuring contentedly. On reaching the harbour wall, Francois opened the throttle a little, partly to give either Henri or Pierre a bit of extra time, scanning the cliffs for whatever was hiding there.

On bearing to starboard, and skirting the headland, Pierre saw the four huge gun barrels jutting out of the cliffs by four feet, at which, five minutes later, Pierre estimated the guns to have an eighteen-inch bore. Swapping places with Henri as unobtrusively as he could, he started to draw a sketch of the cliff, with its nasty crown of thorns. By using his compass, he managed to record the position quite accurately, in relation to the harbour. Looking down at his work, he drank some coffee, while gathering his thoughts on how he could get his important information to England.

In his mind's eye, he saw the face of the cliff below the monster guns, but couldn't remember what he saw. To refresh his memory, he peered around the cabin door, taking pains not to be observed by a German sentry. He couldn't see the cliff face that he wanted, because they had sailed too far round the headland, so they had to stay out at sea for a while, doing some fishing, to give the journey credibility.

Giving Henri a low call, they exchanged places.

'I'm dying Pierre,' groaned Henri, his face green with the dreaded seasickness, 'give all my girls a kiss for me my friend, I know they'll miss me.'

'I won't live long enough to do that', laughed Pierre, then

stepped back quickly, as Henri relieved his stomach.

On reaching the deck, Pierre asked Francois how far they had to go to reach the best fishing ground.

'Another ten minutes, or the end of a glass of wine should see us about there,' Francois said, puffing his smelly, old pipe. 'So start moving the ropes and nets to the starboard side, that'll give the Germans something to look at."

Shortly after the nets had been fed into the sea, they hung suspended on round corks, extending aft, as the boat crawled slowly on its course. With Francois putting port rudder on, and lowering the revs of the engine, the nets formed a big arc, eventually forming a pocket. Closing the net into a circle, Francois shouted to Pierre to start the winch, hauling in the net and sending the fish into the hole. The winch smoked on the rope a few times, but it wasn't a big catch, just enough to make the boat less lively, which cheered Henri.

With the last ten feet of net to come inboard, a pair of powerful engines came burbling behind the fishing boat, causing Pierre to go over the side, into the cradle of ropes, then with the pipe in his mouth, he placed a clip on his nose. On board, Henri was around the net and ropes, making sure the breathing pipe was in the clear of ropes and gear. "It's a pity the boat is designed for two crew," Henri thought, if it were bigger, they wouldn't have to go through this play-acting. The E-boat pulled alongside and a trooper jumped into the fishing boat.

'Ah a good catch captain, perhaps you would like to give us some of your catch?' he said in a strong, guttural Saxony accent.

'Of course,' said Francois, 'please help yourself,' patting himself on the back at the same time, pleased that he hadn't pulled his lobster pots yet.

The trooper helped himself to a box of fish, which he passed to a grinning companion on the German boat, and then climbing back on the German boat, he laughed, and gave a scornful wave to the fishermen. The patrol boat engines roared, and hurtled away, leaving the fishing boat rocking in its wake, on the dark sea. When the German craft was small on the horizon. Henri tapped the breathing tube gently, and reached over the side, and helped Pierre back on board, to put on dry clothes.

Henri looked at the amount of fish the German had left them, and swore, 'Why did you let them take so many fish, Francois?'

He broke off as they heard an aircraft coming over, low.

'A Spitfire,' shouted Henri, and danced dementedly, juggling a bottle of wine with a glass. From the direction of the patrol boat, a big plume of black smoke suddenly rose into the air, curling and rolling up, then the three men heard the boom as the fuel tank and ammunition blew up, filling their ears with the instant violence.

Two minutes later, the Spitfire returned low, doing a very slow victory roll, as the Frenchmen cheered, danced and waved at the pilot.

Stopping suddenly, Henri asked Francois, 'Why didn't he do that, before they stole our fish?'

Francois looked at Pierre, and cast his eyes to the smoke-drifted sky, and shook his head, while telling Henri to go aft with him, and pull up the lobster pots. Looking at their catch later, they were pleased with the lobsters they'd caught, though Henri wouldn't go near them, explaining he only went near them when they were cooked and ready to eat.

'That's made up for the fish we returned to the sea,' laughed Francois, as Henri tidied up the deck and washed the fish guts, blood and scales overboard, Henri watched the gulls for a minute, admiring the ability they had, wheeling around, ready to pounce on any morsel they could get. Finally, with the deck and gear looking a lot better, the boat was steered around, towards the harbour, Pierre and Henri changed places, as Henri told Pierre all the heavy work was done, though Pierre's ribs were on the way to knitting together.

With the headland coming up on the portside, Pierre carefully positioned himself, without being too obvious to get a good view. He was sure he had missed something significant, but what was it?

Musing over his wine, his mind kept flicking back to his wife and daughter on their small farm, as alike as two peas, both in looks and mannerisms, poor, but happy from what he could remember, until in 1940, when a Luftwaffe aircraft, damaged while returning from a raid on England, crashed and obliterated their home, while he was tending a cow in the barn. His eyes turned misty, as he sat on the boat, remembering.

Then the boat became lively, jerking him back to the present situation, and he found himself looking at the rocks at the bottom of the cliff, with its crown of monstrous guns near the top. Asking Francois to slow down a trifle, he scanned the cliff face very carefully, his eyes zigzagging down until he found it – a cleft starting about forty feet above sea level, gradually widening out to about ten feet at the bottom.

"How far does it go back under the cliff?" he thought.

Pierre asked Francois if it was possible to discover the depth of the cleft, or a flaw, but Francois looked at him, in a way that made Pierre think, and feel like a village idiot.

'Oh ask the Germans if they'll run a boat trip out there for you, while the guards look the other way,' he replied scathingly. 'Any boat going too near that cliff would be a home for fish very soon after being caught. Come on Pierre, what can we do with this knowledge? The English are crazy, but not that much. Leave it, please Pierre. I'm going into the harbour now, you are frightening me.'

The boat dipped her bow into the swell, and was soon being tied up on the jetty. Unloading swiftly, Francois was pleased with the price he received, and clasped his arms around Henri and Pierre's shoulders then steered them to the bar he frequented. On the way by the ships' chandlers, they met a German shore patrol, with a lieutenant in command. They put on very glum faces and explained to the German officer what had happened. He flew into a rage directed at the RAF sweinhunds. Afterwards, Henri swore that Francois had tears in his eyes. Pierre and Henri visited Marie's that night, and Henri was well entertained by her, leaving Pierre to draw more accurate maps of the German garrison, approximate position of the arsenal and anti-aircraft guns, as well as the main armament.

The AA batteries were all made up from different people's remarks and sightings, but the size of the arsenal could only be guessed at, by the amount of traffic entering the tunnel displaying the red flag, then re-emerging empty, the wheels and bodies of the lorries bouncing around on the bad track.

Chapter Fourteen

The week went quickly, after a German Naval officer interrogated the three about the E- boat, but when he saw the tears running down the face of Francois, he excused him.

'Very useful things, onions, they give realism to a lie,' Francois burst out laughing as soon as the Germans went down the hill, and towards the jetty.

On being asked by Pierre if he knew any freedom fighters, Francois was vague, but said he would see what he could do about it.

Marie was thrilled with the company of the two pals, and wine flowed freely, with Henri vowing never to touch it again, but Pierre looked and laughed. Marie looked at him, and the afternoons heard the bottles rattling again.

Later one day, Henri went out on one of his numerous errands in the village, shouting over his shoulder that he might not return until the following morning, giving Pierre a chance to read, rest and smoke his pipe.

Marie was able to go out shopping, visiting and gossiping to friends. "I hope her mouth isn't too free and easy with anybody," Pierre thought, giving the log in the grate a kick, to encourage some flames. Away the log burned and glowed, spreading its warmth into the room, making Pierre dozy. He stretched out in the comfortable armchair and fell asleep.

After what seemed five minutes, but was really five hours, Marie came in, soaking wet from the rain, and shivering with cold. Jumping up, Pierre went upstairs to run her a nice hot bath; then returned downstairs to make tea, while Marie languished in her bath. Pierre laid the table, and then warmed the rabbit stew, which was the only meat, apart from the fish.

Eventually Marie came downstairs, with a towel around her, drying her hair vigorously. While he looked at her, she slowly turned round in the firelight. She saw Pierre looking at her. As their eyes met, Marie walked up to him, and dropped the towel. They both reached out, grabbing one another, and with his lips caressing hers, they collapsed on to the sheepskin rug in front of the fire. He kissed her lips and breasts and she pulled him to her, then moaned. They made love, as though it was all there was left to do, sharing each other's pain and ecstasy by the big log fire, before they fell asleep in each other's arms, having found a temporary haven, amidst the chaos of a war they couldn't control. In the middle of the night, they both stirred, with each other in the same position as they were when they fell asleep, pleasuring and loving each other the rest of the night.

The following morning, after a bit of giggling and tickling, the harsh reality of life began, but with the difference of two people, once more enjoying life, and love.

While they were eating their breakfast, Marie remarked that she knew someone that was connected to the Resistance, but she didn't want Pierre taking any risk, as her husband had done, and died, mowed down by a German machine gun, when he was caught stealing weapons from dead guards. While they were sealing the agreement with a kiss, Henri walked in, smiling at the two of them, as they tried to cool down, and return to normal.

Sitting at the table, and producing a bottle of wine, he told Pierre he had found a person who would send a message to England, if he had valuable information. Pierre was glad at last; he'd managed to get someone interested, but was downcast when Henri told him that "they" would be in touch with him soon.

'Still, we are moving,' Henri, said, 'but that's not the only thing that is moving either, I believe we may have a twosome somewhere,' his eyes twinkling as he toasted the couple with his glass of wine.

Later, as Marie, Pierre and Henri walked to see Francois and Louise, they were alarmed to see a new German E-boat tied up. As he gave the boat an inspection via the reflection in a shop window, Pierre noticed the bigger hull, with more weaponry, including AA guns fo'rard and aft. Strolling off seemingly unconcerned, they arrived at Francois's house, and rapped on the door. Francois answered, looked upset so Marie took him indoors to see if there was anything she could do. Poor Louise had tripped and fallen down a few stairs, gashing her head badly. When Francois went to buy some dressing, he was told scornfully, that all such supplies were for the occupational forces of Germany, and French civilians came low in the pecking order. This infuriated Francois, but his neighbours scouted round, and gave him a British Red Cross parcel, with everything he needed.

He asked Pierre if anybody had contacted him yet, and shaking his head, Pierre told him he wanted his information out as soon a possible. Slowly, they walked back to Marie's cottage, each thinking of a nice lady like Louise being treated like that, by the Germans … It was infuriating to both Pierre and Henri, who wished and hoped they could somehow, do something. Marie smiled to herself, as she watched Pierre, burning with passion at this outrage, just like her husband would have done. When they reached the front door she noticed a piece of paper folded into a triangle, just lying by her doorstep. She quickly picked it up and led them inside, where they took their coats off.

Looking at Pierre and Henri, she whispered in a conspiritual fashion, 'Someone will come tonight, so let's light the fire, I'll cook a meal,' then looking at Pierre, commented as to whether there was anything he fancied, and as Henri went out to get some logs, he proved there was.

At nine o'clock, as the three were eating their fish stew, a knock sounded at the door, then as Marie opened it, three men entered swiftly, and silently, guns appearing in their hands as they checked all the rooms, windows and doors. Finally putting their weapons away, one went to the kitchen, lit a cigarette, and then rejoined the other two.

'Well, what's this earth-shattering information you've got,' the leader barked, 'I can't see anything coming from a hovel like this village.'

Instantly, Henri leapt up, his fists opening and closing with temper, demanding to meet the talker's boss. The talker sat down, and one of the other two came over to Pierre and Henri.

'That was the reaction we needed to see, my name is 'erm – Lavell, and I try to lead these German pigs a merry dance, although, I think that's insulting pigs, the crimes that these Germans are committing sometimes. Now give me anything I need, and I will get it to London, but I don't know when the German detector vans do a patrol, so we will send it when we can.'

Pierre gave Lavell his carefully prepared papers with all his measurements and directions, wishing him well, before they drank their wine with a flourish, replacing their glasses on the table. Then on seeing a match strike outside, through the window, as a signal for the all clear, the three went through the door, up the hill, and over the fields.

The three friends looked at each other, smiling, and wishing each other good night. They mounted the stairs, one man in one room, and the other two in another.

Pierre sat on the bed, and pulled Marie to him, his face pressed into her belly, moaning. She rolled on to him and kissed him, her passion for him overflowing with love and desire.

Chapter Fifteen

L ondon looked grey and dull in the dawn, the fog rolling in from the Thames, swirling and twisting, until the fog became trapped in between the high buildings and stayed there, in a blob. Captain Hamilton looked out of the windows at Admiralty House, trying to spot any smoke – the result of the raid last night. Sighing, he used the intercom to ask a Leading Wren if the kettle had boiled. Laughing, Edith said she would go to the galley to chase it up, wishing he would ask for her instead.

Alec sat at his desk, with an RN chart of the French coast in front of him. Comparing the chart with a drawing a navigator made from the message sent from France, the site was easily recognised, but photos were essential, so he noted a request for a photo reconnaissance from the RAF to shoot a film at the target area, if indeed the report was accurate about the guns.

He looked up as Edith came in with his tea, wondering why she was blushing while he thanked her. It was unusual to see a woman blush nowadays, they were out with the Yanks, or other low life usually, not worrying about the immediate or distant future, just riding on the pleasure train, till it came off the rails, which it mostly did. He called in a sub-lieutenant and told him to phone his pal, Squadron Leader Bush, for an appointment at lunch, hoping Nigel could find a suitable aircraft for an hour or so, to do this little job for him. Alec had a feeling about this report, he'd heard of German activity in the area, but nothing definite till now.

Alec drank his tea, wishing he had some rich tea biscuits to go with it. Ah well, he though, the RN issue hard tack biscuits will have to do, and crunched his way into the thick square concoction, after softening it in a steaming hot cup of tea.

Studying the drawings again, he took particular care in sizing up the flaw, in comparison to the so-called gun emplacements ... he found it interesting enough to want to know how far the craft, leading from the flaw, went back into the cliff.

If the guns were what they were said to be, a frontal attack would be suicide, as would be paratroops landing on the top of the cliff. Frogmen? No. Two man torpedoes? Very dangerous.

He had to make an accurate assessment and wait for the 'much-needed photos' and with his report of suitable methods of attack, to Rear Admiral Taylor, the boss of Alec's department, responsible for such expeditions and other tasks.

Alec wanted to go back to sea, but after losing his beloved to a torpedo spread, and losing his right leg, his return was impossible. His input at his desk was, he liked to think, important in its own right, but he liked being at the front end, as his Victoria Cross bore out. His wife and two daughters were so proud when the King pinned the medal on his chest, that his daughters cried with pride, but it all didn't last long, before a Luftwaffe bomb hit the hotel, and all three were killed.

Tears pricked his eyes as he looked at their photos on his desk with black ribbons draped over them, Looking around the room from his desk, the ships from past battles, and officers, long dead and buried, stared back at him. Seeing his walking stick, he picked it up, feeling the names of the survivors of HMS *Hecla* carved into it, realising that most of them had retuned to active duty at sea.

The jangling phone broke his reverie, and picking it up, he heard Nigel's plummy voice, 'What's up Navy, does the Navy need help again?'

Nigel knew this would drive Alec to distraction, but he couldn't resist the temptation, and laughed when Alec took the bait, by saying, 'That definitely is out of order, go and drown yourself in Brylcreem,' then laughing like a drain, he asked Nigel to have lunch, at his expense.

'Rather, Navy never refuse the chance of a free meal,' replied the Air Force officer, 'Will noon be any good at your wardroom in Admiralty House, Navy? See you at noon.'

Alec arranged on the phone for Squadron Leader Bush to be assisted to the wardroom by his steward, who knew the Squadron Leader, and his one leg. "He would have made a good RN officer, if he had used his brain," Alec thought.

The two pals met in the wardroom at noon, and had a couple of gins each, then Alec, eyeing Nigel covertly, remarked how much he would like a photo recce, to fly over a certain area on the French coast. Funnily enough, Alec had the course and bearings in his pocket, would Nigel be interested?

Nigel, jerking his head round, said, 'A Spitfire pilot said something about gun emplacements in that area, the other day, and it just so happens I've had a new Mosquito fly in, fitted with new cameras, so would tomorrow morning be convenient?'

Alec smiled as the two men clumped to the dining room, and after their tinned sausages and powdered potato, Alec bought a bottle of gin for his grinning pal. As they got up to go, the diners saw the VC on the RN uniform, and the DFC and bar on the Air Force uniform. Silence reigned until the two had left the room, then it sounded like a nursery school at a football match.

After a fusillade of 'Navy', and various places to place Brylcreem Alec and Nigel parted with a laugh, and a promise to dine together in the near future, if the war and their responsibilities allowed them to.

The following day started with drizzle, which was good, as the Luftwaffe hadn't flown, giving the giant called London a brief respite, which was better than none, but "a few nights' rest would be nice," Alec thought, checking that the blackout on the windows was pulled back fully.

Sitting down behind his desk and parking his stick, he contacted Leading Wren Taylor, to see if tea was on offer, and with a smile asked if the biscuit tin had been replenished.

Mysteriously, Edith replied, 'We'll have to see what we can see', and giving him a pretty smile, hurried on her errand. Returning shortly afterwards with a tea tray, she placed it on his desk, and was turning to go, when Alec said, 'Take a seat, and join me for a cup of tea,' then looking at the tray, saw the American-made biscuits lying there.

Edith smiled and told him to keep them in his desk, then sitting down, she drank the tea, noticing with pleasure, how much he was enjoying his snack.

"At last he's noticed me," Edith thought, "I wonder if it's too soon after his wife's death... mmm... I think I'll play it as it comes."

Finishing her tea, she chatted to him about the three W's, War, Weather and Winston, which, she could tell, he enjoyed a lot.

Catching up on his paperwork, namely, dates of ship refits, took most of the morning, then he looked forward to not doing much that afternoon, until he saw a despatch rider pull up at the front door. Running up to Alec's office, he gave the package to Edith, as he had a few more packages to deliver and she, knowing this was what Alec was waiting for, ran into his office.

'Whoa, not so fast young lady, if you fell and hurt yourself what would I do without you?' Alec said, his voice joking.

Edith smiled to herself, as she thought about the question, just loving him all the more.

Grabbing the package, he unwrapped the contents, and pinned the photos to a blackboard. His eyes went straight to the flaw in the cliffs on the photo, and he whistled in surprise. The cleft at sea level was measured six foot eight, so the Frenchman was quite accurate. Moving to the next one, he nearly tripped when he forgot the artificial leg, but luckily Edith grabbed his arm. Looking at her in surprise, he saw the worry on her face. Reaching for a high stool, he squatted on it, thanking Edith, and looking at the offending limb, feeling embarrassed. He continued looking at the photos with his magnifying glass, then slapping the blackboard with his hand, he told Edith to look at those "bloody great big guns", immediately apologising, and giving the rest of the pictures a long hard perusal.

Returning, and sitting at his desk, with the aid of a few books and some pieces of paper, he made a very rough model of the target area, with pencils forming the jetty in the village. Standing up, and using his stick this time, he viewed it from different compass points, first of all, from an aircraft's view then from sea level. The puzzle must be solved, Alec thought, guns of that calibre could cause havoc on the RN and MN alike. Looking at his 'model' from an inland angle was quickly dispensed with, and he resumed his views from seaward.

Following up an idea, he looked up the list of ships held in reserve for a variety of reasons: antiquated, too expensive to repair, or waiting to be cannibalised, to keep other ships at sea in particular, destroyers, ships that were built, purely for speed, with either anti- aircraft weapons or anti-submarine equipment, ships looking so badly damaged they just about stayed afloat. Looking at the last list, he noticed a destroyer named *Tempest*. She'd caught a bomb from an aircraft, and looked knackered. Alec nearly carried on reading the list, but going back to her, he found the reference number, then went to the filing cabinet, to get the damage record.

He must remember his bloody stick, he shouted inwardly!

Settling down with the ship's original drawings, and photos of the damage as she is now, he studied her upper deck with the inadequate armament and her four tall funnels, Tracing a copy of the ship from the port side, he worked into the early hours, jumping every time the Wren gave him a cup of Kai, the famous RN drink that watchkeepers through the night enjoyed. Kai is a very thick, scalding, hot chocolate drink, very sweet, and sometimes flavoured with Nelson's Blood.

Time after time, when Edith entered the office, he told her to go home, and get some sleep, or told her that her boyfriend was outside, waiting, but she looked him in the eye, and said 'no he isn't,' and left it at that.

Studying the tracings, he looked away to rest his eyes, and noticed a cutaway of a German destroyer. "Oh, if only *Tempest* looked like that, we might have a chance," Alec thought. Then discovering his cup was empty, and wanting to visit the toilet, he took his stick, and walked out of his office, past his Leading Wren's desk, where he was not surprised to find her sleeping like a baby. Creeping as best he could, he relieved himself, and then crept back to his office. Levelling with Edith, he felt a flood of pity for her, even though she was the admiral's daughter.

Bending over her silently, he gently touched her hair with his lips, and stole away, like a thief in the night.

Meanwhile, Edith kept her eyes closed, with a soft smile curving her lips slightly. Ten minutes later, on "waking up", she went into Alec's office, where he was studying the pictures and drawings, and as she looked over his shoulder, she realised it was the old *Tempest* he was looking at, and pointed out the worst of the damage below deck, which wasn't in the photos. Only three boilers were repairable, and one steam turbine main engine was the same. Alec asked her how she knew. And replying, she said she knew a member of the ship's company, who escaped, but was killed on *Hecla*, en route to Russia.

Picking his stick up, and rising, he turned round, and put his arm around her shoulder and told her to push off home. He would go up to his flat, until he came back to work in four hours, but he gave her a make and mend the following day that is, a day off. She laughed as she wished him goodnight; then they went their separate ways.

Four hours later, Alec entered his office, looking and feeling terrible. Then he noticed his desk was tidy, drawing folded and put away in his desk drawers, and a cup of tea, steaming hot, waiting on his desk.

'Edith, what the hell are you doing here? I gave you a

make and mend, and now you're here, please tell me why,' he said gently.

It's funny, but he was pleased she was here.

Secretly, he thought she was delicious, but who would want a one-legged man of thirty-eight? Sitting down and parking his stick, his desk was like a tip, five minutes later.

He was poring over the papers and his "model" carefully.

Clearing his crockery, Edith suddenly leant forward, kissed Alec's forehead, and then quickly ran out, blushing. 'You're a wolf in sheep's clothing,' he called through the door, then realised, that was it! Deception! Disguise the *Tempest* as a badly damaged German destroyer, limping along the coast, which would be partially true!

Making dozens of tracings of the *Tempest*, even with Edith helping Alec, took a long time. Matching the hull of *Tempest*, to a German equivalent was time-consuming, they were too beamy, or not beamy enough, too long, too short, too light or too heavy.

"We're on the losing side at the moment, there is no hull like a German hull," Alec thought aloud, as the two of them went through Jane's Fighting Ships catalogue again.

Edith shrieked, jolting him out of his thoughts.

'A Blucher class anti-submarine,' Edith yelped, 'Give or take a ton, identical, but a bit more beamy, but if she had a list on, who's going to notice?'

Two hours later, they made a *Blucher* out of *Tempest* on paper, of a typical German design, with two funnels, very fast, and grossly underarmed, carrying only two turrets, each with twin four inch guns and quadruple sets of torpedo tubes, with heavy machine guns scattered over the upper deck. Checking for accuracy for the tenth time, Alec and Edith were over the moon, and nearly danced round the office, when Alec remembered he was light in the leg department so hugged instead, much nicer, Edith thought.

Making an appointment the next day, to see the Admiral was surprisingly quick, thanks to Edith's enthusiasm; her father caught on to things faster than his daughter realised. The meeting resulted in Alec and Edith going to Portsmouth for a week to survey the *Tempest* with a bod from a department glorifying in the title, E(C)5.

Edith puzzled over the title for a few minutes as they drove down to Pompey, but failed to translate it, whereupon the bod, whose name was David Bell, told her it stood for Espionage, brackets, Clandestine, then the floor number the office was on.

'Well,' Edith said, 'of all the stupid titles, that is the limit, you need something more dramatic than that.'

After he had finished laughing, he mentioned that it was also a district in London of unsavoury reputation!

Alec replied dryly, 'That's about right then, they don't get everything wrong anyway,' which set Edith off, while David looked sheepish.

Later, while stopping at a pub, Alec explained to Edith, that David was a full colonel. Looking at him, Edith asked why he hadn't told her at first, whereupon Alec explained to her, that military rank was not important, it's honour because of his intelligence, and the work he was doing, gave him some clout if he needed it.

They arrived in Pompey, just in time to hear the all-clear after an air raid, and stopped on Portsdown Hill to watch the anti-aircraft gunfire from Southsea common. The tracer and the searchlight arced into the sky, tracking the fleeing bombers. Looking to the right, towards the dockyard, flames and smoked belched from the shattered homes near the dockyard, and could be seen clearly, from the top of the hill, The ships had fallen silent, simply because ships in the dockyard never carried a lot of ammunition, obviously because, as would-be targets, if they were hit, Pompey would be no more.

Continuing on to the barracks, they saw some of the awful damage done to the city, amazed, that so shortly after an air raid, people got on with everyday life as though nothing had happened. They didn't notice that the guts were being torn out of their homes. Giving sighs of relief, as they pulled into the main gate a regulation petty officer, and two crushers, inspected the car, and their identity cards, after which Royal Marines escorted them to their different sleeping billets.

The following day, a Royal Marine awoke them, leaving Alec up the creek, because of his artificial leg which had to be fitted, and the time it took him to do it. He knew he had to rush to get a look in for a breakfast.

Fifteen minutes later, he was stomping into the dining room, and found David already sitting at a table.

Alec said, 'Good morning David, oh these damned reveilles, I'd got used to London, no bugles in the middle of the night, and no struggle to get breakfast,'

'Well Alec, the table was reserved for you and me, by Edith I believe,' replied David giving a sideways glance at Alec.

A steward appeared, carrying two meals: powdered scrambled egg on toast, with tinned sausage.

After they finished, and drank their tea, they phoned for Edith to meet them in the wardroom when she could. Phoning the MT section took a few minutes, so by the time the transport had arrived, and the motor launch booked, Edith was waiting in the foyer.

They were off again in the Hillman, looking at the variety of ships in dock for something or other, and also the thousands of dockyard workers, much scorned among RN personnel, but doing a valuable service, by keeping the ships in a fighting mood.

Chapter Sixteen

Getting into the powerful launch, they moved away from the jetty, when cleared. The coxswain adjusted the bucket gear, (Kitchener's steering gear), and the launch shot away towards Fareham Creek. Slowing down by HMS *Excellent*, the RN gunnery-training depot, they came across three decrepit destroyers alongside each other. Discovering that the *Tempest* was on the port side of the amidships destroyer, they motored gently round the sterns.

The *Tempest* looked dead, with one of her four funnels collapsed, and the ship's side grey couldn't be seen for rust. Carefully climbing up the gangway they looked into the gaping hole caused by the bomb. It had done a lot of damage, but Alec and David talked about the possibility of a superficial repair, after all, the ship would only be used for fifty miles at the most, and appear damaged as well, which would save on the repair bill!

Going below, they looked at the wrecked machinery, but realising they would only need one boiler with one main engine and turbine generator, the possibilities were positive, and after stumbling around down below, they emerged to a watery sunshine, then looking down at the launch, they saw the coxswain waving a flask at them. Looking at each other, the three of them nearly broke into a race, but remembered Alec's lower appendage shortage. It allowed Edith the chance to climb down the gangway first, luckily, she was wearing slacks.

Sitting in the cabin of the launch, they accepted the 'swain's offer of a cup of tea, and asked him to stay tied up to the *Tempest* for a while, to allow them to have a discussion, and study a few points, and have ideas accepted, or thrown out. Edith kept shorthand notes, mainly for their own convenience, but she mentioned the fact that they needed lot of photos, to use as a model for the workers who would be doing the job, Alec hoped. As the three and the coxswain were ruminating, the air raid siren suddenly blasted into life, silencing all talk as they put their tin hats on. The 'swain dived into the cabin, offering the others a cigarette. They refused, but he asked if they minded if he had one.

Alec waved his hand, saying, 'Carry on 'swain, I doubt if they'll come over the dockyard, and up in this direction, especially with the naval gunners in HMS *Excellent.*'

The 'swain saw the VC ribbon for the first time, and his mouth fell open as he saluted it.

The cabin on the launch became a sitting room for Alec, Edith and David, all sitting with the coxswain, discussing the war, and the ways to stop it. "It was causing so much misery and pain to the people of England, centuries of war," Edith thought, "and we we're still like children, frightened, and reacting to it by lashing out at the cause." A pompous, strutting peacock had caused this conflict, because of the size of his ego. Edith looked up at Alec, silently loving him and wishing she could tell him via telepathy. Alec, after looking at David, and the 'swain, rested his eyes on Edith, and then wondered if he could ask her out one evening. He then answered his own question with a negative; after all, why should she? He loved the way she blushed, as she was starting to now, and realised she probably knew what he was thinking already, and getting ready to laugh.

Funny creatures, women, they—; the all clear sounded, realising that no bombers had flown over the beleaguered city, so looking skywards, he thanked whoever was around at that moment.

Eventually, they pushed off from the Tempest, and made their way back to the jetty, where, saying thank you to the swain, Alec received several salutes from enlisted men, all from a variety of ships, either working up, or in for refits. Edith scooted off to the WRNS quarters, wanting to walk, while Alec and David meandered back to barracks. David's remarks gave Alec a lot of hope, the temporary work required on Tempest was nothing compared to her next voyage, and the results required from her. All they had to do was sell the idea to the Admiral.

'She loves you, you know,' said David, skirting round some traffic.

'What on earth are you talking about?' replied a stunned Alec, 'I'm ten years older than Edith, her fathers my boss, and I'm short of a leg, so what do you think she sees in me, because I'm damned if I know.'

David looked at him, and smiled, 'Alec I haven't known you very long, but you do your job well, you control people splendidly, but you are blind.'

Alec looked puzzled and David continued to smile as they went into the wardroom to order their drinks and lunch, and consider their return to London.

Phoning Edith two hours later, Alec asked her to organise their car and driver, to collect them all outside the wardroom.

Getting into the car was such relief for Alec, the escapade on the *Tempest*, had chafed, and rubbed his stump, so putting his hand through the hole in his trouser pocket, he loosened the straps a shade, and massaged the stump gently. Feeling a nudge, he turned to see Edith holding some cream out to him, to rub on. Thanking her, he held her hand a bit too long, while Edith blushed; David sat in the front, smiling all over his face!

They had a comfortable ride back to London, arriving at David's home first, then on to Admiralty House. Dismissing the driver, they walked around Nelson's Column slowly, his stump settling down a bit now, with the soothing cream in place. Sitting down on the low wall, he suddenly pulled her down to his side, and gently kissed her lips. They clung together in the darkness, Alec stroking her face, when he was appalled to find her face wet with tears. Apologising profusely, Alec was immediately grabbed by Edith, and kissed on the lips, so exquisitely.

Laughing, she gave Alec his stick, and hand in hand, they walked back to Admiralty House. Phoning for a car, he bade her goodnight, and drew her into the blackness of the doorway; kissing her so sweetly it was eternal.

The voice of the Royal Marine sentry unseen or heard by them, startled them as he wished them goodnight! In the dark, both of them turned scarlet, as Alec put her in the car, and limped back into Admiralty House, where he collapsed on his bunk, after removing his tin leg, and dressing the sore and bleeding stump, but he was happy, in a puzzling way, that he thought could not happen to him again. He was blessed with sleep very quickly, Edith finding her place in his dreams at once.

Chapter Seventeen

lec was so blasé about the air raids, he slept right through until his steward awoke him with a cup of tea, Last night came flooding back, and he vowed to find the sentry who acted as their chaperone. Walking slowly to his office, Edith caught him up, and full of pleasantries, said good morning, looked around, and then blew him a kiss. "She didn't blush," Alec thought to himself, manoeuvring behind his desk, before sitting down. A cup of tea followed a few minutes later, followed by a kiss and a cuddle.

'I'm going to have a serious talk with you young lady,' smiled Alec, as he opened his mail. One letter from the senior WRNS officer informed him, that leading Wren E. Taylor had been promoted to petty officer. Passing the letter over to Edith they both drank a toast with tea.

After a few notes and suggestions, Edith went to her desk, and typed out everything in the minutes book, including the ship to be used, the amount of repair work to be done, and the approximate weight of the explosive in the bow, together with the new silhouette of the *Tempest*. Even the extent of listing to port the dockyard would need to build into the ship, simply by flooding port oil tanks with sea water.

Getting into the lift, he carried on thinking how to get the old man, the admiral, to see his plan, and approve it. The lift jolted to a stop, and Alec stepped out, his stump not hurting as much as it had been.

He walked to the admiral's reception, where, sitting down for fifteen minutes, he was ushered into the inner sanctum. "Surprise, surprise," Alec thought, as he saluted, and seeing David Bell there, sitting, down, and pointing to a diagram of some kind, but, getting nearer, realised it was the Tempest drawing.

'Good morning Alec,' said the old man, 'have you bumped into any sentries lately?' and gave a big smile. 'However, this idea of yours, is it any good? Will it work, and how much will it cost to carry on? The Germans put the guns into commission yesterday, a tanker was bracketed with the things and only got away because it was running light, and washing its fuel tanks out, before refilling them with seawater to stabilise the ship, on its voyage to the USA. So within reason, it would be an advantage to put them out of commission Alec, they're dangerous. David Bell here tells me it's a feasible plan, but two things worry me. The cost of the undertaking, and what would you do to raise a crew? It would have to be volunteers, hell's teeth, you couldn't give jolly jacks a draft chit for this sort of operation.'

Alec's eyes twinkled as he answered, 'Finding an officer is easy. I know of one in a shore billet, who wouldn't hesitate to put his hand up, and if there was any of the crew of his last ship still shore based, they would too. After all, we don't need a full crew, just necessary personnel for the running of the ship. The price, I believe, justifies the end product, and would deprive the Germans of a particularly nasty weapon site.'

David Bell agreed completely, saying the plan was simplicity itself, and the adjustment to the *Tempest* wouldn't be too expensive. Then, if they asked for volunteers from the dockyard workers to do lots of overtime on the Tempest, he was sure the plan would succeed, if they could find a reliable officer to do the job.

Admiral Taylor looked at the two men in front of him, looking for all the world like expectant fathers, studying what cargo was being transported.

He said abruptly, 'Get to it, and if I can help by pulling rank, strings, or anything concerning red tape, contact me and I shall want a progress report every week, but tell me captain. Who is the officer you have in mind for this escapade, and what was his last ship?'

Alec looked the admiral square in the eye and said, 'Well sir, I think you know full well that I shall volunteer, then I will at least be doing something.'

The admiral smiled, but only with his mouth, and leaning on his elbows, whispered, 'If you think I will allow one of the best assets this department has to volunteer for such a mission, you need your bumps read. So you think you haven't done anything? Well who knocked this plan up, and who will explain to my daughter, that the man she's secretary for, is insane, so before you volunteer, don't bother Alec, I'm promoting you to commodore as of now, so being of flag rank, you can't skipper a ship. I understand that Edith has been rated up to PO so why not get her away to training school, and get her commissioned. That way, the two of you will be working together,' and for the first time ever, Alec saw the admiral wink very quickly, he immediately returned the wink, then the Admiral, Alec and David shook hands, vowing to rebuild *Tempest* themselves if they had to.

Alec and David excused themselves finally, both relieved that things had started. Popping into Alec's office, they were surprised by Edith, such a pretty sight in civvies, giving her typewriter a beating.

Looking up, she informed Alec and David, 'The admiral has ordered me to apply to the admiral of Portsmouth dockyard, to supply workmen and materials, to rebuild to an approximate degree, HMS *Tempest* to look like a *Blucher* destroyer, with a built in list and all the unnecessary bulkheads removed, all to the directions as drawn on the superimposed plan of the *Tempest*.

'It will go to the Admiral at Portsmouth, in the morning commodore,' said Edith, her face looking up at him. David walked out, smiling.

Kissing Edith passionately, she was longing for him, as much as Alec was for her, but pulling away from her gently, he whispered in her ear, 'I'm older than you, and what would your father think, a one-legged desk jockey. Edith, I love you too much to spoil your life. When you get your commission, the world will be at your feet.'

'Stop it Alec, I… um… I adore you, and my father knows all about my feelings for you, so he's blessed us. He loves you as the son he always wanted, but never had, so my darling, you see, we are made for each other, we are in love, and so can we be lovers? We haven't hurried like a lot of peo…'

In the morning, they lay alongside each other, not wondering or caring, just loving. Loving each other completely but the spell was broken by Alec's steward trying to open the locked door.

'Just a minute,' Alec called, hurriedly getting up to strap his leg on.

Edith looked at him, 'You dear man,' is all she said as tears of contentment ran wet tracks down her cheeks.

Getting up, she beat Alec to the bathroom, deservedly earning a smacked bottom as she ran past. Squealing with laughter, she shouted, 'I won't be long,' leaving Alec putting his trousers on.

Minutes later, she came out again, unashamedly naked, and started to dress. Alec was looking at her and thinking, what a wondrous sight and she loves me! Making a grab for her, she easily evaded him, causing him to fall on the bed.

'No I don't think we ought to go back to bed Alec, or do you? Personally, I don't think we will have time, although I must admit, it sounds nice,' she smiled, and went into the bathroom, to put her face right.

Meeting her in his office after breakfast, they kissed, then she told him the letter to the admiral in Portsmouth had been signed, and was on its way to Portsmouth by despatch rider.

They kissed, and for days, they kissed, waiting for a reply. When it did come, they read it, and on reading that they would be in charge of all the work, they were overjoyed! A few weeks in Pompey together would be perfect, as good as a holiday. Then they remembered the work to be done, but they would enjoy it they promised each other.

Organising their car and packing their kit didn't take long, and as Alec walked out of Admiralty House, so his car pulled up, with Edith in the back, and grinning like a Cheshire cat, who'd found the cream. Getting out, the driver told Alec, 'PO Wren Taylor will be your driver sir, on the orders of Admiral Taylor,' Alec thanked him, as Edith put their kit bags into the boot, then she opened the door for Alec, and before they knew it, they were off to Pompey. Alec asked Edith about petrol, whereupon Edith produced a full book of petrol coupons, stamped 'on urgent war work', grinned, and blew him a kiss in the mirror. The journey went very comfortably, stopping for a meal at Guildford, where most of the London to Portsmouth military traffic stopped. Restaurants were few and far between nowadays, and the menu was very plain, but so it was for everybody.

Portsmouth hadn't changed, the Germans were still bombing it, but the dockyard seemed to leave a charmed life. Nelson's flagship HMS *Victory* was still a floating storeroom, and a seaman school, people laughing and joking, as though there was peace throughout the world, discussing shops that had, or didn't have cigarettes in stock, of pubs with, or without beer, just like London really but a lot smaller.

The barracks looked grim and forbidding, as the RPO and the crushers inspected the car, and their ID cards. The VC ribbon speeded them up a bit, but King's regulations and Admiralty instructions were King's regulations and Admiralty instructions, and they had to be strictly adhered to, never doubt it.

Driving to the car park, behind the wardroom, Edith carried Alec's kitbag, muttering about lazy bar stewards, but Alec may have misheard.

In the foyer, he gave Edith her instructions for tomorrow, gave his kitbag to a steward, and then went to his cabin, to have a shower, and a rest, until tomorrow, when things would begin to move.

Next morning Alec appeared at the office of the admiral, to discuss the movement of Tempest into dry-dock. He pointed to the mountain of paperwork, and asked Alec, which was top priority. Admiral Boyd was too old for serving at sea, but unfortunately, he felt too old for deskwork as well. The fact that he was making room for a younger man of flag rank, to serve at sea, was the only saving grace, but there was no let up.

Ships entered harbour continually, in dire need of repair and rebuild, or refit, all dry-dock jobs. Perhaps it would be possible to secure the ship to the jetty and start work on the upper deck, and machinery spaces, suggested Alec, a hope springing to mind. The ship needed a bottom scrape, but that could wait until the dry dock was available, he continued, as long as they were assured of the workforce they needed. But did she need a bottom scrape, with the short job she had been earmarked for?

Admiral Boyd smiled at this suggestion, having noticed Alec missing a leg, put it into his mind that this could be his successor, enabling him to retire at long last, especially with the ribbon on Alec's chest. Boyd agreed immediately, ordering two tugs to take *Tempest* from her present mooring, and tying her up near the heavy machinery shop.

Two hours later saw Edith and Alec on board the leading tug named '*Hercules*', while the tug controlling the stern of *Tempest*, was named '*Cyclops*'. These two powerful tugs, usually used for moving battleships moved *Tempest* away from the other two destroyers very easily, and having so much power, were easily in control, nudging the destroyer exactly into where she was required. Edith watched in wonder, as *Tempest* 'curtsied' to her, taking up the slack on the springs.

Boarding the *Tempest* again, Alec and Edith watched as the tugs dropped their tows, and scooted off for stand-easy!

As the dockside crane lowered the gangway on the *Tempest*, a dockyard worker came up it to secure it to the ship. He started to say something, saw the medal ribbon of the VC hummed and hawed, did his job and went ashore, thinking that was the idiot who was putting this old load of razor blades, to sea again. Alec and Edith looked at the ship they had saved from the breakers' yard, and both felt it was their own, so they felt very proud.

Chapter Eighteen

Making *Tempest's* bridge their office, Edith pinned the before and after drawings on a board she managed to scrounge, then with two desks, chairs, two phones and a typewriter, supplied by Admiral Boyd, they broke the work into five phases, and with the drawings in different colours as the work was expected to progress, it was easily understandable, for the dockyard workers, as they sometimes went deaf when it was near stand easy! The work started the following day mainly flame cutting, and removing all weapons and bulkheads that weren't required. Alec kept marching around, like a clockwork toy, but never winding down, checking measurements, making suggestions and arguing, so at the end of the week, *Tempest* was completely flat from the first funnel, all the way down to the tiller flat.

"Work's going well," Alec thought, "I might get a bunk fitted in the captain's cabin."

The reason for this was stump trouble again, gallivanting all over the ship. Edith kept telling him, begging him to take it easier, and as they were talking, he leaned forward to kiss her, overbalanced, and hit his head on his desk. As he lay unconscious Edith phoned for an RN ambulance, then contacted her father in London.

On arriving at RNH Haslar, Alec had his head stitched

and had to stay in the hospital, when they saw the state of the stump again. Then the doctors left the ward in a huddle, leaving Alec in Edith's tender care.

Next day, in swept Admiral Taylor, bristling with anger and worry.

'What the bloody hell are you up to? Edith told me you've been working twenty five hours a day, well Alec, if you want to see *Tempest* finished, you'd better let Edith take care of you, she's told me about you two,' then lowering his voice, said, 'In case you feel like asking her the matrimonial question, I do approve.'

Alec looked astonished, as the admiral finished.

'I don't have time to ask her, until the *Tempest* is finished,' Alec explained, 'but I'm sure Edith feels the same as I do, but nevertheless, I'm grateful to you for telling me, all I've got to do, is convince Edith about *Tempest*.'

Unknown to Alec, Edith had crept up beside him, and when she shouted, 'I'm convinced, Alec held his heart and pretended to faint.

'What a bright pair of lunatics I am most fortunate to know, still, it takes one to know one I suppose,' said the old man, laughing as the two kissed.

After the specialist had altered the tin leg, and his stump had healed up nicely, Alec was taken to the admiral's house, to rest for a week, and as luck would have it, the admiral stayed at his club in London, while Edith was given some leave as well.

Alec didn't moan about his nurse, in fact, most times, if not all the time, she was very obliging. Sometimes Alec used the bath chair the admiral had borrowed for him, so Edith could push him around in it. Sadly, the week went past, all too quickly, his stump feeling comfortable, and snug in the socket. Alec felt confident about returning to work the following Monday, Edith was his permanent driver now and Alec found they frequently went into the countryside a lot, and succeeded in getting lost, especially when the sun was out.

Tempest was a different ship, her bridge needed a little bit of cosmetics, but the two funnels were there, and the dummy upper deck building was nearly finished. A German turret made with wood was in place on the foc'sle, and wooden torpedo tubes were positioned midships.

Tempest was going into dry-dock the following day and Alec as well as Edith, felt very close to the ship. It was their inspiration that had caused the Tempest to rise from the dead, in fact, her name should be Phoenix, but instead of being born in flames, she would die.

Alec continued to inspect, discover and suggest, right up to the Tempest entering dry-dock, but from then on, the dockyard workers took over, working day and night, isolating two boilers that were too badly damaged, and with a dockyard crane, lifted the starboard main engine turbine out. As soon as that was removed, welders moved in to replace the portion of decking that had been removed, for the easy removal of the engine.

Steam pipes were replaced, and two pumps had to be cannibalised form the Tempest's twin, as she was swinging on a buoy. Funnel uptakes were cleared and cleaned. The two boilers had a boiler clean and some tubes were replaced, the first since nobody knew when. One diesel generator was working well, but most of the hydraulics were ruined, so a new system was fitted direct to the rudder, after all was said and done, they all wanted the ship, to answer to her helm.

Flooding the dry-dock, *Tempest* was thoroughly checked for any leaks, then one of her boilers was flashed up, and it was running on maximum pressure of three hundred pounds per square inch. Slowly, so slowly, like an old woman pulling herself up some stairs, *Tempest* dragged herself into the basin, where she enjoyed cheers from the dockyard workers. Tying the "old girl" up, Alec stood on the port wing of the bridge, putting an arm round Edith, and looked proudly on, as their "offspring" bobbed and curtsied alongside the wall.

Finding the right shade of grey for a German ship, she had her make-up put on, but avoided the hole, through which the bomb had gone. Alec thought it labour-saving by using it to his own advantage, the Germans' own work.

Quite apt really, Edith noted, as she typed endless reports for Admirals Taylor and Boyd. It was a shame to put a severe list on *Tempest*, she looked so smart, but sinister, when the swastika was flown for a couple of minutes, to take photos to give to the RN and the RAF for identification purposes. In fact, the workers booed a lot, proving the *Tempest* looked very realistic!

Phoning the draft office, Edith made an appointment for Alec to see the man in charge of the volunteer section. Alec explained what he wanted and the number he needed. He realised the ship was not going on a long voyage, and worked out the minimum he could get by with Mr Henderson, who was in charge of the volunteer section. He asked Alec how soon he needed them, as though he was dealing in cattle.

He got up Alec's nose with his attitude, and Alec wondered why he wasn't in any of the services, but he said loudly, 'About a week at the most.'

Nodding his head, Henderson was about to dismiss Alec, when he noticed that Alec only had one leg. Then, when he saw the VC ribbon, he turned white.

'Listen you disreputable lump of pig's vomit, when you're half as good as the men I will be privileged to lead, you can come to me to beg their forgiveness, but until then, you're answerable to me to find these volunteers, which obviously, you will do,' roared Alec, leaning on his desk, his face, three inches from the pig's vomit.

Straightening up, he tapped his stick on the desk in front of the quivering man, and said in a normal voice, 'Don't forget will you. I need them in a week.'

He nailed Henderson to the wall with his angry piercing eyes.

Reaching the pavement, Alec cooled off with a pint of beer in the first pub he came to, where Edith, worried as she waited in the car, found him. They drove home, where they got down to the business of – where were we – oh yes I remember, and Alec gave her a kiss to see if she could remember.

The following week consisted of refuelling *Tempest*, and loading the cargo, all of it fo'rard of the boiler room. Two torpedoes were fixed to the bows, three feet below sea level, the brackets clamping them very tightly to the hull. The percussion caps, easily fitted just before the *Tempest* sailed, waited in their boxes on the bridges. Alec checked and rechecked everything, comparing the *Tempest* with the *Blucher* class destroyers in every way. *Tempest* was hidden from prying eyes, in case a German pilot got through the anti-aircraft fire, and managed to return to Germany.

Edith and Alec had a lazy weekend, listening to the wireless and drinking what they could bring home from the local.

'You know Alee, if there wasn't a war on, life could be wonderful,' Edith mused, sitting in the huge lounge. 'The *Tempest* is all ready, apart from the crew, so did you mean it, when you said we would get married when the *Tempest* project was finished?'

Alec looked at her, a flood of love and tenderness rushing to his lips, as he transmitted his feelings on to Edith, and she, on receiving them, bounced them back.

When they reached her bedroom upstairs, feminine clothing formed a line from the door to the bed, leaving Alee in no doubt as to where she and he wanted to be.

'This is my promise,' Alec said, caressing her shoulder and breast, 'I shall marry you as soon as we can, after the *Tempest* saga is over and finished,' then they continued with what they where doing.

Chapter Nineteen

Monday morning brought Alec and Edith the letters they were waiting for. The drafting officer had found the volunteers they needed to form a skeleton crew.

The men's names were as follows:

Lieutenant Commander	Rogers
Lieutenant	Chambers
Stoker PO	Brown
Leading Stoker	Hall
Stoker	Denton
Stoker	Forbes
Seaman PO	Riley
Leading Seaman	Thompson
AB	Dawson
AB	Cooper

The letter then went on to ask Alec when he required to meet the men at the *Tempest*, they were all in barracks, and keen to know what was expected of them. After a brief discussion Alec phoned the drafting office, and suggested Wednesday at 0815. The office said they would contact and confirm later that day.

Alec mentioned that no kit would be required, just clothes

they wore at sea, on watch, which for stokers was overalls and for seamen, number eight's. The ship was in the basin, having her boilers steaming, and the generator producing *Tempest's* power, partly to bed in all the valves and pumps, and give the dockyard workers a bit of overtime, but *Tempest* was alive again! The list hadn't been put on yet; the CO would flood the port tanks when the *Tempest* neared her destination. Tuesday was a day of nerves for Edith and Alec, checking the "cargo" was all fast, and couldn't move. Both were amazed at the amount of explosives that was carefully packed into the bows, all ready to go forth and give the Germans, both a surprise, and a headache; the most lethal weapons were particularly destructive. Alec had high hopes of them entering the flaw, and exploding, widening the gap, thus enabling *Tempest* to ram into the gap more, then with the rest of the nitro-glycerine, and jellied petrol mixed with high explosive exploding, surely some damage would be done. Alec hoped he and David Bell had calculated the force accurately.

As Edith and Alec left the *Tempest,* she looked down at the bows. It would only add to the realism, for when, or if the Germans saw her, she would have the look of being badly damaged.

Alec was early on Wednesday, and while Edith made a big pot of tea, Alec waited on board by the gangway, for the Tilly (utility bus), to bring the men to the ship. When it arrived they fell in on the jetty, waiting for Alec to inspect them. As Alec came down the gangway, the waiting ranks saw that he was missing a leg, and they all looked at each other, all wondering what a German destroyer was doing in Pompey.

Calling them to attention, PO Riley saluted Alec, and with Lieutenant Commander Rogers, escorted Alec down the two ranks. Eyes saw the ribbon on his chest, and mouths either fell open, or lips pursed together, wondering how he'd earned it.

'Right men,' said Alec. Then turning to Lieutenant Commander Rogers, he said, 'Bring them on board will you, I'm not prepared to explain what we're up to, or trying to do, here on the jetty. Anyway there's some tea in the bridge.'

Looking at his list, Alec asked, 'Do you mind if I call you by your Christian name? Not in front of the men of course, but as you can imagine, I'm not keen on being formal when we are not in public.'

The "crew" of the *Tempest* filed on to the ship, and made their way to the bridge, where they all sat down for an informal chat on the task to be undertaken.

'If anybody doesn't fancy going for a quick sail to France, and back, they can walk away now, and nobody would make them feel guilty. You all have a right to get up and go. I would rather know now, this mission is urgent, and it will hurt the Germans.'

Alec prayed nobody would drop out. They didn't!

Nobody moved, only Edith, as she passed mugs of scalding hot tea among them.

'Well that's the nasty part done with, but it applies all the time, right up to sailing time, but I'm sure you would like to see *Tempest* as she is down below,' finished Alec, drinking his tea and appraising the men in his mind, while consulting their service records.

The machinery spaces were first, being the means of getting where they were going, then the cargo was last, the reason why they were going. The stokers talked to the dockyard workers, asking them if she was steady, and the condition of the pumps, as well as the sprayers, and the accuracy of the gauges, for oil pressure, and steam pressure. Realising the water tanks would be full of seawater; fresh water would be carried for washing or tea. The *Tempest* wouldn't have time for anything else.

Calling them all together, Alec asked them what they thought of the job. Bob Rogers brought up the problem of getting off before *Tempest* hit her target.

'There will be a twenty foot launch, with two Rolls Royce engines, swung on the davits on the starboard side. You will have a practice, to find the quickest way to abandon the *Tempest*,' said Alec.

Bob Rogers came up with a brilliant idea namely to light a fire on the quarterdeck, to distract the Germans' eyes from the launch being lowered on the other side of *Tempest*.

'Terrific, Lieutenant Commander, that's what is needed, ideas to make the ship look genuine to the Germans, any silly little thing, so let's have them, and there might be some neat rum going around, unknown to me of course,' Alec said, the last remark in a stage whisper. 'So let's get you victualled in barracks, separated from everybody unfortunately, because we don't want too many ears to hear too much,' Alec warned, 'The walls have ears as they say.'

Sitting in the bridge together after the men left, Alec wrote down his thoughts on the volunteers, while Edith made tea, and tidied up around the bridge. Drinking the tea, and kissing, they eventually typed and sent by despatch rider, the final report to Admiral Taylor, knowing he would be pleased with what Alec said about the men. Alec glanced at his copy of the list of the men.

Lieutenant Commander R Rogers
Reliable, and takes his work very seriously, someone to rely on.

Lieutenant D Chambers
Ex-submariner. Known to hate being ashore. Trustworthy and very easygoing, good to have on your side.

Stoker PO Brown
A typical Stoker PO. Knows the RN wouldn't exist without 'Stoker PO's', Very fond of drinking, but a good hand.

Leading Stoker Hall. (Nobby)
All his family were killed in a bombing raid in London. Knows his job and hates all Germans, bar none.

Stoker Forbes
Strong as an ox, and capable, his last ship had been sunk. The joker of the pack. Another Londoner, he'd gone home on leave, to find his wife in bed with a Yank, who he promptly put in hospital, very seriously injuring him. Funnily enough, there were no charges!

Seaman PO (G) Riley
A gunnery instructor to the core, usually called gob 'n' gaiters' to his charges, hated, but his 'lads' would follow him down a gun barrel.

Leading Seaman Thompson
Very ambitious man reads ships' manuals every spare minute he gets. Good power of command.

AB Dawson
Considers himself far too good for this menial work, a bit of a lower deck lawyer, but reliable when needed.

Able Seaman Cooper
Totally irresponsible, but could be relied on to do his work. Likes to drink.

Admiral Taylor was invited to see Alec's brainchild, his bride-to-be, and he himself sat in the bridge for a while, talking excitedly about the dream, that had materialised. With their enthusiasm so infectious, it was nearly a plague!

Chapter Twenty

That evening the stokers met the deck apes, (seamen), at a pub in Old Portsmouth. The two branches, never, under any circumstances, met on a mutual basis. "The *Tempest* had a lot to answer for," Bunker Hill thought, as he bellied up to the bar, still, they couldn't all be bad. Rejoining the table, the six asked each other what they thought of the commodore in charge, as they all agreed on the Jenny Wren, that she was well worth it, but her being a PO put her out of their sights.

If only they knew her before. Commodore Hamilton was, it was concluded, a bit of a "glory hunter", but he was a good bloke, even though he was an officer.

'He's gotta have a bit 'o' class, to wear that ribbon, Bunker,' someone said.

They all nodded in agreement, then looking round, they all shook hands, while holding their glasses tightly. The six got back to barracks, well pissed, and past it, but they were all shipmates to the end, as they sang all the way to their billets.

PO Brown and PO Riley met in the NAAFI to talk about the job to be done, and the men they would be in charge of, coming to the conclusion, that they had found a place where they could put up the flag, gape at the young ladies serving them, and wobble off to their cabins, shouting "night, night" to all and sundry.

Alec met Bob Rogers and Harry Chambers in the ward-room bar, and asked the two of them, what they thought of the *Tempest*, the job they were all looking forward to, and the men they were going to do it with.

Bob said, 'The work on the ship was done to a standard where it would fool Admiral Doenitz himself. Now the job, well let's face it, it's a peach really, because it'll hurt their pride, oh yes, I'm looking forward to it, sir.'

Harry committed himself by saying casually, 'It's about time I did something on the sea, it's terribly noisy ashore sometimes, when those Luftwaffe chaps decide to infringe on our privacy, especially when a fellow is feeling fragile. Stout chaps we've got too you know, they would scare the hell out of me, if I met them in a dark alley at night, and that's the truth.'

After they stopped laughing, they turned to a more serious matter, the serious matter being, how to drink gin and tonics very fast, while eating corned beef sandwiches, commonly called "dog hammocks", as they always turn up at the corners.

Alec made his way back to his cabin, reflecting on the past few months, comparing the time before *Tempest,* and now, with *Tempest* and skeleton crew getting ready to weld together, get into action, and complete the mission successfully. Alec felt everything was starting to hang tightly together. Even his love for Edith, and her's for him, sometimes, looking back, he wondered how it all happened, at the same time. He felt a very lucky man, a smile creasing his face, as he remembered the admiral's reference to the sentry outside Admiralty House.

Then, stinging shockingly, he remembered the agony of his wife and children, snatched away from life because of this war. His face was turning ugly as tears raced down his cheeks. As he reached his cabin door, he thrust it open and fell, straight into Edith's arms. She, holding back her tears, laid his head into her lap, and stroked his face softly like a cobweb.

Alec, looking up, said, 'Hello lifesaver, you will be more than a little surprised to know, that your ancient old husband-to- be is drunk! Are you sure you want to spoil your lifeblood, by marrying an old drunken fart like me?'

Edith, her tears flowing freely by now, whispered, 'I'm marrying you, you old fart, because I love you, I would be worse than useless without you,' then she went off to make a pot of tea.

The tea went down well with his hoard of biscuits Edith had bought for him, and then as he kissed her forehead, she undid his tie and shirt, slipping his jacket off easily, then she suddenly realised he was undoing her blouse buttons. The rest was pure enjoyment for both of them, as Alec laid back, pulling Edith on top of him, kissing her neck and shoulders, then slipping her undone skirt off, and caressing her beautiful thighs. So they lay there, savouring each other, until dawn. Edith stole away before reveille, not wanting to be discovered in a flag officer's private cabin. But when they were married, watch out!

Appearing at the ship the morning after, ten white-faced senior ratings and ratings stood at attention, to be inspected. Alec called down to Bob, 'Wheel them on board please,' then in a quieter voice, 'We don't want, or need any of that bull this morning, anyway, PO Taylor is making the tea.'

It was a familiarisation day today, finding out where everything was, which was vital for anything like the success the RN so badly needed. Alec was waiting for a civilian wireless operator, who spoke fluent German as a second language. Time was marching on, with the weather and tides as normal as they could be for the time of year, heavy seas were a definite no, with the artificial damage that was going to be inflicted on the ship. The radio shack was already fitted, and made a lot of difference. *Tempest* was looking very spartan now, not that ships like destroyers are comfortable, but *Tempest* was a wreck. The decks and bulkheads had all been weakened, so that when she hit the cliff, she would telescope as much as they could arrange it, then the charges, timed explosives and the torpedoes meant curtains for the guns.

Didn't it sound simple?

It all meant calculations and calculations, checked, then rechecked, a lot of prayers for all the work to be right, and for the weather they needed, for a job to proceed with no hitches.

Meanwhile, in London, Admiral Taylor was asking his secretary to inform Commodore Hamilton he was on his way down to Portsmouth, with some news. The secretary knew Edith very well, so was able to tell her he was in a worried frame of mind, and to be prepared!

Edith ran off to find Alec, somewhere on the *Tempest*, working something or other out, she was sure, when she found him having a cup of tea, with the watch-keeping dockyard men in the boiler room. The heat was terrible when you got out of range of the big steam-driven forced draught fan, she thought, so she waited under the fan until he'd finished.

Pointing upwards, Alec and Edith went up the ladders, through the airlock, and into clean air. Well, as clean as you would expect, in the middle of a bomb-torn dockyard, full of ships in a variety of stages of work, and damage. Taking their time to enjoy the air, they walked to the bridge, where the information from the admiral was passed on to Alec, after a kiss and cuddle.

'Those ladders hurt my stump something awful darling, I can't go down there again,' gasped Alec, as he felt the socket of the leg. It was bleeding, not a lot, but he must reline it with cotton wool, so that he could safely show the admiral around, although Bob would have to go round the machinery spaces, because Alec felt sure the admiral would want to see them and everything else come to that. But Alec would be responsible, if anything went wrong.

The admiral pulled up at the gangway, three hours later, telling his driver to return in two hours, as he walked along the jetty, looking at the *Tempest*.

'My word, if I saw her at sea, I'd sink her,' he said to himself, looking in at the refashioned upper deck. 'Let's get on with it then, but she looks more German than the *Bismarck*,' he thought aloud, as he strode up the gangway, looking down the bomb hole in the upper deck cautiously before going to the bridge.

'Good afternoon sir, how are you today, impressed by the *Tempest* I hope?' asked Alec nervously.

'Well Alec, she worried me at first, I thought the Germans had invaded Portsmouth, and taken the dockyard over. She looks magnificent, but what is she like below?' as he picked up his tea which had been supplied by Edith.

Alec explained everything he thought was relevant, including the steaming crew, and how pleased he was with everything. Admiral Taylor explained he would not be viewing the machinery spaces, he'd seen the dockyard report, and the machinery that was needed for the short mission, would be more than adequate for the task facing them, it was a shame it was all going to be destroyed but with a purpose that would deprive the enemy of a major weapon, and lowering their morale as well.

Walking fo'rard, he saw the huge amount of cargo fitted on sliders, so that when the ship's bow hit the cliff, the two torpedoes fired into the flaw, and the jolt would cause the cargo to slide forward by momentum, and explode, hopefully cracking the cliff in half, making the Germans, minus one weapon against Britain.

'Yes Alec,' as the two officers walked along the jetty, 'you've all done an excellent conversion job, and you'll be pleased to know, it's tomorrow night,' smiled the senior officer looking at Alec out of the corner of his eye. 'Two MTB's will escort *Tempest* to ten miles from the target, and then I'm afraid she is alone. Tell the crew to get into the launch when she is a quarter of a mile from the impact point. I presume you will tie the wheel, but you and I know she will wander a bit, though the weather boys say it'll be flat, and dead at twenty three hundred, the tide being on the turn. Wish the men the best of luck; we'll see they get some leave after this, as well as you and Edith. But,come to see me, both of you, when it's all over,' the last being said with a smile on his face, 'but try not to damage yourself any more, leaping up and down ladders like a lunatic.'

So getting in his car, Edith shut the door, and the admiral was off, back to London.

'You minx,' laughed Alec, and taking the minx in his arms, he kissed her neck, her hair, and then her lips. Instantly, Edith melted into her man, loving him forever.

Chapter Twenty One

Calling the men and officers together, Alec explained to them the plans, and the departure time, 2130, stressing to them, 'If there is anything you don't know, or you are unsure of, ask me or your CO Lieutenant Commander Rogers. If anybody is doubtful about the job, or wants to unvolunteer, please do so now without any prejudice to their service record,' then Alec waited. No reply was the answer, so continuing, he said, 'Good, now the lot of you can go ashore tonight, but I want you here at 0800 tomorrow, we're refuelling the ship, and swinging the launch on to the davits, with full tanks I hope. PO Brown, it's your responsibility I believe to check them. One more thing, have a good time tonight, but keep your mouth zipped about what you are doing. Right, carry on.'

As Alec and Edith watched the men marching to barracks to going ashore, they looked at each other, Alec was hoping nothing would go wrong, and Edith, thinking how much she loved him but knowing full well, he was worrying about the mission.

'I think they will be alright,' he said half to himself, 'I wish it was me going all the same, but how could I get down a rope ladder, and into the launch, from a destroyer doing fourteen knots or more? Stupid to think of it really.'

Edith agreed completely and wholeheartedly, reminding

him, among other things, what her father had said, and forget about returning to the sea, otherwise she would think he was trying to get away from her!

He looked at her, shock all over his face, and slowly shaking his head.

Telling him to sit down, she pulled his trousers off, leaving his artificial leg exposed, and then undoing the belt, she noticed he was grimacing with pain.

Removing the leg quickly, she saw the blood around the socket of the leg. After covering and dressing it as best she could, she knew she had to get him to Haslar, so arranging for an ambulance to meet them on the Gosport side, she phoned the MT office, boat section, to take them, explaining why. An ambulance boat came quickly, with two male nurses to stretcher Alec down Customs House steps. Edith was lifted into the boat, and away it roared, the P6 engine grumbling all the way to HMS *Dolphin*, in Gosport.

Unfortunately for Alec, he saw the same doctor he saw previously, and after inspecting the damage done to the stump, insisted on Alec staying in.

Alec was worried now; he had to be on the jetty, at least to wish them a safe return. It was his and Edith's baby, who indirectly, was responsible for Edith and Alec's bliss. He must be there. His stump was treated first with cream, then powder, and then it was securely bandaged up, the bandages having to be changed every three hours, day and night. Gangrene was frightening the doctor and Edith, so the treatment was going to be forced on Alec.

Edith stayed all night with him, bathing his face with a cold flannel, and keeping him comfortable, Alec's leg had been taken away to be altered, so when he woke up, he told

Edith he'd be legless for a while, but Edith could see he was desperate to watch the *Tempest* and her men off, so thinking, she phoned her father, Admiral Taylor. At noon, when the doctor came to look at the wounds, and the dressings, Alec told him his stump was wonderful, so before it was redressed, the doctor looked at it again. It was better, but it had a long way to go before he would be happy with it, and Alec had to wait for the leg to be repaired anyway.

However, the doctor allocated a bath chair to Alec, and if he could arrange a boat, there might be a chance of him seeing the *Tempest*, but he had orders from above, not to risk Alec's health in any way.

Alec spent a miserable four hours, until 1600, praying and waiting for good news. Edith had to leave him, and go to the ship to meet someone, as well as the men of *Tempest,* who didn't look too bad, after a night on the town. All of them were saddened by Edith's news, without exception, but she explained a plan she had cooked up with the Admiral. 1630 arrived to a sudden influx of ten visitors, rushing into the ward.

Alec was thinking just a minute, I know those faces: the bilge rats! In walked all ten of *Tempest's* crew, laughing all over their faces as they crowded around him, lying in bed. From somewhere, came his uniform as if by magic, then they all turned their backs on him, enabling Edith to help him with dressing. There was a sudden absence of hospital personnel, and his bath chair appeared. After Alec was lifted into it, they all started to sing a famous RN song, about a young lady, whose name was Eskimo Nell, while the men wheeled him out with Alec hidden from sight, in the middle. The doctors and nurses all had a quiet laugh, as they watched the performance.

It was much funnier this way.

Getting to the jetty at HMS *Dolphin*, he was surprised to see the launch allocated to the *Tempest*, so at least, he was going in style. Edith watched him looking at the destroyer, knowing his dreams, never to come true, but at least, he would see his baby steam out of Portsmouth, for her final voyage. On the upper deck, there was a canvas awning, with three stewards waiting, and the man from London, the admiral. Carrying Alec up the gangway in his chair. Hill and Cooper pushed him to the admiral, and turned to go to their duties, but the admiral managed to talk them into having one drink! The POs and ratings looked at each other, with a quizzical look on their faces for a second, but it was washed off with a pint of bitter.

Later on, the launch was hoisted on to the davits, after having the fuel tanks and the oil level checked. While the clamps were tightened up, a civvy strolled on board, saw Bob on the upper deck, and told him he was the German signalman, and could he be directed to the wireless hut. After studying his ID card, and his credentials, they welcomed him, and pointed him to his domain, where he would spend all the duration of the one-way voyage. The team worked very easily, and professionally together, they practised lowering the launch with the artificial list on. Everything went well until the wireless operator, Les, proved very nervous, climbing down the scrambling net, but he'd get over it, everybody hoped. The fuel tank of the *Tempest* had enough fuel to get her to France, and a little bit more, but fuel was at a premium, and tankers were being sunk all the time by the Germans to bring Britain to her knees, Alec repeated his advice about the door still open if anybody wanted to drop out, but nobody took him up on it, so they all sat around, smiling, and looking at each other, with a funny look of relief, and panic on their faces.

When darkness fell, two sinister looking MTB's heaved to, fo'rard of the *Tempest*, then some mates slipped her mooring lines, furtively and invisible under the mantle of night, led by her consorts. Alec, Admiral Taylor and Edith waved them godspeed, at which she flashed her Morse lamp once, then faded from sight, slowly leaving a crowd of people on the jetty sure with the knowledge that if all went well, she would never see Portsmouth again, but would fly the hated swastika flag very briefly. Looking at each other, the three clasped hands, and said a silent prayer for those brave and foolhardy men.

Trying to hide his face from the other two, Alec was shocked to see the old sailors' eyes moist, and red, still looking for an invisible *Tempest*, remembering, just remembering.

'Right you two,' Admiral Taylor whispered, 'Let's organise some food and drink. Oh by the way Edith, did Alec ask you anything, you know, um, well anything really?' He finished lamely, 'Because if he did, that's something else to celebrate!'

'You old fraud, of course we're getting married, you just want a party,' Edith said laughingly, and joyously, then kissing Alec's lips, she held him in her arms, and cried with happiness.

Chapter Twenty Two

HMS *Tempest* steamed out, past the forts that had been built in the Napoleonic wars, and then slid past Southsea Pier, to the open sea. The seamen flooded the port fuel tanks and water tanks, until she had just the right list on, while the MTB's scurried about, hoping an RN ship didn't see the *Tempest,* and fire on her. German ships were another problem for the MTB's, because *Tempest* flew the German flag, and they were flying the White Ensign; it could turn very awkward to say the least.

Down below, in the boiler room, Stoker Denton was brewing the kai for all, the delicious thick, sweet scalding hot chocolate drink was quickly disposed of, and very shortly afterwards, more was asked for, proving that stokers made the best kai in the fleet, 'cos Carnation milk was invented for kai, by a stoker, it's in the stokers' bible, so they say.

As the trio of warships got to the limit of their escort, the MTB's peeled off, then flashed a quick Morse message, telling the *Tempest* crew to do something humanly impossible, but they promised to meet the *Tempest* crew in the Barracks Tavern, then they roared off, back home to Pompey. "No doubt they'll be drinking, and meeting girls, well, we won't go into that, but I expect they will!" thought AB Cooper.

Lieutenant Chambers, being the navigator, did all the magic that navigators do, and soon their course was sorted out, and the mission was on. Leading seaman Thompson, with AB Dawson, got ready to light a bundle of rags on the quarterdeck, then on getting the signal from the bridge, lit the rags, then both went to the davit, ready to help with lowering the launch. In the boiler room and engine room, the stokers jammed the throttle on the turbine, then blowing kisses to the screaming turbine, went topside to the launch.

Stoker Brown lashed the main stop valves open, then wedged the safety valve shut. After flashing up all sprayers, then adjusting the water feed valve and air pressure, the stokers went up top. Seaman PO Riley was on the wheel, steering the *Tempest* to her destiny, wanting to be precise more than ever, the whole mission depending on his ability as a coxswain. The fault in the cliff was rapidly nearing the ship as he lashed the wheel, holding it for a few seconds, stroking the surface of the wheel, partly in pity, partly in joy at a job, perfectly executed, thus dealing the enemy a serious blow ,hopefully.

Suddenly, he felt somebody standing next to him. It was Nobby Hall, asking if he could help in any way.

'Get down to the bloody boat you idiot, there's hardly any time to get to it,' growled PO Riley, jamming on his hat, and lifejacket.

Hall left the bridge, to wait on the boat deck.

As he waited, he heard the PO tell the Captain, that with one turbine thrusting to one side, namely port, it was wandering a bit off. Bob realigned the ship to the starboard side of the flaw, then, as it seemed all right, gave the order to abandon ship.

As the men clambered down the scrambling net, they looked fo'rard to see the cliff only two hundred yards away.

The launch was quickly manned, and with both engines

bellowing, left the hull of the *Tempest,* and setting course for Portsmouth, pulled away on course. Bob took count of the men in the boat, and finding them all there, wait, no, where's Hall? Turning to the *Tempest*, and the cliff, they thought they saw a figure on the bridge, but Hall wouldn't do that would he? Then the ship's siren blew, leaving them in no doubt, all faces shocked at what Hall had done. He'd overheard the talk about *Tempest* possibly missing the target, so Nobby, thinking of Ada and his family, made sure the ship didn't miss.

The flash as the torpedoes blew, for an instant, turned night to day. The explosion rolled around, and then with no warning, the main cargo went off. The effect was truly amazing, so brilliant, it hurt the eyes as the men in the launch watched. It continued for a terrible length of time, ripping through the cleft in the cliff, better than it was supposed to. To top it all, the German arsenal blew, after the flash got to it. The watchers in the launch swear the cliff lifted in the air, before returning to earth as a pile of rocks at the base of the cliff, where the *Tempest* lay, broken, and still.

She filled her part in RN history, but would she have done it without Nobby Hall? His hands steered her to her place in the history books. The bows of the ship hit the cleft perfectly, with the speed of the ship estimated at twenty-seven knots, she was rammed into it, where she telescoped. The cargo took a terrible toll on German lives, infuriating the Fuehrer, vowing vengeance on the RN but failing dismally.

A Mosquito recce plane flew over the smoking ruins of the site, took lots of photos of the damage, and the hulk of the *Tempest*, lying dead in the chaos she caused, but happy with her one-man crew. The damage was unbelievable on studying the photos, the guns, nowhere to be seen, the top of the cliff looked like a volcano, and recently erupted; it was total destruction.

The remaining nine men went to a memorial service for LME Hall VC where his parents were met, and made welcome by the *Tempest's* tiny crew. They had been to Buckingham Palace, to collect the medal from the King who offered them his condolences, and thanked them for sacrificing their only son.

Alec and Edith went on leave, and surprise, surprise, got married, then went on honeymoon, receiving a good send off from the *Tempest's* crew.

But before going, Edith received her reward, she had earned it, her commission, enabling them to go to Navy bases, and live as a normal couple, if you can live as normal in a war as in peace. Edith's father Admiral Taylor retired after the *Tempest* mission, enabling Alec to step into his shoes, hoping to mastermind more missions.

The explosion woke all at the French fishing village. Pierre and Marie looked out of the bedroom window, saw the wrecked gun emplacement, and the carnage all over the cliff, which prompted much laughing and dancing. Then back to bed, where they could discuss the name of their child, which would be born in three months. The *Tempest's crew* went their different ways, to seagoing commissions, or barracks, but they all received a month's leave. Except for LS Hall VC, one day, they may serve together once more; war was like that, the most unlikely bedfellows.

Several of the *Tempest's crew* thought of Nobby, and wondered how many of them would pay the ultimate price, before there was peace, but like Nobby, and millions of others, they would steadfast, only interested in winning this war, and going home, if they still had one.

PO Riley walked to the end of his road, and stopped, surveying the damaged, flat totally devastated area, where his house once stood. Painful memories crowded his mind.

Memories of pushing his son Clive on the rope swing he had tied on the apple tree at the bottom of the garden, and the look of delight on Clive's face, followed by shrieks of delight. Neighbours tried to give him solace with some food, telling him Flo' and Clive didn't suffer, it was very quick.

Joe Riley picked up his case, and walked away, tears ripping his heart out, as he turned around for the last time, and wishing he was dead, returned to barracks. Three months later, he got his wish, running to meet Flo and Clive as his destroyer sunk in the sullen gray very angry Atlantic, unmourned, and in an unmarked grave, as most RN members died.

Chapter Twenty Three

Alec smiled at Edith, his wife, and secretary, as she brought a tray of tea and biscuits into his office. All three RN commanders sat at the long table, waiting in silence, as she poured the tea, and handed the plates of biscuits around.

'Gentlemen, I am not one for foolishness or snobbery, when we are fighting for our very existence in this war, so I would like you to meet my wife Edith, the best person I know, to get a good deal on biscuits.'

The officers introduced themselves, and feeling a little more relaxed, settled down in their chairs to drink their tea.

'We have a problem with swarms of E-boats so I understand, what can I do, and what suggestions have you got, to put on the table so to speak? I know the speed and capabilities of these boats; they are efficient, and so damned fast. To top it all, they are so accurate, these new torpedoes the Germans are using, I know all this. What can we do?' Alec partly murmured to himself. The E-boat scourge was virtually a missile, firing a missile, once they left harbour, with their engines giving a peculiar booming noise, and as yet, nobody knew why. The speed a which the E-boats appeared, was frightening, one minute, a clear sea, the next, there were swarms of them, causing havoc.

The three men, Alan Jones, Frank Stewart and Rob Hunter,

were all destroyer commanders, and all three knew the damage the E-boats were doing to both merchant ships, and the convoy protectors, that were too slow to do anything, being both old and under powered, which is why their commands were all at the bottom of the North Sea. The dreadful fate of American troops on exercise in Cornwall, prior to the landing in Normandy, still rankled in every one's minds, knowing that five E-boats caused the deaths of eight hundred crack troops, for no loss to themselves. All three produced folders, each with their own ideas on the beating of the E-boats, but nobody knew where the things were based even, so as yet, it was all guess work, and that, at a time of war, was not the thing anyone needed in a situation like this. The harbour the boats were based in, must be large, and easily supplied with weapons, fuel and space for repairs and maintenance as well as the moorings of the boats, and living quarters for the crews. So in front of a large map of France the four men scoured the coastline for such a place. It was a poser that defied the men trying to find such a place.

'Commodore Hamilton,' a commander started, but was cut short with a smile.

'Call me Alec, if you please, while in conference anyway,' said Alec, delicately passing a hint to Edith to make some more tea, by giving her a crafty wink.

While drinking their tea, Alec phoned a friend in Air House.

'Good morning Nigel, it's the Senior Service here, what would you say to a spot of lunch today, with some pals of mine? They have a problem. See you in our wardroom, at noon.'

'How are you Navy old man? You know my religion; if the

meal is free, accept it, even if it means being asked to help the Navy at any time! Bring your wife, or else!' replied Squadron Leader Nigel Bush, putting the phone down quickly, as a WAAF gave him a note marked URGENT.

They all met in the wardroom at Admiralty House, Alec as usual sending a steward to the front door, to assist Nigel past the Royal Marine sentry. His tin leg was squeaky for some reason, so Alec told him to get it serviced at the garage. Nigel took the banter as he always did, by explaining to the three men sitting with Alec and Edith, that, 'he'd broken one tin leg, looking after the RN' let out his famous yell of Tally-Ho, and then scuppered his gin and tonic.

The three commanders sat there, amazed at the commodore and the squadron leader, one a VC and the other, a DFC and bar on their chests, laughing and joking about each other's tin leg.

Then Edith pleaded paperwork panic, and begged their pardons, and hurried away, returning a few minutes later, calling it a false alarm. The meal went smoothly, Nigel wondering what the Navy wanted, and Alec wondering if Nigel could find three Mosquitoes.

On completion of the meal, all five men and the lady, stomped upstairs, each arguing about the way to win the war, and leaving the wardroom in a complete turmoil, the majority blaming the RAF fellow with the gammy leg, though I suppose he's done his bit.

Sitting down at the table, Alec explained to Nigel, that the planes that were available to the Navy, were too few and far between, they were all desperately needed for protecting the much-needed convoys. Alec wanted the Mosquitoes to run up and down the coast, and try to spot a harbour big enough to accommodate a lot of MTB size boats to use. Pulling down the wall map of western France, all crowded around, wondering, where on earth were those bloody E-boats based? At length, Nigel left the office, promising he would help if he possibly could.

Three different plans were looked at, discussed, then shelved, the meetings going on for several days, but the problem could not be solved, until they knew where the base was. Then photos from Nigel began to arrive, of all suitable harbours along the French coast. Some of the photos were taken from different compass points. Nothing was given away; heavy AA gun emplacements were all the way along the coast, so that didn't give any clue either. Life on the English Channel was quieter since the Germans had lost their major warships; these E-boats only disturbed it. French fishing boats were always out, the German occupation of that country was draining its resources to keep its civilians going, consequently, the whole country suffered, as they always have done, through several wars with their neighbours and always being on the losing side.

French freedom fighters did what they could for information to send to England, sometimes defying the grip the Germans kept, and maintained on them, with fear. If one German troop was killed, the Gestapo killed ten French civilians, all in a variety of lingering ways. Nevertheless, Alec made a request to the authority controlling the areas concerned, sending messages out via the BBC using specific call signs, and coded messages.

The slow reaction was to be expected, the Germans having radio detector vans, which made it uncomfortable for the French, to say the least.

Meanwhile, any Mosquito flight on PR or Spitfires fitted with cameras, snapped the coastline, both outward and homeward, making it possible for Alec to build up an extremely accurate overall view in its entirety. The floor of the banqueting hall in Admiralty House was eventually covered in all the suitable looking bays and harbours. Alec studied these photos minutely, but one detail on one photo, was sticking out. An old merchant ship that was aground on the coast.

A Mosquito flew over it, identifying it by the name on the stern. She was the *Scorpion,* quite a common tonnage of ship, built in 1921, of ten thousand tons. Curiously, after checking the newly photographed coastline, which included the *Scorpion,* it seemed to differ from the old chart. The cliffs were slightly higher, and more land jutted out into the channel, looking like a cliff collapse, but if that had happened, the cliffs would be lower, while the ship was aground, where the cliff curved out towards the sea, away from the coast.

There was no beach, so the ship's main mast was the same height as the cliff. Looking at more photos, the signs were that she was well aground, apparently driven there by one of the infamous Channel gales that were not very frequent, but very nasty when they did occur.

Slowly but surely, the freedom fighters in France sent reports back to England. No E- boat activities were seen, except in the approximate area where the *Scorpion* lay, then they lost sight of the boats. Noticed by some fishermen working around the *Scorpion,* was the fact that three buoys had been moved into deeper water. Some German seamen had been seen hauling the buoys into a launch, where they were repainted in the same colours, taken out further into the deeper water, and moored there. Perhaps the *Scorpion* was carrying explosives that were becoming unstable. The Germans wouldn't worry about a detail like that though, Alec opined, and wondered if the *Scorpion* was all that she pretended to be.

Sending a man out to the *Scorpion* was going to be difficult, and very unattractive to do, being in the position she was in. It would be a wonderful base to use for inspecting the coast more intensively, so looking at the available photos of her, Alec studied her, to see if she was too badly damaged to hide on, or prone to the Germans using her as a target for practice with their weapons.

One day, a French fishing boat, motoring along the coast with his nets out, saw an E- boat, then looking down at his nets, he saw that he had a very good catch, so expecting the E- boat to claim it, or most of it, he glanced up at the E-boat, it was not there! Rubbing his eyes, he looked again, knowing he saw one of the German fast patrol boats, but it had just vanished.

Returning to harbour shortly afterwards, Andre sat in a bar, after unloading his catch, then worried about the E-boat. Andre was not a drinking man, everyone knew him as an unimaginative, stolid worker, and drink was not a problem. It was today.

Customers in the bar heard him saying, 'Pouf, gone! It was there then pouf, not there.'

Francois was there in the bar, listening, and wondering, so he sidled over to his pal Andre.

'Hello old friend, what's all this, pouf it's gone? Are we talking of the Germans? If you are, don't moan, just rejoice they have at last left us.'

'I am talking of the German pigs, but not men, their stinking E-boats, that's what. It was there, on my port side,

I looked down at my nets while I was pulling them in, then looked up and there it was, gone, pouf!' replied Andre, his eyes rolling, because of the unusual cargo he was taking on.

Francois took Andre home, putting him to bed, more like a corpse, than a living person. The following day brought Andre and Francois out fishing in the area of the vanishing E-boats, but that day, neither of them saw anything of the boats, but the *Scorpion* was there, silent and dead. Francois studied the hull of the merchant ship, and hardly recognised the immediate coastline; it had changed where the *Scorpion* was beached. But there was no beach along this exposed coast. Violent storms cleared any rocks or sand away from the cliffs, with undercurrents and eddies, which were so dangerous for fishing boats, which is why the fishermen kept outside the buoys. But why did the Germans move the buoys out? That fact, coupled with the changed coastline, was intriguing Francois, but with the *Scorpion* undamaged as far as he could see, apart from upper deck damage that is, what had made the ship run aground?

Gathering the nets and the lobster pots in, they took stock of the catch, which they decided was good, so the boat headed for the jetty, to sell it, before the Germans claimed it as theirs. Wallowing along, the steady rise and fall of the boat gave Francois and Andre time to look and think.

While Andre was rock solid, the vanishing E-boat caused him to think, and then suddenly, a particular vision came to him. A section of the *Scorpion's* hull seemed to be moving. Then it stopped; leaving the hull complete and unblemished. He explained to Francois what he thought he'd seen, which gave Francois a sudden thought. Explaining to Andre that he had a date with Veronique, he must get to Dabertique, all clean and tidy. On hearing this, Andre added revs, to the engine, casting a sly glance at Francois, accompanied with a lecherous smile on his face.

'Francois, you are the limit, with all the girls you see, it is a wonder you can remember who you are meeting,' roared Andre, an animated look on his face.

Reaching his mooring on the jetty, his catch was soon sold off to the villagers, without a German seeing it. The two men strode off to the bar, Andre drinking coffee, while Francois drank wine, while talking to a pal of his, sitting in the comer, about the fishing trip, and the *Scorpion*.

'That ship doesn't look natural in that position, the crew must have been blind to run her ashore like that,' Francois mused partly to his pal, and partly to himself, 'The problem is, we cannot keep a continuous watch on her, because of the position of it. The only place to be unobserved, is from the sea, but how? I'll explain to the Englishman with one leg, he's good at what he does, considering he's English.'

Alec received the signal two days later, and remembered the *Scorpion* had been mentioned quite a lot, by the photo reconnaissance pilots, so studying all the photo evidence of the ship, and the slightly changed coastline, he got the magnifying glass out of the desk drawer, and gave the hull of the ship a very close scrutiny. As he rang the intercom to Edith, she walked in with Squadron Leader Bush in tow. With the aid of his sticks, he managed to move into the armchair, where he said, 'Hello Navy, any help needed on this French coastal search? I'm puzzled about this bloody freighter that's aground, it apparently appeared overnight, from nowhere, and superficially damaged, nothing critical you know, so what have you decided Navy if I may be so bold?'

Edith and her husband looked at each other, then burst into laughter, causing the RAF officer to ask what he had said, that was so funny, damn funny types, these RN officers, and guffawing loudly, he accompanied the married couple for a meal, and a drink, where both armed services entertained each other with outrageous stories and jokes, reducing each other to a laughing mess.

Retreating to his office, Alec and Nigel reviewed the photos again, the merchant ship being the main focus point.

'The ship's hull is plenty big enough, for some form of door of sorts, but where are the E boats, and how do we watch the *Scorpion*?' asked Nigel. Alec's eyes swept over the photos again, as they had many times before, when he saw the solution, so simple, so easy, and right under the German nose

'The buoy!' Alec says, at which Nigel looks out of the window, and asks, 'Where, Navy?'

'Come on Nigel, this country is in trouble for the second time this century, this problem must be solved,' returned Alec, his good humour leaving him sorely deflated, like a dying barrage balloon.

'Well look at it this way Alec, this war has made heroes more heroic, and cowards more cowardly. You and I know one side of the coin, and neither of us are cowards, so the answer is to make light of this Austrian house painter, and treat him with the utmost contempt. He is not fit enough to clean the boots of a British "Tommy", and never will be.' Striking Alec's tin leg with his walking stick, Nigel continued, 'You are still fighting the war with one landing wheel missing, in case you haven't noticed I've lost one as well. Douglas Bader hasn't any legs, but he's taking the fight to the Germans, even as a prisoner-of-war. All right Alec, your loss was cruel, but I think you are the sort of man that has the ability to rise above your physical and mental damage. Edith makes me envious of you, you lucky Navy!'

Alec smiled, Nigel's long speech had moved him greatly, as with tears just below the surface, the memories flooded his mind, then cleared when he saw Edith's worried face looking at him.

Tea was the medicine at this moment, for all three, she decided, and called through to the PO Wren to detail Alec's steward for the job. Edith eased Alec's mind with a kiss and a squeeze of his hand, mouthing, and 'I love you,' to him. 'I say you chaps, steady on will you. You'll make me blush next,' twittered Nigel in a falsetto voice, then shouting, 'Tally-Ho,' as the tea appeared. 'Make an exact replica of the buoy, but with an entrance or exit clamped on, and room for two men, also a capability for the men to take photos. Being able to stay there for a period of four days, before being replaced with two other men, at night obviously, via a French fishing boat,' Alec thought aloud, looking at a photo showing the buoys and the Scorpion.

'The E-boats have been seen in this area, and the bloody things disappear here according to a French fisherman. I think it's worth a trial, to see what happens, after all, we have to start somewhere,' Alec concluded, looking at Nigel, to see and hear what he thought of the crazy notion.

Nigel nodded his approval at the audacious plan, and grinned as Edith gave him a bag containing some biscuits he loved.

'You know Navy, you're getting clever in your old age,' Nigel said, and ducked his head as a piece of chalk hurtled in his direction.

'Not only do you rob me of my food, you pinch my biscuits as well,' returned Alec, a smile on his face.

Chapter Twenty-Four

Alec arrived at his office to find the report from Dover. The PO Wren looking excited, as she asked, 'Is this the one we've been waiting for, sir?'

Looking at her with a smile, he replied, 'Yes, I believe it is PO so would you ask my wife to join me, and perhaps you could rustle up some tea?'

PO Wren Kendall saluted Alec, saying, 'Certainly sir,' and shot out of his office, excited that the E-boats were maybe coming to the end of their reign.

As Edith sat with him, Alec talked to her about methods of attacking the E-boat pen. There were only two methods open to him, one by air the other by sea. The RAF were up to their eyes in bombing the Reich, and the surface fleet had obligations in the Mediterranean, Atlantic and the Pacific, a lot of square miles to cover and very hostile all the time. That left submarines, or their counterpart, midget 'X' boats. These crude but effective weapons were towed near to their target by a submarine, then the 'X' boat, with its three-man crew, crept the rest of the way on the electric motor. On reaching their target proper, one of the crew released powerful explosive charges that were strapped to the 'X' boat's hull.

After carrying out their mission, they got away back to the mother boat, hopefully, and returned to base.

"No," thought Alec, "torpedoes will be the most suitable

weapons to use. I hope I can borrow a submarine for a day or two". He started to think of the beautiful capital ships and cruisers like his beautiful *Hecla*, and all the men and families, destroyed by this unseen weapon. He sensed, and then felt, Edith next to his arm, then finding his face wet with tears, he smiled into her face, and then his body rocked, as he sat sobbing at his desk.

Edith held back her tears, put a tough face on, and then said, 'So the tea is cold, what do you expect? There is a war on you know.'

Recovering his composure, Alec rose from his desk, picked up his stick, and kissed her long and tenderly, leaving Edith gasping for breath. With her face hot and flushed, she whispered, 'Alec, please, later.'

Looking at the submarines in harbour for refits, repairs or replacement crews, and some, too badly damaged to bother with repairing, didn't leave Alec with a lot to choose from; he only wanted one, just for one day. Then he hit pay dirt – HMS/M *Avenger!* There she was! A new crew, and she was off shortly, to work up, and get rid of any rough edges in the performance of both the boat, and the crew. Perhaps she could cut her teeth on this operation, and do him a favour too. Eagerly, he grabbed the phone, to call Submarine Command in Portsmouth, Discussing his requirements with Admiral Hewitt, he discovered *Avenger* would be free for two, perhaps three days... She already had a fully experienced boat crew, who only needed a day of familiarisation with *Avenger*, leaving Hewitt confident that a job like the one proposed by Alec, would sharpen them up nicely.

Telling the admiral he would let him know the precise date as soon as he could, Alec phoned the department Ted and

Pete worked for, asking their boss, if he could see them at Admiralty House, at 1400.

'Certainly sir, I'll send them over, then they can carry on with their new assignment they've just been given,' said Mr. Weller. He put down the phone, and called for the pair to give them the instructions.

'The Navy want to see you two at 1400 today, at Admiralty House. Try to be sober will you?' He then continued to look at the noticeboard, plussing and minusing people in Europe.

Alec met the two men at the door, congratulating them on a job well done, then led them to his office. Drinking the eternal drink of England, tea, he discussed the photos they had taken, and measurements of the sliding hatch on the *Scorpion*. Ted estimated the width of an E-boat and decided it was definitely too narrow for a submarine to enter. It was a death trap with torpedoes fired from the buoy area. Measuring on the map marked with the word 'Wreck', it looked very difficult. It was like firing a torpedo down the throat of a surface target, but a lot smaller. Thanking the two men for their help in this important mission, Alec wished them good luck on all their missions, and saw them out. Later he wondered what they would be up to next. To put the record straight, they were both captured, and tortured to death by the Gestapo, while on their next mission.

Phoning Admiral Hewitt again, Alec explained what he needed, but not why and thought of the big poster downstairs, showing a wall with ears growing on it. He did however find that arranging an appointment with the *Avenger's* commander to come and see him was much easier. As always, while planning an operation, his stump was sore, very sore, so sometimes he took his tin leg off while sitting at his desk. This simple action relieved the pain no end, until he put it back on. Then he would find the stump swollen beyond belief, so he allowed Edith to push him in of all things, a bath chair. Degradation upon degradation!!

The following day, a lieutenant commander met Alec in his office. While studying all the photos, he gave Alec his opinions about methods of destroying the base. The final decision was to get as near to the buoy as possible, at periscope depth, watching and waiting for the hatch in the *Scorpion* to open, then the submarine. *Avenger* could then unload her highly volatile load of torpedoes. The commodore and the boat commander went for lunch downstairs, after deciding to put *Avenger* on standby, until she had fired some practice torpedoes through a target, approximately the size of the *Scorpion's* hatch. Nothing must be left to chance in this instance, the state of the war was critical now, and all ships were at a premium, as all the rescued destroyer men would testify. Lieutenant Commander Kent was really overjoyed at landing a peach like this. His charge, the *Avenger* was fully fuelled and armed, ready for working up that all crews hated. It was boring, with no real challenge, but plenty of monotony. Practice, sleep, practice, sleep, boring, but in reality, so essential to any armed force, and more so in times of conflict.

Kent took the *Avenger* to sea the following morning, to meet the target-towing tug, praying the workup would go successfully, and the *Avenger* would be accepted into the fleet, but that decision would have to wait until Commodore Hamilton was satisfied with the boat, and the efficiency of the crew.

For the next three days *Avenger* fired, practised torpedo after practice torpedo at the wooden target, with a motorboat ready to retrieve them, after they floated to the surface. Mediocre tests soon improved to seven out of ten firings, but on the third day, after ten perfect shots, Alistair Kent knew his boat and crew were ready for anything that came their way, so everyone had an extra tot of rum. After using the wireless to send a signal to Commodore Hamilton, the *Avenger*, and her triumphant crew returned to her base, allowing her port watch a few hours ashore, followed by the starboard watch.

Alec and Edith met Lieutenant Commander Alistair Kent on board *Avenger* the next morning, offering their delight at the submariners' success, achieving the highest possible hit rate they could get.

Luckily, Edith was wearing slacks, so they were able to go down the conning tower ladder, into the tiny wardroom, where the officer's steward served the obligatory cup of tea.

'Now Alistair, we've jumped the first hurdle, and we are fully conversant with the job to be done. The E-boats leave the base in the early mornings, which is understandable. The Germans want to keep their base a secret for as long as they can. The weather boys tell me there will be no moon in three nights' time, so if you haven't any complaints about either the boat, or the crew, your sailing time is 2100 on Wednesday. Here is your course and the latitude and longitude, with your code book for that night only,' concluded Alec, secretly wishing he was in command of this boat, of the latest design and class. The Submarine service was beginning to get some decent machinery, so the Germans had better watch out!

Eventually, Wednesday 2100 came, and the carefully calculated ETA at the buoy, was to be at the first chink of dawn, when things were not as clear as they could be, which would be to *Avenger's* advantage. The crew were like coiled springs, ready to snap into action at a moment's notice, but finally, the *Avenger's* diesels flashed up. Then clearing the jetty, she slowly moved out, showing nothing but her running lights.

After passing the forts and the Isle of Wight, she changed course, to pass Brighton still on the surface, but fully prepared for diving should any German ship on patrol spot her on the surface, when a submarine was at its most vulnerable. Diving time came and she did her job smoothly, as the sinister shape slid into the element where she was very dangerous for the Germans. With the electric motors humming, it was so much quieter, giving Alistair time to talk to his navigator about the cross tides, and currents, that at times could play havoc with a navigator's workings and estimates.

The three hours soon passed to shoot the stars, so Alistair surfaced the conning tower, enabling the navigator to do his job, and find the exact position of the *Avenger*. The submarine continued with her conning tower just above water, both to give the boat a blow with fresh air, and as she proceeded, for quick identification of the target. One mile from the buoy, the *Avenger* hid her tower under the water, her periscope the only communication with the surface.

Hanging in the water, the submarine waited for its prey to appear out of the side of the *Scorpion*. The tension throughout the cigar-shaped hull was like electricity charging through the men, who watched their commander studying and watching the hull of the *Scorpion*. Men stifled coughs, and moved around the boat very slowly, their nerves stretched like violin strings, and ready for instant action; the tension everywhere in the boat, like a living, breathing thing. The outboard torpedo tubes were open, the noses of the torpedoes ready to be launched at their unsuspecting target, at the whim of Alistair.

The hatch moved so slowly, Alistair waited a couple of seconds, before whispering to the crew to prepare for firing. Seconds ticked away, and then a small light from the innards of the *Scorpion* appeared, with a mass in front of it. Slowly, the E-boat came, like a fox leaving its earth.

'Fire one,' five seconds, 'Fire two,' five seconds, 'Fire three,' five seconds, 'Fire four,' five seconds 'Fire five!' Alistair shouted, looking through the periscope, with a stopwatch in his hand.

Air hissed through the pipes to the tubes, throwing the underwater missiles clear of the *Avenger*, slashing to the target. More seconds passed, then the first torpedo hit the E-boat, causing it to disappear in an orange flash. As the other torpedoes exploded, the flashes and the eruptions raged, the *Scorpion* changed from a tidy shipwreck, to a battered hulk, as rippling explosions reached the fuel tanks, and the ammunition stores, as a torpedo hit the main switchboard. The huge man-made cavern collapsed, smashing to eternity any dreams the Germans had, of haunting the RN. The long rumble eventually rolled to a halt. And Alistair, still looking through the periscope, gave a yell when the dust and debris settled, bringing a peace of sorts to the scene.

After turning *Avenger's* bow towards Portsmouth and the beer, and the ladies of the city, Alistair thanked his crew for doing a good job, and the first round was his!

Alec had the photos, and the report on his desk, the following day, from an RAF Mosquito, showing the complete devastation of the E-boat base, never to be a threat again. *Scorpion* was a load of junk lying amid the rocks and rubble of the cliffs, plus the wreckage of the E-boats, scattered like chaff in the wind. '

While Alec was looking at the photos, a messenger came into his office, from of all places, Downing Street! Inside the official envelope was a note, thanking him, and all concerned, for their diligence and bravery in carrying out this attack successfully.

Alec was starting to think about taking Edith over to the USA where they could forget the war, and work, and enjoy life for a while, and take it easy, the way only the Americans could.

Chapter Twenty Five

As the lifeboats made their slow progress from the stricken ship, so the cargo ship settled itself into the sea, a bit like a hen getting comfortable before laying eggs. Then the bow dropped quickly into the sea, very slowly at first, and then rapidly increasing its speed to the seabed, catching the crew members still on the upper deck, condemning them to death, by drowning in a mixture of seawater, and furnace fuel oil. Looking back at the swiftly dying ship, the crew remnants said 'cheerio' to pals, clothes, and their home, some with tears in their eyes, others, with a devouring hatred of U-boats, and Germans.

Finally, the *London Pride* slipped into her grave, one of the countless victims of U-boats. The convoy scattered when the wolf pack fell on it, but not before four ships had taken that final plunge, taking men, and tanks with them.

The men in the lifeboat rowed, leaving the wreckage, and burning oil behind, all wondering what to expect next. Three hours after the sinking, a long black steel tube, with a conning tower surfaced, causing two boatloads of men, both angry and anxious, as the hatch opened, and an officer appeared.

'Is the captain with you?' he yelled into a megaphone, 'I need to speak with him. I was not aiming for you men, but the war supplies you were carrying. Now please, your skipper if possible.'

Captain Evans stood up in the rocking boat, and proceeded to call every German under the sun all the filthy names in his wide Merchant Navy vocabulary.

'We have food and water that will last you a few days, so with what you've got, you should be alright. Did you get an SOS out? Perhaps one of your escort destroyers picked it up. If you would like to row to our submarine, you may pick up the supplies,' then turning round abruptly, Lieutenant Lindner went below after organising some of his crew to supply the lifeboats.

The U-boat seemed to want to hang around after the supplies were handed over, it stayed with the boats a long time, which really worried the lifeboat's occupants. Captain Evans nodded to his lads, and said, 'They're waiting for a destroyer to rescue us after they received the SOS we couldn't send,' and laughing, they watched the Germans, who were watching them.

On the second day, alongside the U-boat, surfacing so rapidly, it caught the lifeboat sentries unawares, a second U-boat appeared. It was easily twice the size of the first, and had camouflage, instead of black. The U-boat crews cheered, and slapping each other on the backs, welcomed each other, like long-lost friends.

Telling his men to keep quiet, and continue rowing, Taffy Evans watched the U-boats. He started to draw as best he could the biggest of the U-boats, trying to get an approximate size, and measurement. He watched some of both crews appear, carrying what looked like hoses, and passing them to the smaller U-boat, then connecting them to deck fittings.

'My word, she's a U-boat tanker, to keep them bloody things at sea longer. Well, of all the nerve, I wonder if they carry food and torpedoes, to supply the square headed bastards?' Taffy Evans moaned, as the lifeboats made little or no headway in the sullen gray Atlantic swell. His question was answered later, when twelve of the deadly missiles made their way over to the hunter, as Taffy called it.

'Listen mates, we have to get this information back if we can, it may be very important, and if the proper people know about it, we could end this short cut to long cruises by these bastards,' said Taffy, who then suggested lashing the two lifeboats together. Everyone looked at the sea, and the colour of the sky, and how efficiently, and professionally the German crews attacked the work they had been assigned to. As the bunkering and rearming ceased, so the food supplies started passing between the boats, making Taffy think about how much diesel fuel, and torpedoes these fat sausages could carry, or perhaps a German freighter supplied the suppliers. The sausage looked like two conventional U-boat hulls, welded side by side, with an extension fo'rard, and another aft. "A very big boat," Taffy thought, and then wondered when the two U-boats would sod off.

The tanker U-boat went first, submerging as it went, giving the British something to cheer about, but before the hunter sailed, the U-boat commander shouted over, that he would send an SOS on behalf of the lifeboats.

'Yeh, and I'm the Queen of bloody Sheba as well, you lying pig, 'replied Taffy, thanking God the U-boat commander hadn't seen fit to search the lifeboats, because the emergency wireless and compass were still intact in their boxes. 'Well Fred, were you able to plot the course of them buggers? You are the navigator, so let's hope you did,' said Taffy.

'Of course I did, you saw me plotting on this bit of paper,

but we'll have a long wait, before we're rescued. Sparks sent the SOS out yesterday, but now we can put a longer aerial up, we might send a better signal,' replied Fred, who was quite a good navigator really, and took the leg-pulling easily.

'Are you going to keep that Kraut food for yourself Taffy, or are we going to starve until we don't need it?' added Fred, an air of innocence on his face, just like a choirboy.

Taffy kept two lookouts, fo'rard and aft, both with strict instructions to waken all eighteen as soon as a rescuer was spotted.

The following day, they saw a smudge of smoke on the horizon, but Taffy didn't fire a flare because identification was impossible. Two of the crew weren't handling it very well, the fuel oil being in their eyes, and lungs, it was a wonder they lasted so long, but eventually, first, one sad bundle went over the side, gradually, and slowly spinning out of sight. Then his mate surrendered to his fate, and his body went the same way, leaving the remainder looking at each other, and wondering who was going to be next.

The food and water had nearly run out, when the destroyer, HMS *Ursa* heaved to alongside the lifeboats, and took the survivors on board, then sinking the lifeboats with rifle fire. As the *Ursa*'s doctor examined the men, few of them needed medicine or treatment, while they were at the mercy of the U-boat. Its commander did them an especially big favour, when it was explained that good U-boat commanders were few and far between.

Taffy Evans couldn't get the big U-boat out of his mind, knowing it was a replenishing boat for the hunter U-boats. The fact that the U-boats could stay at sea a lot longer, had given the Germans a major propaganda point, making the

Allies think the Germans had more U-boats than they did. It was a point that made the RN and MN very nervous on the Atlantic convoys, seeing periscopes when none were there.

'The crafty devils, they must be kin to the English,' growled Taffy, his mistrust slowly melting, as he was being cared for by the *Ursa* doctor, and the SBA.

Later, the Welsh captain went up to the bridge, to talk with Commander Woodward, taking care to explain the picture he'd drawn while he was in the lifeboat: the extra large hull with huge ballast tanks; no deck gun, and as far as he could see, no torpedo tubes, but a peculiar contraption lying on the upper deck, just for'ard of the conning tower.

The two men sat at a desk, and with the enticement of some liquid from the wardroom, Taffy drew the supply U-boat better than he did in the lifeboat.

On completion, he called the survivors of his ship to the bridge, one at a time, and with Commander Woodward's permission, a drink at the end.

The length of the contraption was grotesque, being between twenty and twenty five feet long. The submarine as whole, was ugly to the extreme, but was most odd with the bulbous hull with the peculiar hook sticking up three feet from the deck of the boat... All the officers studied the drawing, nobody coming up with a reasonable, or feasible use for the hook.

Portsmouth appeared on the horizon three days later, the *Ursa's* fuel tanks very low, down to the thick black sludge at the bottom of the tanks, but there was enough to get it into harbour.

HMS *Ursa's* ship's company, and the *London Pride's* survivors said their farewells, each swearing never to do the other's jobs, and swapping addresses. The merchant seamen were loaded into a launch, to be transported to RNH Haslar, for their final check-up and treatment. Taffy Evans looked at his drawing, "It's a bloody mystery alright," he said to himself, folding the piece of paper up, and putting it in his inside pocket, wondering what to do with it, and worrying whether his drawing was accurate.

As the seamen were debriefed in Haslar, they were sent home on leave, with Taffy standing outside the office last, all by himself. "Not all Englishmen are bad," he thought, but they bear watching, thinking of the pain and discomfort his men had suffered in the lifeboats, and the families he'd have to write to, hoping they would understand what sort of man did this job, at time of war.

An RN rating appeared round the corner, asking him to go in the office. On entering, Taffy had his hand shaken by an RN commodore, who was wearing a VC ribbon. Taffy looked around for the King, but no, there was no sign of him.

'Captain Evans, my name is Hamilton, and I'm very interested in that fat U-boat you saw. Incidentally, did you know, the skipper of the U-boat that sunk you sent the SOS signal on the German wavelength? Well it's lucky we happened to be listening in, but I'm sure, not very lucky for your crew members who died. My God, the Merchant Navy have suffered badly, and have given too many lives already.'

Alec paused a minute, then signalled the two other officers out of the office, but not the WRNS officer, to whom the commodore was kind and considerate.

'I would like to introduce you to my wife. Now, this object you saw on the U-boat casing, it's causing our boffins here a lot of sleepless nights,' Alec concluded, giving Taffy a cigarette. Pulling out his much-thumbed drawing, Taffy explained the length and diameter of the tube, mentioning the odd hook and ball.

'Could you see if it was connected to a lifting mechanism, or a block and tackle, or just stowed on the casing, and fixed with brackets?' Alec asked, sipping his tea, and leaning his walking stick against the desk. Seeing it, Taffy got excited, and holding his slightly cupped hands under the handle, said, 'That is it. Put a ball in my hand, which we will call the basket, what it was made of, I've got no idea, but I have never seen anything like it before, and if it's only on U-boats, I do not want to see it again,' Taffy's Welsh brogue was coming through very strong.

They stared at the walking stick for a long time, each man trying to visualize what the thing on the U-boat did. They knew it existed, but for what purpose? The Germans were a methodical race, and wouldn't have objects on their U-boats, for no reason.

Alec sat at his desk in Admiralty House, thinking about his opinion that the Germans did not waste time with useless items. They did not think like that at all.

'I'd write and ask them about this unidentified 'thing', but I don't think they'd tell me. I wonder why, after all, we are in the same war, you must agree,' Alec said, looking at his audience, who were hysterical with laughter, his straight face completely breaking them up.

As Alec's secretary brought some tea in, the three recovered their composure, and concentrated on drinking the tea. Alec cocked his head to one side as a toilet cistern upstairs was flushed, then closing his eyes, he thought. The flash of inspiration didn't come, yet it was gnawing at his vitals. There is some use for the 'hook', as Taffy called it, yet why was it a pipe? It must be water-tight, air-tight and of some use. It was fitted to a monster enemy U-boat, but Taffy mentioned that he hadn't seen it used in any way when the two U-boats were tied up alongside each other, transferring from one to the other.

'Well gentlemen, I think you know what we need, and that is this. We have got to find out what this wretched thing is for, so put your thinking caps on, let's crack this puzzle, it might be a way of stopping these damned supply boats from doing their job. You don't need me to tell you that this U-boat war is seriously damaging us as a country, both with the loss of lives, and the loss of the war materials, as well as the food the Americans are sending over the Atlantic, but I'm sure you don't need me to tell you that, and I'm positive you'll do me proud.' After ending his speech, Alec watched them as they filed through his door, all deep in thought, and some praying.

Simon Lee, a lieutenant commander in Alec's dream team, thought of the 'hook' and the length of it all night. Coupled with the sound of the toilet cistern he had heard in the commodore's office, the day before, he could not get out of his mind, that the 'hook' was like a U-bend and ball cock on a cistern, but obviously, water was not inside the pipe. The Royal Navy were trying to sink their boats, without them trying to do it themselves. If it wasn't for water, could it be for gas or air? Diesel engines needed air, but they also needed to be vented into the atmosphere, sea water down an exhaust pipe was fatal to any engine, so it wasn't that, such a big bore pipe for a U-boat to carry, then while doodling, he drew an oval, about a foot across. Studying the drawing, and thinking of the length, it couldn't do anything in its position on the casing, but what would it do if it were upright, similar to a periscope? The ball in the cage, at the end of the U-bend would fall down in the cage.

Slashing his pencil across his drawing, in disgust, he noticed the line his pencil had made, halved the pipe lengthways, and then he looked at it from another angle. Diesel engines, and petrol engines for that matter, needed air, and they needed to vent their exhaust at the same time, but they couldn't clear their exhaust under water, which is why submarines had to surface, to recharge their batteries, after using them while the boat was submerged. Any submarine was very vulnerable when she was surfaced, and running on diesel engines, but what if the 'hook' could supply both air, and vent its exhaust while at periscope depth?

Alec and Edith were sound asleep in their flat at Admiralty House, when there was a hammering at the door. Waking instantly, they thought simultaneously, AIR RAID! Edith helped Alec with his leg, then, in dressing gowns, went to the door.

They were puzzled to find Simon Lee there, with a folder of papers. 'I've got a use for the 'hook' sir, and I'm sorry to waken you, but this could be the breakthrough we're looking for,' Simon gushed. Alec waved him in; he couldn't trust himself to speak, without using some RN language, and more! Edith, genius that she is, decided it was a very nice time for a cup of tea.

'Do you realise what the time is?' Alec enquired politely, 'this better be nothing short of brilliant, and to prevent me from killing you very slowly Simon, I'll give you a chance, then you can drink you last cup of tea!'

Simon Lee was white, as Edith came in with tea and

biscuits, then quietly chided Alec with her eyes, and poured three cups of tea.

Nervously, Simon proceeded to explain his theory of the 'hook'. Using the tabletop as the casing of the U-boat, he stuck a tube of paper together with sticky paper. Adding a U-bend made out of paper, he stuck it on top, then holding his hand loosely around the end, with a rolled ball of paper inside his loose hand.

'Well sir, think of the pipe as two pipes in one, and imagine the ball of paper as a ball-cock, to shut the sea water out. Stick it up behind the conning tower, similar to a periscope. It would be capable of supplying air, and vent the exhaust gases. The fresh air pipe could have a fan for a steady supply of air. The same system could apply to the other side. When it was not in use, for extra security, shut a valve on both sides of the pipe; then stow it flat on the casing,' Simon finished, looking at his shoes, then the commodore and his wife, very nervously. Alec stared at the paper contraption, seeing how it could work, for work, it must.

Slapping Simon on the back, Alec bellowed, 'You've got it Simon; it's all it could be used for. Now I want you to draw it for Portsmouth Dockyard to make, and as soon as you've got it ready, and working to your satisfaction, let me know. I'm putting you in complete control of the project; you are responsible to see the thing made as you visualize it. Well done Simon, I promise, I will not touch a hair on your head, please believe me.'

Simon replied that he appreciated the promise, and then, begging his boss's pardon, he felt he needed some sleep.

The next morning saw Alec in the office early, wondering how Simon was getting on. On entering Simon's office, he found Simon crashed out, with his head on his desk, sleeping as soundly as a baby. Creeping out, he made himself a pot of tea, and sat at Edith's desk in the corner. How ingenious of Simon Lee to work it out, with only Taffy Evans's drawing of it to work with, then thinking back to what he said to Simon, he wanted to crawl into a hole, and fill it up! Even if Simon's idea weren't right, it was a bloody good idea, and resolved that Simon would get full credit for the 'hook', he wouldn't put it into a brain team, and everyone getting a slice of Simon's 'glory'.

Three hours later, with Edith creeping around, and Alec drinking tea, and worrying, Simon woke up, and with his eyes barely open, received a cup of tea.

'Hell,' asked Alec, peering at Simon, anxiety etched in his face, 'Any luck with the task?'

Simon wearily handed him his sketches, thoughts and drawings, then asking Alec's forgiveness, made his way upstairs, where he promptly collapsed with exhaustion on his bed. Alec studied the paperwork, thinking how simple the system appeared to be. As he looked very closely for any sort of flaw, problem, or drawback, he couldn't find any whatsoever, so Simon's idea had to be tested on an RN submarine.

Phoning the Admiralty technical office upstairs, he asked Captain Foster down, to give his opinion and advice, if any were needed, on Simon's wonderful idea, or problem. On entering Alec's office Captain Foster saw the paper contraption on the desk and asked Alec if it was too early for Christmas decorations.

'Very funny you silly old goat, now get this fixed in your mind, if it's available that is,' Alec retorted with a grin, and then went into great detail with the 'hook' fitting. On finishing, Cyril Foster was ecstatic at such a simple but brilliant idea, and declared his support for Simon all the way, and being an ex-submariner, had the ability to pull strings in the right quarter and ran off to collect Simon, to go to Portsmouth dockyard, and the submarine base, HMS *Dolphin*, talking all the way about measurements, and capabilities, but the key word was effectiveness, and usefulness to Britain's submarine fleet.

Alec, now a desk jockey, was frustrated at the new twist in events, being used, in the past to leading all the runners from the front, but his anchor, Edith, gave him that smile of hers, and wiped Alec's face clear of frowns, producing a smile big enough to sink a battleship.

Though there was an inkling in mind, that the day of the capital ship, the long vaunted and feared battleship, would soon be replaced by the aircraft carrier and the submarine. He wondered if his thoughts would be proved right or wrong one day.

These supply U-boats were causing him, and a few other senior officers, grave concern, and Edith sat down after her teeth bit Alec's ear gently, realising the dangers our Atlantic convoys would be in now.

'No wonder our tonnage loss is getting worse Edith, they can put fresh crews on, and stay at sea, but they must either rendezvous in a predestined area all the time, or signal their position, compared to the nearest supply U-boat, and go from there, depending on the amount of fuel left in their tanks.'

Alec suddenly remembered Bletchley Park, full of the best code breakers in the country. They'd cracked the top secret German 'Enigma' code, two RN destroyer crew members having boarded a sinking U-boat, at great danger to themselves, to grab the 'Enigma' machine and code books before taking the plunge to the seabed. Bletchley Park decoded all the U-boat messages, the same day, so that if the RN destroyers knew the U-boats' rendezvous position, without giving away the fact that we had 'Enigma', they could stumble on the U-boats purely by luck, and perhaps sink two at the same time. Phoning Bletchley Park was not easy, in fact, only the Prime Minister's office could even talk to them, so the long windy road of red tape was started. After the 'hook' contraption was fully explained, and the value of destroying the supply U-boats, the PM Winston Churchill, being such a knowledgeable leader, realised the importance of ending the U-boat menace, and the Atlantic sitting-duck syndrome, asked Bletchley Park to cooperate with Commodore Hamilton as fully as possible, leaving Alec wondering how far, 'as fully as possible', would stretch.

Chapter Twenty Six

F our days later, really in the morning, a nondescript Austin met Edith and Alec, at the door of Admiralty House, to collect them for a ride to a very big house, in the heart of the country. Three civilian men met them, and proceeded to give them some information about 'Enigma', and the way it worked.

'Each German armed service has its own code, the Luftwaffe, SS Army and the U-boat arm. We have been very lucky with breaking the different codes,' said Mr. Brown, 'but so far, the Germans are not aware that their code has been broken. What we don't want to do is, bring this fact to their notice. We don't want them to change the codes. We are at a critical point, having just broken the supply U-boat code. They have changed the codes in the past, which is why our convoys are vulnerable, but I can say with absolute certainty, that with any luck, and a few destroyers, we can slow them down, if not stop them. We have worked out that they have five of your supply U-boats, the German mentality lives in straight lines, so the five U-boats send similar sounding signals, differing very slightly for each U-boat they need to supply. It's a foolproof system, each individual U-boat commander is aware of the minute difference in the signal. Now have either of you any questions or suggestions, even objections, taking into consideration that if we can knock out all five of these supply U-boats Jerry is going to put his thinking cap on, and do what we don't want him to do?'

Mr. Brown, accompanied by Mr Smith and Mr White, showed the amazed Alec and Edith, some of the work that had been accomplished, with 'Enigma', showing a very old 'Enigma' machine to them. Looking like an antiquated typewriter, it didn't look capable enough to carry all the military secrets of Germany's war machine. But it did.

Drinking tea in a beautifully decorated Victorian room in the splendid house, Alec and Edith talked about what they'd seen, not realising until later that they were whispering.

Looking at her, Alec said, 'Very unusual names don't you think?' then burst out laughing, Edith quickly following him. The driver called for them shortly afterwards, and the three civilians escorted them to a Hillman this time, and not as comfortable as the Austin, but the heater worked a lot better. But it had been a peculiar day; the civilians explained a lot, by not revealing very much.

'Perhaps they swap names sometimes to confuse people,' Edith whispered, and then shrieked with laughter, as the car pulled up outside Admiralty House. Returning the Royal Marine sentry's salute, Alec thought he recognised him as the sentry on duty, the night that Edith and himself were hugging and kissing next to him, and neither of them not knowing he was there, until he said good night. Alec knew he was right afterwards, when on entering the building, and stepping into the light, he saw Edith's face, a brilliant scarlet. Smiling, he kissed her nose, and holding her hand, he led her upstairs.

The following morning was busy again, a message from Simon Lee, requesting Alec to go to Portsmouth, to inspect the device that the pipe workshop in the dockyard had made.

'You try keeping me away,'' threatened Edith, before he had asked her if she wanted to come with him. So off they went again, after telling the motor pool that his wife would be driving.

On arriving at Copnor on the outskirts of Portsmouth, they found the city had suffered an extremely heavy air raid, and the roads were mostly blocked with debris from North End into the city and dockyard. So they went through Fratton and Eastney, towards the dockyard, through Elm Grove.

Alec knew where he was, his memories going back to that terrible morning, when he found his wife Sally, and their two daughters. Once again, he saw the grief and agony in the faces of the fire brigade, and others who had tried to help, in the ruins of the hotel. His memories worked overtime, as he remembered his desire to join his family, lying under a dirty blanket, on the earth. Edith saw him weeping, and stopping further up the road, comforted him, and holding him close, explained that she would never replace Sally and the children, but she loved him, and was for him only.

Looking at Edith, Alec realised she was right, just for him, and hugged her, causing her to whisper, 'wait a few minutes, we're near the Barracks, perhaps we can manage a cup of tea, anyway, there's some folk giving us some funny looks!' Playfully, she pushed him back into his seat, and completed the journey quicker than normal.

Apologising profusely to Edith, Alec vowed he would never hurt her again, and with tears gathering in his eyes as Edith pulled him toward her, declared, 'I will love you until I die, you are my reason for living, I would expect you to mourn for Sally and the children, it wouldn't be natural if you didn't,' then the couple linked arms and walked to see Simon

Lee, to see his interpretation of the 'hook'.

The 'hook' was standing on its end, as though fixed and jointed on to the casing of a submarine. The tube had been made in two halves, similar to roof guttering, then divided with a flat piece of thick steel. Putting heat insulation between the two halves was essential, as hot air entering a boat was awful, but heated up by diesel exhaust would be deathly. Simon explained the working of the ball-cock valve on the U-bend, how, when the boat submerged, the float would lift, causing a valve to shut, stopping any flooding. A valve fitted inside the boat, would be an extra safety precaution, in the event of the air pipe being damaged at all.

'How can we prove it works, apart from fitting it to one of our own boats?' pondered Alec, and then noticed Simon smiling like a proverbial Cheshire cat.

'Well sir, a pal of mine, Brian Dale, has expressed his desire to help us out with this problem. He's in command of a boat, being refitted at the moment, so he's in the right place, at the right time. I've written a letter to Flag Officer (Submarines), who is giving me his full cooperation and help, if the boat commander is willing,' Simon finished, grinning from ear to ear.

He'd had a problem with the joint at deck level, the tube was hauled erect by an electric motor, and held steady, simply by locking the motor. Inside the boat, the motor with the worm drive, fitted below the valve, completed the watertight integrity.

'We hope, sir,' Simon added wryly.

Alec was amazed at the speed and single-mindedness that Simon had demonstrated, and his enthusiasm was catching, with Alec telling Simon to organise transport down to the recipient boat. Alec's car rushed Edith and Alec, down to the dry dock, where there were two boats being worked on, with rivet guns and air-driven hammers competing with each other. On meeting the commanding officer, Lieutenant Commander Brian Dale, Alec was impressed with his calm, and his 'hands-on' attitude, though when thinking about it, was essential in Brian's very dangerous profession, and Brian himself choosing it as a volunteer, as were all submariners and always would be.

On the way back to London, Edith noted once again, the spark of fire, in the eyes of her husband, his natural excitement in his job bubbling through, and affecting Edith because of it. He'd found another crusade to fight.

Getting back to a routine in his office was difficult after the eagerness of the boat commander, and Simon. Alec's phoning every day was obviously a very bad case of the nerves, so Edith tried to channel his enthusiasm to the problem of hunting and killing these supply U-boats, succeeding only when he managed to get six destroyers, all equipped for anti-submarine warfare.

They were all old American ships, designed for another kind of war, but fitted with the new electronic wizardry called Asdic, and modern torpedoes. They already had the turn of speed. They were very "wet" ships, that is, they weren't very good in a strong running sea.

As a Jack would say, 'They'd roll on damp grass.'

Cannibalising guns and torpedo tubes from irreparable or older ships had been going on for quite a while, ever since the RN had received the old destroyers from the USA but they were serving their purpose, Alec's six had been given priority for Asdic to be fitted to all, hoping it was as good as they said it was. Radar was already fitted, and though not the latest type, it had a range of twenty-two miles. So if they streamed in a formation of two lines of three, thirty miles apart, with luck, they may catch boats surfaced at their rendezvous "accidentally". The work forged ahead, the dockyard workers working around the clock, to get these "tin cans" off their hands. Soon, all six were working up at Portland, aided by a submarine commanded Lieutenant Dale, who was happily testing the breathing/exhaust tube, very confidently and successfully, as soon as the crew became competent at raising and lowering it.

'You don't own them you know,' Edith noted, looking at her husband, as he looked at the destroyers, tied up on the wall in pairs.

'My word, they are old, but they do look terrific,' Alec replied, and before Edith could stop him, he was walking with his stick up the gangway. Following Alec, Edith was pleased to see two of the ship's company helping him off the gangway, and thanked them for their patience, whereupon they saluted Alec, and went back to their duties.

Strolling on the upper deck, Alec hoped they were good enough ships to catch these U-boats, although, remembering Taffy Evans's account of the U boat commander giving the lifeboats some food, and sending the SOS made him think. Stories of U-boat machine-gunning survivors while still in the water, infuriated all three of the armed services, but apparently you couldn't paint them all with the same brush, and he thought, he'd like to meet that skipper one day.

Bletchley Park phoned Alec four days later, giving the latitude and longitude of a rendezvous at sea (RAS) in a week's time. This message had a lot of people travelling in two directions at the same time, ordering fuel, food, and ammunition for six destroyers. Two days later, the six "brothers" pulled out of harbour at night, and steamed for the Atlantic, and all the dangers it involved.

The breathing mast, or schnorkel, as it was called, worked on the submarine perfectly, and work was started to fit all RN boats with the idea. Simon Lee was amazed at the success, and was promoted to commander and put in charge of the project at HMS *Dolphin* at Gosport. Alec and Edith were both very proud of discovering him, and sometimes burst out laughing, remembering how he got them both up that night.

But the destroyers were Alec's main interest now, and he talked his worries over with Edith, who had her fingers on Alec's pulse so to speak, all the time.

'Did they work their fuel consumption out correctly? That bloody Asdic stuff better work as well, or I shall put a rocket right where it's painful,' Alec muttered, thinking of the lives in jeopardy.

Meanwhile, the much-maligned destroyers were stretched out in their search pattern, with the weather quite affable, for the Atlantic anyway. Asdic, and radar sets amazed the operators, picking up shoals of fish on the Asdic, and more importantly, one could see its companion, covering all the sea between them. As they sailed on the weather got dirty, and Captain Simms, the overall commander of the flotilla, ordered twenty-four hour action stations. He knew the importance of this sortie, and he also knew it was the first time destroyers had such a big number, purely to hunt U-boats. He had vaguely heard of some place called Beeches Park, or something, which declared they knew all about the U-boats' movements.

'Quite honestly,' Tony Simms explained to his number

one. 'I think the boffins and Churchill are all going gaga. They'd tell us anything to put a show of force on, purely for the Yanks, and if these destroyers are an example of their building skills, its no wonder they gave the bloody things to us,' and then both of them stomped off to the wardroom for a meal, and a wet.

It was fourteen hundred hours, and the heavy gray Atlantic swell found the destroyers making their way slowly in formation, waiting. Waiting for the familiar ping on the Asdic sets, the operators sat, soaked in sweat, headphones clamped on their heads, frustrated and angry with the hidden enemy. Eyes, sore with both sweat and fatigue as they watched the small screen, wishing they were able seamen and not this new branch of the RN. At least the seamen worked in the fresh air, although, in the ocean they were in, perhaps not. Strong black sweet tea was plentiful in all six ships, as they ploughed through the angry gray black sea, always there, and ever will be.

Fred Townley was scribbling on his pad, when the Asdic pinged, and back came an answer! A good one, nice and strong.

Yelling what he'd heard up to the bridge, on the intercom, the No 1 came down so fast, Fred though the was going to complain about a short tot! Listening on Fred's spare set of headphones, he heard it, he didn't believe it, but the boffins were right; it worked. Running back to the bridge, he told the CO everything was on, who then shut the ship down to action stations, all this happening while signalling his companions, giving them the bearing, and course of the contact. Slowly, as the destroyers turned he thought he heard a contact. Ummm, maybe not, and started to write again. Yes! It was a contact towards the target, all quietly loading depth charges into the throwers. Suddenly a second contact was on Fred's screen, on a collision course with the first one.

'Oh Lord, give us some good luck,' whispered Fred, as he tracked the two echoes, knowing that other sets were doing the same. Fred was feeling bone dry when two torpedoes tore the ship's side and bulkheads out of his ship. His last thoughts were, "What a way to end it all."

The destroyer sank very quickly, going down in two pieces. The U-boat responsible tried to escape between two destroyers, who were closing on each other, both echoes on the two ships identical.

Commander Cole, on HMS *Attacker*, fired his depth charges, and ordering the guns loaded, waited, maybe hours, but in reality, fifty seconds, then the sullen surface was ripped apart with explosions, then calm followed briefly, then wreckage was finally spewed from the depths, including lifebelts, and bodies; more dead as sacrifices to war. Andrew Cole looked at the few bits and pieces, floating on the surface, and realised there must have been three contacts, so why didn't his pal Tony Simms ping it? What a bloody waste!

'Asdic to the bridge, two echoes converging on us,' the excited metallic voice shouted, forcing Andrew Cole to put his monitor headset on, noting the positions, and telegraphing to the engine room, 'Full speed ahead hard-a-starboard!'

'Hard-a-starboard it is, sir,' repeated the coxswain, spinning the wheel as fast as he could. Echoes were coming faster now, until they were as one.

'Fire depth charges,' shouted Andrew Cole as the quarterdeck bounced with the violent turn and the torque of the propeller shafts. HMS *Foxhound* fired her depth charges a few seconds later, then quiet reined, except for the hiss of the ocean against the hull. Then the sea erupted into a turmoil of screaming noise, and tortured water, as it hurled itself to the sky, then returned to its proper place, with such force, it forced the U-boat wreckage below the surface, before it returned, floating in diesel and seawater.

Chapter Twenty Seven

HMS *Agility* and HMS *Alacrity*, in company with HMS *Alliance*, turned to starboard, to meet their prey, which appeared to be two U-boats, very close, or tied up together.

But the good news was that they were surfaced.

The fading daylight was made worse by the sea, now behaving as only the Atlantic can be. The destroyers, their depth-charge throwers all loaded, had the initiative so closing down to silent routine, they approached the boats.

Using his night glasses, Commander Matthews saw the U-boats transferring from one to another, so working out that the Germans would be slow to react if they saw the destroyers, he telegraphed slow speed ahead. Matthews ordered a shallow setting to his depth charges, and then crept up on the enemy. Manoeuvring to the starboard side of the U-boats, he signalled,' Full starboard,' bracing himself for the movement of the ship, as she put her quarterdeck near to the two enemy vessels, waiting in the darkness.

The right second came, yelling, 'Fire,' into the bridge to quarterdeck linkup, he caught sight of the depth charges leaving the throwers. Seconds later, six depth charges exploded on the two U-boats. Simultaneously, they exploded, lighting up the stem of the ship that had killed them.

The release of tension was an audible thing, with

Commander Matthews congratulating his officers and men, piping 'Up Spirits' as a thank you, after they had tidied the upper deck, with everything battened down. No 1 saw the torpedo track first, realising it was too late to take evasive action.

The torpedoes hit the destroyer in its engineering spaces, giving her a fatal wound. Settling herself very quickly, the crew managed to get two lifeboats into the water, but she slid beneath the surface, going faster as all the heavy machinery ripped free, tearing holes in her hull, as she fled to the seabed. It was as though the *Agility* had never existed. The third U-boat had claimed her final victim.

Seeing the two remaining British destroyers, the U-boat commander ordered the periscope down, and smiling, said, 'Ein Englander kaput!' The submariners cheered, a bit raggedly, their U-boat had not been replenished with food, and she was so low on fuel and no more torpedoes. The commander explained that they could porthole the boat, or surrender to the two remaining destroyers that were destroyers straight away, that they wished to surrender.

The destroyers hove to, one on each side of the U-boat, which was covered with machine guns from both. Six seamen climbed into the U-boat, and with no trouble relieved it of its Enigma machine and code books.

The two destroyer commanders decided to use mooring lines from the fo'rard ship, aft on the other destroyer, placing the U-boat between them very securely, each destroyer sharing the German crews between them.

The trip back to Portsmouth was very long and slow. The two old ships made hard work of it, and were a bit nervous of Coastal Command finding them and perhaps mistaking the

American ships, for German. The *'Sunderland'* that Coastal Command used was very good at dealing with U-boats, and U-boat commanders dived as soon as one appeared on the horizon.

On entering Portsmouth Harbour, the ship's sirens hooted, and Old Portsmouth was covered with grieving and cheering people. On tying up on the jetty and tugs had placed the U-boat alongside at HMS *Dolphin*, a Royal Marine band played 'Rule Britannia' as the Germans were loaded into lorries, and transported to a debriefing centre, then to a POW camp.

Commodore Alec Hamilton, VC viewed the two crews of the destroyers, and spread some medals around, but the 'Up Spirits', and a month's leave was so much more appreciated.

Simon Lee was allowed on the U-boat after the Enigma machine and code books were taken to Bletchley Park. After removing and inspecting the schnorkel, it was found that the German standard of workmanship was slightly better than ours, but eventually, we copied it, and fitted it to all our submarine fleet.

Looking at the list of the dead, Edith cried. She cried at such a waste of young men, and the pain and suffering of the stricken families.

'Edith my love, those men who gave their lives, have in all probability saved countless lives, now that we know how the Germans have been doing it, staying at sea so long, and that hook thing, what is it, the schnorkel thing? Do you know what that saves U-boats doing? No surfacing for air, and no surfacing to run the diesels, to charge the batteries. Mind you, I don't think we'll use supply submarines, but depot ships with workshops new crews, and plenty of stowage for torpedoes and ammunition. Big galleys to cook for the boats, now that's something I'd like to see,' Alec replied, then kissed her lips so gently.

Picking up his stick, he suggested quietly, 'Let's go home darling, let's make up.'

Edith looked at him, her eyes wide open, with her lips in a small '0' and an index finger nail touching her lips.

The following week, everything was back to normal, Alec sitting at his desk, remembering and wondering. Edith saw him as only someone in love sees. The passion, the grief and the sorrow, the way his nose wrinkled when he laughed.

'The war must end soon Alec,' she whispered, wanting to see him laugh a bit more. 'Oh and another thing I'd like to talk about, my doctor has told me I'm pregnant.'

'What did you say? I thought you said you were pregnant,' he roared, 'I haven't done something right have I?'

Alec phoned his father-in-law, and all his pals everywhere. They thought he was insane. Yes, Alec thought a holiday was in order after he recovered from Edith's news, his father-in-law agreeing entirely, booked a passage to America on the *Queen Elizabeth*, in three weeks' time, for them both,

'To do some relaxing and some shopping at leisure,' he said. The three weeks went by so slowly, Edith looking forward to it, Alec wondering what horrors lay ahead of them on the huge liner, returning to America with American serv-icemen, wounded and mutilated in the European theatre of war. Then after seeing the look of happiness on Edith's face, he couldn't, wouldn't spoil it in any way. He could only hope and pray that Edith didn't see what was preying on his mind: invasion of England.

As Edith and Alec boarded the *Queen Elizabeth* at

Southampton docks, they noticed the ambulances and buses parked on the jetty. On reaching their state room, Edith remarked, 'I know the ship is going to be full of wounded men you know Alec, so don't treat me with kid gloves, darling ... I have been aware of the American losses as well as ours, and I promise, I will rest.'

Alec looked at her, feeling relieved that she didn't need any explanation from him, and then taking their coats, he hung them up on a hat stand, before talking her into having a rest on the sumptuous soft bed.

Edith woke up just in time to go on the upper deck, and watch as the great liner slipped out of harbour. She looked away from the disappearing England, and she noticed Alec trying to help some Americans see the shoreline going over the horizon.

Edith smiled, thinking of his "peg leg", and gambling the Yanks didn't know anything about it. In fact they were travelling in civvies, after all, you don't want to wear uniform, while you were on leave.

Alec waved to her when he saw Edith watching and she walked over to the group of men he was talking to.

Introducing her, they were all very gracious, and made her feel like a queen, treating her so nicely. 'He doesn't do bad, considering he's only got one leg,' said Edith, slipping her arm through his.

The Americans were amazed at this news, and congratulated him on hearing of his exploits on HMS *Hecla*.

'Gee sir, this is a great little boat ya got here, why she can outrun anythin' the Krauts have got, 'n' that's goin' some,' one of the Yanks said, waving his handless arms in the air.

The *Queen Elizabeth* was gradually increasing her revs.

To increase too quickly, would lower the steam pressure in the boilers temporarily, and the *Queen* wasn't a destroyer.

Strolling along the upper deck after breakfast, they talked to the wounded men, who were "topsides" for the fresh air. These casual meetings of the men gave such a varied outlook on the Americans. The variety of injuries they had suffered, some indescribable, it made Edith dash back to their stateroom, to try and compose herself. She was feeling nauseous in the mornings now, and that didn't help.

One particular man, who had been blinded, seemed to brighten up whenever Edith and Alec met and talked to him. He was the son of a preacher, based in Texas, and longing to get into the US Army, so joining the bombardment group, he was sent to Europe. The howitzer next to him exploded, robbing him of his sight.

'But ah guess God has a task fo' me, otherwise ah would be dade, ah surely would, jes' like mah buddies,' he remembered, tears from sightless sockets running down his face.

Edith would have spent the entire voyage with the wounded, picking out the ones who looked lonely or frightened. Frightened of their future in their country, but Alec thought she was getting too attached to the "work", and pleaded with her to rest. Eventually, Edith capitulated, and rested in the sun, while the *Queen Elizabeth* outran any U-boats or other German opposition. The huge bows parted the water of the Atlantic, leaving a bubbling white wash behind her four enormous propellers.

Alec worried about Edith's health and well being, knowing that most pregnant ladies felt sick in the mornings, but he believed Edith might be feeling homesick as well. Alec admitted to himself that he missed being a desk jockey, but he was thinking of his successful "escapades", at the Germans' expense.

He thought of Sally and their daughters, dying, as well as their unborn baby, his grief, then his salvation by Edith, who loved him with a ferocity that made him so content now, especially with the addition on the way. He was determined to give Edith a good holiday, a thing very rare for British people in these stressful times.

Arriving at New York was a blessed relief for Alec, no more worry of Edith getting attached to the wounded Americans through sympathy, and pity. Although he did feel pity for them, the war had been going on for two years before Pearl Harbour was attacked by the Japanese, forcing them into the war, but to line so many battleships up in neat rows, Alec thought, was criminal.

The holiday passed them by so quickly, both enjoying the American lifestyle, compared to Britain, but good things must surely come to an end. Edith was hankering for home, to settle down and prepare for her baby.

Arriving back on board the *Queen Elizabeth*, into the same stateroom, they both relaxed, to prepare for the work in Admiralty House.

Alec groaned as he said to his wife, 'Edith my love, I'm dreading to see what's been going on at the office, it's not such a busy place, but it would be now, while I'm not there, that something will crop up. Then there is the addition as well. Well I think you ought to take some leave, and go and stay with your father, after all he's as excited as we are, but the air raids, and those infernal flying bombs would not be any problem for you, what do you think?'

'I think you are trying to get rid of me Alec Hamilton, but

I can tell you now, that you will not get rid of me, EVER! But you are quite right about going to stay with Daddy. He is by himself now, so I can see that he's cared for, while I am a lady in waiting,' Edith replied, her eyes sparkling with humour, as she saw Alec's face, stunned at her outburst. Then he saw the laughter in her eyes, and they both roared with laughter, several young American soldiers looking at them, alarm showing on their innocent faces.

'You have a wicked sense of humour, but I love you for it,' gasped Alec, wiping the tears from his eyes.

The *Queen Elizabeth* was full of American troops, all eager to show the "Krauts" how to fight a war, and win! Never mind that the '"Krauts" were mostly battle trained, what was this Waffen SS that they'd heard about? The enthusiasm was infectious, until the liner was mid Atlantic, when there was a spate of the usual very bad weather, that was part and parcel of the awful Atlantic at times.

The main target of all U-boats, was the two *Queens,* always full of troops on both crossings of the Atlantic, but when the lookout on watch shouted,'U-boat, fine on the starboard bow, approximately three miles.'

Slamming the phone down, Bert scurried down to the bridge, where he pointed out the direction of the U-boat. A klaxon sounded, declaring a state of alert, then the hull hissed in the water, as the master ordered evasive action. The liner put her stem towards the U-boat, by turning to port, thus making the target so much smaller to the U-boat, but able to use her superior power and speed for escaping the danger she was in.

Alec said, 'Usually, U-boats try to turn their fast targets into the path of another U-boat., The Master has done the exact opposite to what the Germans intended. He's turned to the ice of the Arctic, which is where the U-boats don't want to be.' Looking at his watch, Alec asked to be excused, and went to the bridge, where he showed his identification.

'I suggest you zigzag at irregular times captain, he has no chance of catching you, but I think there may be a pack of them ahead, with a string of the blighters to your port side, hoping you'll turn into them,' said Alec. The captain agreed, putting the necessary orders into motion.

The upper deck was full of troops, with the weapons and equipment needed for making war.

'Gee Chuck, I guess I know what these sailors feel like, going over this man's ocean,' said a voice from the back, who was instantly shouted down.

Queen Elizabeth carried on through the night, leaving the U-boats behind strolling on the deck as the ship flew in her haste leaving a broad white scar in the sea at her stern, but the sea will ever be, what else will?

Chapter Twenty Eight

L ondon seemed almost peaceful, as both Edith and Alec walked around Trafalgar Square, before entering Admiralty House.

'Back to the old grind,' Alec muttered to himself as they walked from sunlight, into the dark interior, after receiving a salute from the Royal Marine sentry. Edith and Alec looked at each other simultaneously, wondering, and both bursting out laughing, thinking if he was the sentry who said goodnight to them, such a long time ago it seemed.

While they were recovering in the foyer, the Royal Marine marched in and halted at the signing in desk, where Alec and Edith stood, gasping for breath.

Looking at them, the Royal Marine deliberately winked, and said, 'Good morning once again, sir,' smiled, and marched off to his destination, leaving the two of them helplessly laughing again.

Eventually, they opened their office door, where Edith asked the new WRNS secretary to make a brew, thinking of when Alec had kissed her hair when he thought she was asleep, the tears of joy threatening to flood her eyes, but blinking quickly, she opened the mail which had piled up over the leave they had enjoyed.

'What are you thinking about darling, you look so sweet and vulnerable,' said Alec.

Edith looked at him long and hard, squeezed his hand, and said, 'Thank you.'

Alec scratched his head in wonderment, and started on with reading his mail.

"Good grief," Alec thought, all these Officers and men volunteering for any mission Alec's department inspired. He had an impressive reputation which, he had to maintain, otherwise the extraordinary' missions would grind to a halt, due to lack of volunteers.

His mind returned to his family, all standing so proudly before the King, all wiped out, if it hadn't been for Edith, Alec knew he would be no more by now. But he had a new wife and baby

He read all the volunteers' applications first, remembering the old Royal Navy saying, 'Never volunteer for anything, except more leave'!

Asking Edith to file all the names, he mentioned there were two official letters, so after a cup of tea, she could help him read them, in case he was in any sort of trouble. It was the first brown envelope that was interesting, in fact so interesting that Alec walked over to the wall map of Europe and the UK.

According to the admiral's letter, some sites were being occupied by the Germans, involving their vengeance weapons, so the admiral "asked' in his quaint way, if Alec thought a few photos taken by the superb Mosquito, would be beneficial.

Alec sat at his desk chatting to Edith, wondering if the admiral thought Mosquitoes grew on trees, when his secretary put a signal on his desk. Opening the official letter, he was amazed to find that two Mosquito PR aircraft with pilots were at his disposal. Stationed at Waddington in Lincolnshire, the main Lancaster base, they were fitted with long range fuel tanks, the most up to date cameras, and painted pale blue underneath, with camouflage on top.

'Well I'll be, Edith, see what they've supplied me with now!' Alec laughed, as Edith read the letter.

'Oh dear Alec, you'll never guess who they've put in charge Nigel Bush! I'm leaving. He'll have us as batty as he is within a week, and that laugh!' Edith shrieked.

'Control yourself,' answered Alec, in mock severity, 'Is there anybody else so stupid as to do this job? There you are then,' he finished, smiling at Edith's glee, and his own pleasure. The word invasion, kept in Alec's mind, throughout the day, the perfect answer to Hitler's dilemma. It would catch the British forces with their trousers down again. Alec just hoped and prayed Hitler wouldn't think of it.

He had...

Chapter Twenty Nine

A lec phoned Nigel the following day, asking him to put an irregular patrol up, looking for any build up of forces, ships and landing craft. He also mentioned the fact that German troops seemed to be building up in three coastal areas. His Mosquito could "accidentally" fly over them, to see if there was any Panzer build up, associated with tugs and barges. Alec was hoping against hope that invasion wasn't in the German mind. Another factor seemed to be, more U-boat patrols than normal were being carried out in these three areas, so perhaps they were there for the protection of these sites, from the Royal Navy blockade ships.

The worst nightmare the Germans could have was Mosquito and Spitfires fitted with cameras. The air in Europe belonged at last to the RAF – and as Nigel's leash was slipped, so the patrols and photo-shooting flights would start. Nigel's plan of fitting very loud howlers on the Mosquito engines' exhaust ports was shelved, unlike the German Stukas.

Alec immediately tackled all the intelligence gathered from the French resistance, and attempted to match the intelligence to the wall of photos he started to collect, one site after another, all coming under the close scrutiny of the huge cameras fitted to the Mosquito anti- aircraft guns were amassing around a particularly big natural harbour, but seeming to protect nothing but a railhead. Why? Alec wondered. Admittedly there were fishing boats working from the harbour, but not enough to warrant being so well protected from aircraft attack. The Germans would not entertain that anyway, protecting the French, when their own forces needed the protection more. All this was flashing red lights in Alec's mind, as he stared at the map on the wall, wondering why a backwater received such a big protective blanket.

'Alright, there is a few landing craft there, but the Germans would need hundreds of barges, for any sort of invasion. There is a rumour that Field Marshal Rommel is in charge of western France, and its coastline. Now we know he's the best they've got

'Nigel, so why have the Germans placed a top soldier in charge of nothing?' Alec mused as they both drank tea and studied, then restudied the map.

'Look at this Nigel, there seems to be a lot of haystacks being built, now I understand it's the season for it, but are the French geared up sufficiently to harvest so much, in so short a time,' Alec wondered, then ran as fast as he could to the map, with a huge magnifying glass in his hand.

Swiftly passing over the haystacks in question, he stopped, causing Nigel to bump into his back.

'Look at those bloody big gun barrels sticking out of the haystacks, Nigel! The crafty bastards, they've filled the countryside with dirty big panzer divisions, and we've been here, twiddling our thumbs. Nigel old man, have you any Hurribomber COs that you're still pals with? Just to hit a couple of those stacks, to prove we're right,' said Alec, the adrenalin pounding through his body.

'Certainly Alec,' replied Nigel, 'but these things take time to set up, aircraft are so scarce. 'However,' and a crafty look came over Nigel's face, 'we could use a Mosquito, after all, they're more heavily armed than a Hurribomber, but we already have a Mosquito, so we can take the external cameras off, and refit the eight inch rocket launchers, and there's your problem, solved,' Nigel finished, hoping that Alec would approve of his idea. He wanted to get some flying hours in too, so what a superb way of killing two birds with one stone.

He was silently laughing when Alec said casually, 'Who'll be the pilot Nigel?' then seeing Nigel's heaving shoulders said, 'Oh no you bloody well don't, you crafty sod, but let's go to the wardroom, and have a meal. Perhaps you've got some ideas or plans to show me?'

At the mention of food, Nigel's moustache bristled at the pleasure he was going to indulge in and was off down the stairs like a two-legged carthorse. Alec followed, chuckling to himself over the discovery of the panzers, hiding in the French meadows, waiting.

On reaching his table, Alec's train of thought didn't change at all; he wanted to know where the landing craft and barges were, and where were the troops?

Suddenly, he had a brainwave, dashing upstairs as fast as he could to his office; he grabbed his magnifying glass off his desk, and went to the wall map. Looking through the glass intently, he went over every minute detail, both in the buildings, the woods, and the green rolling hills, so verdant at this time of year.

Nigel entered the office forty minutes later, fully sated, and happily went to Alec's side by the wall.

'You know Alec, an official translator would be able to see what you can't see, why not call one in? Your secretary will do the honours while we discuss a plan I've got rattling around in my head,' suggested the RAF man, 'which is quite simple.'

'I must agree with you on the first count. The second I'm pleased about, and the third, about you being simple, well never mind Nigel, I'm still pleased your on my side,' Alec concluded, a smile on his face all the time.

Nigel's plan consisted of crossing the French coast thirty miles north of the target, thus avoiding the anti-aircraft fire the Mosquito would draw, attacking the target from the inland direction. The Mosquito would have to carry extra fuel tanks. While the Merlins that powered the Mosquito were the ultimate in aero engine design, they were not economical.

'But the Germans,' Nigel reasoned, 'would not expect an attack from the east of France, mainly because they're occupying it,' and released his laugh, so distinctive, so loud.

The following day, an RAF photo translator arrived at Alec's office, ready to study and measure the items in the photos on the wall. Within two hours Sergeant Becket had confirmed the fact that the haystacks were disguised German tanks, and after measuring, decided they were fitted with the deadly cighty-eight millimetre gun. After a cup of tea, and two hours later, Alec started to get agitated, and wondered what Becket could be looking for.

Sergeant Becket said, 'Hell sir, the fields are covered with camouflage nets, of a quality I've never seen before because of the good workmanship, and brilliant colour matching with the whole area, but you have a problem. There's room for a lot of troops under those nets, they're covering a multitude of sins, sir.' Becket finished, then pointed out all the tell-tale signs to Alec and Nigel, such as badly hidden tank tracks suddenly ending at a haystack, and colours, appearing out of place in their surroundings.

Alec was amazed at all the signs he had missed, and congratulated Sergeant Becket at the ease in which he'd found the camouflage net.

'But Sergeant, if there are all these troops here, and Rommel in charge, where are the invasion barges if they exist? But if they don't, how are the Germans going to invade?'

Perhaps the Germans were not going to invade, but why the military build up, tanks, and a man like Rommel, who is a tank man, all lined up in France? The only thing missing were the invasion barges and landing craft, although, there were a dozen or so landing craft moored in the shallow end of the harbour. The three men eventually left the office; Alec off upstairs to his flat to wish Edith was with him, and the two RAF men going their separate ways from Trafalgar Square.

As always, Edith phoned at nine o'clock, giving Alec all the latest gossip, how she felt, and how she wished they were together, as they needed to be, always. Alec didn't mention what had been discovered in the French countryside, it would worry her too much; especially if she knew Nigel was thinking, and hoping, of flying the mission.

The next day saw a sortie flown by Nigel, and everything went according to plan, except for a bit of cannon fire after a tank hiding place was destroyed, with its occupant. But Nigel reasoned, they couldn't use that direction of attack any more, and photos taken the following day, confirmed the two lines of anti-aircraft guns on the backs of lorries, mixed with "nebel-werfers", German rocket concentrations, also highly mobile, thus destroying the RAF ability to do low level attacks.

As Alec worried and fretted about the problems, who should walk in, like a light breeze over the Sussex downs, but

Edith, immediately putting a smile on Alec's face.

'Your forehead looks like a ploughed field darling, and you haven't kept me up to date with this-er, um, stop it Alec, someone might come in,' she paused, then said, 'But why should we worry, we're married!' then launched herself into Alec's lap, where they both introduced Alec to the bump.

'Of course, in three weeks' time, I'll be slim again, and we'll be three,' whispered Edith, as Alec nibbled her ear.

'Well I'm blowed,' said Alec, 'is it on us as quick as that? Well that's eight months of the war gone, but I wish it all went fast, then we could all go home. But old Nigel has landed us with a bit of a problem. The Germans have got Commander, tanks and men, but no bloody invasion barges.'

'Perhaps the barges are under the camouflage Alec, after all with the railhead so convenient, what could be easier?' asked Edith, looking at the map on the wall, where Alec had spent so much time, looking and studying.

'Of course, the best place to hide so many barges, is in the sea, or somewhere, disguised as jetties' Edith mused. 'There, I'm getting as twisted as you, my darling man.'

Alec smiled at her tenderly, and said, 'You are my life Edith, I just want you to know that,' then carried on measuring the area of the harbour.

The seabed of the harbour was most irregular; it had an effect almost like corduroy, with peaks and valleys covering most of the shale bottom. Phoning Nigel in Waddington, he wondered if there was any chance of getting some clear photos of the complete harbour, taking into consideration, the German defence, so complete in its effectiveness. 'Well, Navy can I have some time to study the photos we've got? We've taken delivery of an eighteen- inch camera, for high altitude work, and I'm itching to use it,' Nigel ending with a guffaw, and the eternal, 'Tally Ho!' before Alec replaced the receiver.

Edith and Alec went for a meal in the West End, the quality of the food being greatly restricted by the rationing, that rationed food to the absolute basic of basics. 'At least, one of us is slim,' Alec, remarked, preparing to duck before Edith hit him.

'You pig, you made me like this, then you say a thing like that,' Edith seethed, but before she could leave the table, at a nod from Alec, the little band, that had been having a rest, began to play Glenn Miller's *'String of Pearls'*.

Alec reached over and caught her hand, placing a slim box into it. Edith's eyes jolted open, when she saw the contents, a beautiful double string of pearls. Her tear-streaked face swung from the pearls, to Alec, who was looking at her anxiously.

'Oh Alec you fool, fancy buying this at a time when food is more important, especially with Alice here, waiting for the day to come,' whispered Edith, as she tried the necklace on.

'Am I forgiven?' pleaded Alec. 'The whole scene had been set up, by me and the band, and I thought you'd be amused.'

'Well Alec Hamilton, it's a good thing I'm a forgiving person, but I shall laugh again in three weeks, when I will be half the woman I am now!'

The mediocre meal ended as usual, with everybody looking for a taxi in the blackout, but somehow they were lucky, and a drive around the diversions, to miss the bomb damage and rubble, took them to their flat at Admiralty House. Edith played with her pearls all the way home, the way all ladies do when they're happy and content with their lives.

'Ho hum,' she sighed and looked at her husband as they

walked to the imposing doorway. The Royal Marine presented arms, and wished them, 'Goodnight sir, and your lady.'

Edith shot her head round in unison with Alec, saw the sentry, looked back at each other, and scurried through the portal as fast as they could, before erupting into a fit of laughter and giggles, then settling down to the occasional whimper as they climbed the stairs. 'That poor man, he'll think we're laughing at him,' gasped Edith, as they sat on the bed, looking at, and loving each other.

Simon from Portsmouth appeared at Alec's office, his face eager, his eyes sparkling with enthusiasm.

'Good morning sir, the team have come up with a good scheme, to keep the Germans wondering exactly how many submarines we have actually got in active service. Hell we thought, if we submerged them, and rested them on the bottom, with the schnorkel raised above water of course, they'll be hidden with a few sailing boats, or fishing boats, anything that looks innocent and nondescript. Four men to each boat would be sufficient to enable to do this. Then blow the tanks at night, then tugs could move them back to different jetties, that way, fooling the Germans as to how many boats are in harbour and at sea,' Simon finished his explanation, which had found Alec silent and listening, all the time.

Congratulating Simon and his team, Alec walked over to the map on the wall, and looked carefully.

'Simon, would you step over here please, there is something I want you to look at,' Alec murmured.

Simon stepped up next to Alec, a worried look on his face.

'What does that vaguely resemble?' wondered Alec, giving a sideways glance to Simon, a man he greatly respected.

'Well sir ...'

'Alec in private, please,' interrupted Alec.

'Well...er...Alec, it looks to me that someone has been digging trenches, or something underwater, though I can't be sure. It's either trenches, or something or other buried there,' replied Simon, a little hot under the collar with calling a commodore by his Christian name, even at his request.

'Thank you Simon, a great idea for the boats, carry on with the good work, let's polish off this German corporal as soon as we can,' Alec finished, as Simon put his gas mask over his shoulder, and put his cap on, at a saucy angle.

Wishing each other safety in whatever they did, Simon left, bound for Pompey, and his "babies", his submarines.

Could it be barges, sunk in shallow water with a view to being ready to hand when needed? Alec pondered, and if so, how would the barges be brought back to the surface, ready and fit for use? He wondered if Nigel's latest camera was up to the job. Unless, as one Mosquito flew high over the target, to draw the flak, the other Mosquito could fly in low, taking as many photos as he could, of the harbour.

Excitedly, he phoned Nigel at his base at Waddington, putting the question, theory, and answer to him in one breath, 'So what do you think?' Alec ended, with a deep gasp of breath. 'Hell Navy, ha! I'll give it some thought, this camera can snap a fly, having its way, in the desert, from twenty thousand feet,' and with a bellowed 'Tally Ho,' he put the phone down, his enthusiasm bubbling over, giving Alec cause to smile.

His problems were wearing him down, plus the slight chance that Edith might have the usual complications that are associated with childbirth. But if it was the barges under the surface of the harbour, how could they be resurfaced? Barges were single-hulled vessels, with one basic use, to shift cargo, or to shift troops.

He walked to the wall map. "It seems to rule me at the moment," thought Alec, then he thought of Simon Lee, and his latest idea of hiding submarines during the day, from any enemy aircraft that flew over Portsmouth, taking photos the same as the RAF did – if the barges were fitted with ballast tanks like boats, it might. 'Just a minute here,' said Alec to himself.

'Just a minute, that idea would work, barges fitted with two independent ballast tanks, one fastened to each side. Release the barge from the tanks, and the barge floats to the surface! 'Where's the phone?' Simon was soon answering the call from Alec, who told him to use his imagination again, and visualise a barge underwater, held by a ballast tank on each side. On release, it would surface, or wouldn't it? Could Simon build a model barge and try it? Then if the secret of the harbour was barges, a method of destroying them was on the cards, very much so. Putting the phone down, he picked it up again to phone Nigel, telling him of his suspicions, and that Simon Lee was making a model, and if the barges were there, how could they be destroyed.

'Hello Navy. We have what we call delayed action bombs old man, mind you, the Navy don't use them, they still use, what are they called? Oh yes, they use cannon balls don't they? Tally Ho Alec, we'll crack this nut, don't worry about it, go to bed,' yawned Nigel, and put the phone down.

Alec looked at the time, and thought of Edith in her bed.

"Ye Gods," he thought, then looking at the map, he smiled, hoping he had found the truth at last, then turning, he climbed the stairs, realising by now that he was exhausted, completely. He got into bed at three o'clock in the morning, his wife sound asleep, his slight noise covered by Edith's measured breathing.

As soon as Alec woke up the next day, he looked at the clock. It was half past two. Never, and looking at his watch, discovered it was right. Putting on his tin leg and trousers, he had a wash and shave. Returning to the bedroom, to get dressed, he found Edith sitting on the bed, looking at him with a worried expression on her face.

'Any problems?' asked Alec, 'Please tell me, and I can organise transport for you.'

'Alec, I think I'd better go home to Daddy. I'm having funny things going on now, so rather than disturb your work, on this invasion thing, I've got a car and driver to take me home. I'm so sorry Alec, but our baby is very important to me, and you, so until I've had Lucy.'

'Alec is his name,' said Alec. His eyes looking at her so gentle, and loving, then he kissed her long and tenderly. They stayed like it, until the doorbell rang a couple of minutes later. It was a WRNS driver, to take Edith home, sadly away from Alec. As they said goodbye, their fingers, lingering together for those last few desperate moments, before Edith went down the stairs, as though she was going to her own execution. Looking up at Alec, with her tear-stained face, she gave a weak smile, and her hand fluttered, like a dying bird. Trying to cheer her up, Alec gave her a big smile, and blew her some kisses.

Entering his office, his secretary brought in a pot of tea, and of course his biscuits, which Edith had told, he was most partial.

Trying hard to forget Edith for a while, he stood, looking

at the photos making up the wall map.

'What is your secret?' he said to the wall, 'is Simon's system for the boats, the same, or is it something else? Or is it an ordinary coincidence?'

Returning to his desk, he phoned Simon, to see if things were going well with his vanishing boats. 'Yes sir, it works perfectly so as we fit the boats with schnorkels, we can lose them so to speak. How is your harbour problem, sir? Seeing the seven boats down as it were, I must admit there is a similarity, in fact, they are very noticeable from the air so I've been told, I'm thinking of dragging a camouflage net over them. Underwater of course, then Portsmouth harbour will be the same as it always is so to speak, to our Luftwaffe chums on high altitude reconnaissance.'

'Thanks Simon, I appreciate the effort you are putting in. By the way, you've been promoted to captain as of now, congratulations, we'll have to have a drink,' replied Alec, thinking over Simon's idea, with a net spread underwater, would alter the shape of a solid object, due to the tides and currents, causing the netting to move and sway.

'Very clever indeed Adolph, but I've got Simon Lee and Nigel Bush on my side, and we are going to f—'. Mary, his secretary, came in with a tray of tea, just as he was going to finish his sentence in his RN vocabulary.

'Oh thank you Mary, I'm sorry about that, but I was getting carried away.'

'Sir,' said Mary, 'to be quite honest with you, since I've been in the service, I've learnt a whole new language, and its really opened my eyes,' then she gave him a saucy wink, and went back to her desk.

The day was drawing to a close, when a motorcycle

despatch rider came into his office, and handed Alec a thick package. Asking Mary to make the rider a hot strong cuppa, with some of Nelson's blood in it, purely for medicinal purposes of course! Damn! Damn! Why do they do these parcels up, to withstand the blast of ten battleships broadsides?

At last, the photos were revealed to him, so clearly, the bloody Mosquito must have gone underwater!

Alec whooped at the images, 'Got you, I've got you,' and carried on studying.

Mary came in, her hair awry, and her uniform jacket being done up. 'What's the matter sir? You frightened me and Bert, the despatch rider. He's finished his tea sir,' she finished lamely.

'You can leave now Mary, go and have a nice night out, but ask Bert to look after you, on that motor cycle,' Alec said, giving her a knowing wink. Blushing, Mary thanked him, and left the office, hoping Bert knew a nice place to go.

Chapter Thirty

When Alec phoned Nigel to ask him for lunch, his body was burning up. He was living on adrenalin and nerves and didn't sleep the previous night.

Nigel, as keen to eat at somebody else's expense, showed up at noon, greeting Alec with a raucous, 'Hello Navy, 1 believe we've got your target worked out correctly. Very clever, it's a pity it's wasted on the losing side. Still, what with taking on another front against Russia, and the rumours about these camps, old Adolph has got to be insane,' said Nigel, striding over to the wall map, using his stick. 'I think the easiest plan is to use delayed action "eggs", to make sure they reach the bottom before going off. Navy, it'll have to be high altitude as well. Bomber Harris doesn't want any of his Lancaster squadrons to be short, believe me.'

While waiting for their meals to be served, the two officers discussed both Simon Lee, and the harbour, of which the latter had occupied their two minds for a long time it seemed. 'He is an excellent chappie, that Simon fella of yours, fancy him coming up with the same idea as our pals over the Channel,' Nigel remarked, which was high praise indeed, coming from this volatile man.

'Well Nigel,' started Alec, 'would Bomber Harris be in any way interested in this job? After all, we are talking about the invasion of England, which presumably he doesn't want to see,' Alec said quietly 'I can't attack the target from the sea obviously, and a land attack is out of the question, so I'm afraid the RAF are the only ones to deliver.'

As he finished, the steward brought the meals, whispering to Alec, 'Excuse me sir, but there is a Danish officer over there, but nobody knows anything about him, and nobody trusts him, I don't wish to be rude, but be careful.'

He finished dusting crumbs off the table, and hastened away to the galley.

'Good Lord!' Nigel said, 'you can have him moved out surely, foreigners always cause wars you know,' and attacked his meal with a 'Tally Ho.' Alec nearly fell, laughing at his friend.

Eating their meals didn't take long, wartime meals were nothing compared to pre-war ones, but they were adequate, supplying all the vitamins and energy a body needed, but no luxury at all.

Returning upstairs to Alec's office, the discussion went on, Nigel was to put the idea to Bomber Harris, in charge of Bomber Command. Alec had a more daunting task, giving the plan to the Prime Minister, Winston Churchill. Four o'clock saw the two men, one saying cheerio, the other, saying 'Tally Ho', each feeling they had had an enjoyable few hours, an oasis in the barren world of war.

* * *

Phoning the admiral, his father-in-law, he put the idea to the wily old fox, knowing he would be enthusiastic, to get on with the raid. In fact, the admiral suggested borrowing' a cruiser for two days, to lay a barrage down on the AA gun emplacements, but soon forgot that, when he realised the U-boats did regular patrols, sweeping down the English Channel. The Germans would know they had been caught out, if a lot of attention was paid to the area. So the final decision was the RAF's and high altitude bombing.

'Give me two days Alec, I'll have words in the right ears, at the right places, and at the time,' the admiral said confidently, 'just have a bit of a make and mend.' After a chat about Edith's health, and each other's, they said goodbye, the admiral grateful for something to do, Alec, grateful for a powerful ally, but he knew he'd worry, he'd fret, until he found out if it was on or off.

In HMS *Dolphin* in Fareham, Simon's plan was proceeding successfully, joking, 'The Navy don't know where their submarines are, they have to ask me,' which caused Alec to laugh so much, Simon darted forward to help, but it wasn't necessary, and Alec waved him away, tears of laughter streaming down his face.

'Simon you swine, if you carry on like that, I'll put you on the stage, the first one out of town', then Alec had another spasm of laughter, as he saw Simon's face, not knowing how funny he'd been; it was as straight as a gun barrel.

Travellling back to London through Guildford, he stopped the car, and Alec, with the driver, had a meal, then after finishing, returned to the car, where he asked the driver to drive a bit slower, to gather his thoughts and ideas. Then he thought of Edith, feeling so uncomfortable with Alec junior, or Alice, he didn't mind really, as long as he or she was healthy, then feeling his eyes pricking with tears and the driver glancing at him through his mirror, he sorted the papers and photos out, and put them away in his briefcase, distracting himself.

London was quiet as they passed Croydon airport, now an RAF base, and avoiding the bomb damage still waiting for re-emplacement, soon rolled to a stop outside Admiralty House. Sitting in the car for a few minutes, he looked at Nelson, standing atop his column, and wondering what he would have thought of modern warfare: ships without sails, and machines that could fly.

"I don't know Nelly, I think you were better off somehow or other,"Alec thought, and climbed out of the car, saying good night to the driver, and signing a chit mentioning that the driver had finished at ten o'clock, entitling him to a day off work. Then entering Admiralty House, he was so exhausted that he hung on to the banister and dragged himself up the stairs, to bed.

When he looked around his bedroom, his uniform had disappeared, and he discovered a bandage on his head. He started to fit his tin leg, just as Edith came through the door.

'What the hell happened? I didn't have any drink, so why am 1 like this? I feel awful.'

The steward had come into the room by then, and over-hearing Alec's questions, answered, 'Well sir, as you climbed the stairs last night, I'm afraid you fell down. Now at first, I thought you were p—, intoxicated, but as you rightly say you weren't. Well I got the duty scab lifter, and he put the bandage on yer barnet, head sir. Then I phoned your lady wife, an' that's it sir,' Simpson the steward concluded.

'What's the time man, I—,' then he saw the clock, two thirty!

'Has there been any phone calls, at any time?' Alec asked anxiously, knowing the answer was to the negative.

'Yes Alec,' said Edith, and then waved Simpson out. 'Its

been passed as positive, and you have, or will have fifty dirty big Lancaster bombers at your disposal, as soon as you want them. You must call Tally Ho Bush, and get it organised.'

She looked at her husband, a big stupid smile on his face, frozen in the middle of putting on his tin leg.

'Oh Edith, I needed this so much, it hurt. I could taste getting those planes for the job, and now it's fact,' Alec quietly remarked, 'Who do I thank?'

'Well I think it was you, and having the nerve to suggest it,' replied Edith, gently doing the last buckle up on his tin leg.

'I must see Tally Ho tomorrow I think I'll go to Wadding ton wherever that is,' said Alec, 'where's my uniform by the way? Its gone missing.' 'I know, I've been sewing it up, and pressing it up tiddly again, so you owe me,' Edith told him cheekily, holding her head on one side, the way only Edith could do.

Phoning Tally Ho, Alec told him he would be in Wadding ton tomorrow, at noon, for lunch on him.

Tally Ho's laugh came down the phone, as he said, 'I see Navy, you want to see how the poor live do you? Well you bring that stunning wife of yours, and we will allow you in, but if you don't, you won't get near the main gate! See you tomorrow. Tally Ho!' roared Nigel, and the phone was silent.

Chapter Thirty One

'Come on Mrs Hamilton, time to get up, wakey, wakey,' Alec murmured. 'Go away then, I was having a lovely dream, I was putting my arm around your neck, and—', Edith blushed, and cuddled the lump.

Alec laughed, gently kissed her, then putting on his tin leg, got up to go to the bathroom, and then make the two of them, some breakfast of tinned sausages, and powdered eggs,

Edith slid in behind him, saying, 'You've pinched my job now you brute,' and laughing, laid the table, gaily chatting to Alec about everything a baby needs. 'I've got a chest full of cast offs and knitted things, but it's so difficult what colours to knit, so I've done so many of pink, and the same with blue. That way, the colour we don't want, we can give to somebody less lucky than us,' she finished, then drinking her tea, began to get herself ready for the drive up north to Waddington.

Alec, as always, looked very smart in his uniform, as they stepped into the car, a nice big number, not very old, and consequently was the flagship of the fleet. Car production had closed down at the outbreak of war, turning the factories over to the production of tanks and weapons of all sorts, but the Humber looked brand new, as it whisked them away from smoky old London town, leaving behind streets blocked with rubble. But one incident came to Alec's mind; he remembered a double-decker bus, standing on its rear end, with its front wheels resting against a building.

The air became fresher as they travelled, and by the time the car had reached Cambridgeshire, it was nice and bright. Asking the driver to pull over and stop somewhere, the three had a cup of tea from a flask, rested a minute, then off they went again, reaching the main gate of Waddington aerodrome, an hour later.

Standing by the gate, was, yes. Tally Ho!

Jumping into the front seat, he directed the driver to the officers' mess, and asked a steward to look after the RN driver. The driver, Alf, had been in the Navy eighteen years, and this jumped up f—, so he smiled sweetly, and said, 'Ta,' then lurched off the NAAFI, still mumbling under his breath.

On entering Tally Ho's office, they were amazed at the state of it. Photos of German and RAF planes, a lot of pictures of young men, some of the pictures having a black ribbon on. Bits of airplane were strewn all over the floor, accompanied by a flying helmet and jacket with a parachute hanging on a nail above the chaos. A microscopic desk seemed to be covered in wet cup rings, and numbers scribbled in chalk.

'Good Lord Nigel, how the hell do you work in this terrible mess? Let's get it straight.'

Nigel looked at Alec steadily, a smile on his face, then slowly sat down.

'Well Navy, my batman went on leave, and got himself killed in an air raid. My secretary got let down by a Yank, after she fell pregnant, and walked into a prop of a Lancaster, two weeks ago. That is why. But she never knew I adored her, much to my shame.'

Edith went forward to hold him, his shoulders heaving, as

he sought solace in his grief. Jerking himself out of his well of self-pity, he suggested tea, before calling the officers' mess for a batman to bring some.

'So sorry Nigel, I didn't mean to be so insensitive, why didn't you tell me? I would have understood old man, please, we'll return to London, and do this—' started Alec.

'Never in your life,' Nigel said very quietly, 'we've got to move on with this raid, before the Germans get stronger, and they invade. Anyway, it's my turn to buy you a meal,' Nigel interrupted, back to his breezy self.

Looking at Edith for a second, he said, 'Thank you dear Edith, I think I feel better now, in fact, if Navy over there upsets you, tell me, and I'll sort him out,' a smile on his mouth, his eyes still wet with tears.

Eventually, they went to work, fitting in where fifty bombers would be available. The final decision was the twenty-eighth, and then an RAF jeep took them to the officers' mess, for lunch. Looking around, Edith and Alec noticed that most of the aircrew consisted of young men, vital, laughing and essential in the lives of all present.

Nigel saw them looking around, and when Edith and Alec looked at each other, he said, 'Don't say it, go on board any of your warships, and they're all the same, young and oh so innocent, but they do the work they were trained for, that's all they're expected to do.'

Meeting the station commander after lunch, Nigel and Alec asked him if the twenty eighth was convenient.

'Of course, as long as it hurts the Hun, but the bombs you need, you say delayed action would be perfect. Well, a one-minute delay would give the weapon too long, it could bury itself in the sea-bed before going off, so I would think ten seconds would send them off, just above these barge things you say are sunk there. Damn funny way to fight a war, what?' he finished, and strolled off to see his adjutant and organise everything needed for the raid. Alec followed him with his eyes for a second, before asking Nigel if he was always like that.

'We're all as batty as hell, but that's what keeps us on top of the Germans,' he replied. Then guiding the pair round the corner of a hangar, he introduced them to two Mosquito fighter bombers. Painted pale blue underneath, and camouflage on top, they were beautiful machines.

Edith explained that she didn't like the colours on the top, but it was a nice blue.

Nigel and Alec peered at each other, and carried on, Nigel saying to Alec, 'They're yours, one is fitted with cameras and cannons, and the other has machine guns, cannons, and a bomb bay.'

Getting closer to the aircraft, Edith saw her name painted on one Mosquito nose, while on the other, was Alec 2. She rushed to Alec; her arms open wide, and said tearfully, 'Isn't Tally Ho nice?' Then turning to Nigel, said, 'You know Nigel, you are always welcome to stay with us, now, and after this war is over, either way. But you will always be Tally Ho to us, understand?'

'Yes ma'am, I do believe your transport is waiting, so Tally Ho, Navy, and his wife!' and chucked his cap in the air.

The journey back to London was nice and smooth, the big Humber rolling away, eating the miles so quickly. Alec and Edith were both sound asleep when the car pulled to a stop outside Admiralty House, not realising they were home.

The two weary people got out of the car, and thanking Alf,

the driver, made their way upstairs to the flat, stopping off in the office on the way, to see if any messages had been left, but no, the pair of them could relax. They decided to have a cup of cocoa, then a read in bed, where they went out like a light. During the night, Edith started to have pains, and then the contractions started.

'Alec, Alec, get the ambulance here now. It hurts,' then Edith started breathing deeply. Alec called the duty scab lifter, knowing he'd get quicker action than he could, then tried helping Edith, trying to remember how he'd helped Sally, all that time ago. He must remain strong, he must for Edith and Alec 2 or whatever. The ambulance driver and assistant rushed into the room, while Alec was trying to make her comfortable. But they were so quick putting Edith into a chair stretcher they'd brought, they were away in seconds, with Edith shouting, 'See you tomorrow,' and leaving Alec shocked and exhausted. He then turned round and went to bed, glad in a way that the time had come. As he was nearly dropping off, he remembered the admiral. He'd phone him in the morning, he wouldn't want to be woken up at this time of night, and off he went.

Tally Ho, Simon and the admiral knew, before breakfast, and Sally's parents were told. They were very pleased, in fact, they all were, and all of them asked to be told when the baby was born. Saying yes to everybody, he had to get to St. George's Hospital. He called for a car and went the short distance, but it seemed like a million miles, and Alec found he couldn't keep still. The car eventually got to the hospital, where he was shown the way to Edith, and baby Alec.

'A boy,' he whooped, and gave his wife a hug, making her gasp so much, he said, 'I'm so sorry Edith, but thank you so very much, and I do love you so.'

'I think you'd better get back to your office Alec. Women have been having babies for all time, but it's not often that you get the chance to stop an invasion,' Edith replied surely, but weakly. Alec saw she needed rest, so touching her forehead with his lips, he whispered her name, and left as quietly as he could, Alec knew she was right.

After telling Tally Ho about the baby, and Edith's health, he asked casually, if he could go on tomorrow's raid, in a Lancaster. Nigel immediately burst out laughing, saying, 'Why? Have the sleepless nights and endless nappy changing got you down already? Alec, you've no chance in the world, ever, of going on this mission, I'm sorry Navy, I'm more frightened of Edith, than I am of you, but I'm going over about an hour after the raid, to take photos for the records. I'll let you know later,' said Tally Ho.

Alec thought to himself, "No I don't think so. Edith and Alec deserve more thought than that, I would love to, but I must say no."

Telling Nigel of his decision on the phone, Nigel said, 'Yes Navy, that is the decision you should make but I'll bring back some good photos, for you to show Alec, Tally Ho!' he bellowed before slamming the phone down.

Alec stayed in his office most of the day, his last memories of HMS *Hecla*, and his dragging those crew members from below decks, and he could vaguely remember a man screaming from somewhere nobody could reach. Alec imagined the ship, going on her death dive, eventually thudding into the seabed, coming to a final stop where she was still, that beautiful ship and all those men. As Alec remembered all this, he knew he was in the grip of self pity, a terrible state to get into, so he'd better shake himself out of it, and asked his secretary if tea break was near. Smiling, she walked in, thirty seconds later with a tray. She was making it at the time. Asking the girl to take a seat, he told her about Edith and the baby, feeling very proud of himself, then thought, Edith did the work, making Mary laugh.

'You know sir, the Royal Marine sentry said he phoned Hitler to tell him about your baby,' Mary told him, between laughter and sips of tea.

'Well sir, I must go to finish my typing, but ta for the tea,' then stopping at the door, asked, 'Would you or your wife mind if I visited her tonight sir? Hospitals are miserable places, especially if you're young, and just had a baby.'

Alec felt quite touched, as he said, 'Of course Mary, I'm sure she would love to see you, that is very sweet. It's very kind of you.'

Chapter Thirty Two

At eleven o'clock the following day, at Waddington, two hundred Rolls Royce Merlins started up, making the wings of fifty Lancasters tremble, with the power of the beautiful engines. In Vic's of five, they roared off into their natural element, the sky, rotating around the airfield, until they were all airborne, and then climbing all the time; they left for the French coast. Flying time was one hour, forty-five minutes, so the crews settled down to drink from their flasks, and look nervously at one another. From the windows, Lancasters were all over the sky, the four spinning discs on each, powering their way forward, and hopefully, back.

'Ten minutes to target time,' the pilots called, 'test all machine guns,' after he made sure there were no more Spitfires protecting them.

The air gunners duly fired, and reported all weapons OK, 'Five minutes target time, bomb doors open. The bomb aimer in the perspex nose of the Lancaster, looked through his bomb sight, waving his left arm, "left, right a bit more, right, steady, steady, bombs gone".'

The Lancaster, relieved of so much weight, shot up a few feet, then more agile than it had been, turned to starboard, and started to climb. The crew saw the anti-aircraft shell bursts, just below them, which caused all the aircraft to buffet like they were shaking to pieces, jolting about, as the four propellers clawed their way upwards, for safety.

As the last of the bombers left the target, nobody noticed twelve Focke Wolfe 190 fighters screaming out of the sun, down like wolves, on to the big slow Lancasters, three going into their death dive, before the German machines were spotted.

The Lancaster's commander, shouted, 'Lancaster's huddle now!' The remaining aircraft closed into a very tight formation, each aircraft, offering his neighbours covering fire from his twelve machine guns. The 190s persisted, and two more Lancaster crews died in a flaming coffin. Luckily for the Lancasters, the Focke Wolfe 190s didn't carry a lot of fuel, so after they all did victory rolls, they returned to base, for more fuel.

'Head for home,' came the shout through all the Lancasters, 'Biggin Hill is sending us an escort of Spitfires!' The shouts of all the crews couldn't be heard, but the commander, Group Captain Hill, heard his own as the Lancasters rumbled on for home at Waddington. Fighters with RAF roundels joined them. They appeared on the wing tips of the bombers so fast, one minute, the space was empty, the next, the space was full with a beautiful Spitfire. In a few minutes, the fighters surrounded the Lancasters, the whole armada, with the fighter pilots telling the bomber pilots, to get a stronger elastic band fitted to all the bombers.

On their way home, nobody noticed the solitary Mosquito going to where they had just left. Tally Ho was the pilot, as always, singing his head off, but stopping as soon as the target neared. Sending his Mosquito down, in a vertical dive, to confuse the German AA gunners, he levelled of at twenty feet above sea level, firing his three cameras continuously, while he flew over the bay. He gave his two engines full boost at the end of the run and climbed almost vertically, frightening a pilot of a Focke Wolfe 190 into a dive, soon returning on the tail of the Mosquito as it levelled out.

Tally Ho was worried, he had no guns, only cameras, so he had to rely on speed and cunning to get home. He had the first, but the latter, he would soon find out. With his throttles wide open, the Mosquito bellowed its way home, weaving sideways, and up and down.

The Germans put a line of holes into the tail, but not really serious damage, it left the control wires still operable, so diving, he gained some more speed, the German plane gradually losing way, and drifting back to shortly disappear, as he turned for home. Tally Ho relaxed as he crossed the Suffolk coast, opening his cockpit canopy a couple of inches, to cool off, after his dice with death again. A few minutes saw him lowering his landing gear at the base at Waddington; noting the Lancasters had only just been dispersed to their protective bunkers.

Landing the Mosquito, then spinning it around in the dispersal bay, he shut the engines down, while ground crew emptied the cameras of their films. Glancing at the name on the nose, Alec 2, he slapped it with his hand, and hollered 'Tally Ho!' then his batman helped him off the wing of the Mosquito, then giving Tally Ho his sticks. Looking at the damage the Germans had caused, he went to the mess to have a few drinks, and telling whoever would listen, about his being bounced and getting away with it very easily, all listeners having seen the damage to the Mosquito.

Alec received the photos the next day. Obliterated! Bits

and pieces of barges all over the area.

"Well done, lads," Alec thought, holding a glass to the crews who would never return, being very glad it wasn't he who would be writing all those awful letters, about their valiant relatives, who gave their all.

Chapter Thirty Three

Next morning, as the long line of humanity crawled to its labour site, at the camp gate, the five dead bodies were left on show, frozen in grotesque positions, proving there was no dignity in death.

Otto grunted an answer as they moved through the dockyard gate. A guard looked at them carrying Joseph as they staggered past him.

'Halt, come here vermin, and you two, stand back, let him stand by himself,' grated the guard. Poor Joseph instantly fell at the guard's feet, who, accompanied by another guard, proceeded to kick Joseph to death, then pulled his blood-soaked rags, and broken body to one side.

'Schnell, schnell,' the guard shouted, waving his Schmeisser menacingly at the long line, who all glanced at the remains of Joseph, whose crime was that he was a Jew, and in Germany, where he was born. Felix, Otto and Carl quietly mourned among themselves, as they worked that day, doubling their sabotage activities, and delaying tactics. Slow in delivering rivets to the riveters, the rivets not hot enough, and losing time, getting mixed up with which riveters they were to supply rivets to. The gray dawn, clawing its way into day, found a stream of men trudging into the gray-stoned dockyard.

The only colour in the drizzle was the huge flag, with

a swastika in the middle of a red circle. As the men went through the gate, with the words, Ein Volk, Ein Reich, Ein Fuehrer over the gate, and under the flag, armed guards of the SS prodded at men, digging the barrels of the Schmeissers into the 'untermensch' ribs, and backs moving them, by fear, to their work places.

As the prisoners walked through the dockyard, hunger, and lack of sleep caused three of them to fall, finding their eternal peace, being kicked to death, in the filth and grime of a German dockyard, dedicated to building warships over the dead bodies of Jews, Poles and Russians, all finally realising that as they died in filth, others were there, to be thrust into their places. Until history repeated itself over and over again, it was accepted as the way of life, and death.

Eventually, after walking and slipping over the wet cobbles, the slaves reached Hull Number Ein hull.

Hull Number Ein, when completed, was going to be a huge seagoing airfield. An airfield equipped with the most modern aircraft in the world, the Messerschmitt 262. No other country in the world had an aircraft like the 262. No propellers, but two jet engines, such a simple engine, with only one moving part in its entirety, yet so much more faster than Spitfires or Mosquitoes. England was thought to be experimenting with the revolutionary concept, but didn't have an aircraft to put them in yet, whereas the Reich had them flying! When the aircraft carrier was finished, it would be called the *Adolph Hitler*, the flagship of the Kriegsmarine. Built by countless dead, the workforce being formed like a coral reef, each unit taking over from another. So the never ending line of slaves, at the end of a flickering whip, or an axe shaft, worked for their masters in the building of this monument to the Third

Reich, for a bowl of cabbage soup, and two slices of black ersatz bread, with coffee made with acorns.

Felix Liebermann did his job as well as he could, on his diet, or as well as the next man. But Felix was always thinking. Always thinking of small acts of sabotage that could be caused by his circle of friends, who believed in the same thing. Stop the Germans at all costs! Felix knew that his lives, and all the other slaves, were virtually ended. It wouldn't take long before their suffering came to a stop, yet until that moment came, they all felt they had to do some small thing. Anything to stop the German scourge from destroying all the good, and leaving the decay, and the rot of the bad. The work the slaves were allotted, were all menial jobs, supplying the German riveters with rivets, by keeping the furnaces full, so the rivets glowed white as they were hammered into the hull.

Greasing the three huge propellers, and the twin rudders were the worst, on the rivet job; lots of men got burnt, or fell off the scaffolding that ran the length of the hull. But when it was raining, the poor quality grease was washed off by the rain, on to the creatures putting it on again. They would be covered in a mixture of grease and rainwater, making them ill, and ghastly to look at. Somebody one day remarked that the grease came from a place called Auschwitz. Felix often wondered if it was true, he'd heard what Auschwitz was, and always felt sick when he was on the greasing.

So the days rolled by, working twelve-hour shifts, day and night, but having a brief chat to the three men he knew, with the same feelings as him. That three knew more of the same ilk, but not one man knew them all, which was less than ideal, but the security they could think of.

In the lunch break, which consisted of black ersatz bread,

and acorn coffee, the four conspirators sat under the hull, enjoying these delicacies.

'Well Joseph, what have you thought of today, I'm still trying to think of a way to fix rivet heads over the holes, with wax, so they'll fall out when this thing is floating, but it's very hard to get near the holes, the Germans watch us like hawks all the time. He must get a message out to England, but how?' asked Felix, studying the three faces around him, eating their food greedily.

'We've got to wait until an opportunity presents itself, then take advantage of it, I don't think we can look out for a chance, we've either got to make one, or wait for one,' said Isaac, his bread and coffee eaten, but filling a very small portion of his belly.

'Felix, what happens when you put sand or fine gravel into lubricating oil tanks, or gear boxes?' asked a little voice quietly.

Silence reigned for a few minutes, the four friends contemplating with awe what would happen.

Felix looked up, a slow grin emerging from his dirty face, shouting inwardly, how easy, how incredibly easy!

'You are a genius! Now we have an aim in life, be it so short, but we must always have sand or light gravel in our pockets. By itself, it won't damage anything, but it'll block up the oil filters and separators. Then the damage occurs!' exclaimed Felix his eyes flashing with force they hadn't possessed for a long, long time.

Shortly afterwards, an SS guard, his whip hissing through the air, got the four back to work, all of them with a spring in their step, and looking forward to the first act of sabotage. The rest of the day passed by, as it always did. Two men died, and were thrown into the back of a truck, ready to be thrown into a quicklime pit, especially built for the purpose. To the old, and infirm, this was the easiest way out, rather than suffer hunger, pain and degradation.

Marching back in the dark to their billets, the guards, with their Dobermann pinschers, were laughing and joking with the German civilians, about the way some of the slaves were walking, or about the condition they were in, but Felix, Joseph, Otto and Carl, had that thing about them, that told the other slaves they might be up to something or other, so whispering, 'Don't look as though you're enjoying it, look normal,' Felix urged his group on, knowing that later on the information about sand and gravel would be distributed among his three friends' groups, no whole group knowing the others.

Walking through the barbed wire gate, and past the armed guards, they stood in a long line, waiting for their supper, dished up on to filthy utensils, by German manipulated stool pigeons, ready to get anybody executed, so they could keep their plum job, and walked among the slaves, trying to find information to give to their masters.

Felix ate his supper, and then strolled around the compound, looking casually for light gravel, and putting it into his pocket. Otto and Carl were doing the same, while Joseph had some already. His view was that too many men doing the same thing, would be vary suspicious to the Germans, and problems would be created.

Before Felix fell asleep, absolutely exhausted, he thought of his wife and three children, killed at Belsen death camp, and quietly kissed their memory, as it lingered on forever in his mind.

Chapter Thirty Four

After breakfast, they were marched to the shipyard for their day's labour. Trudging in the rain, over the gray cobbled streets, they passed Wilhelmstrasse, where Felix noticed a Wehrmacht soldier, his eyes staring at Felix. To Felix's amazement, the soldier winked, turned, and walked next to Felix for a few minutes, before turning off down a street turning to the left. Felix didn't think any more of the incident, nor did anyone else, even if they saw the incident happen.

The work progressed, causing the aircraft carrier to be altering her appearance almost daily. Pumps, diesel engine generators and steam turbine generators were being installed into the ship, before the flight deck was put into place. The boilers and main engine steam turbines were all having steam pipes fitted, but unknown to the Germans, sometimes a big bolt, or nut or in several cases, spanners were introduced into the pipes, before being closed and sealed tight.

The speed of the construction worried the entire labour force, the German carrier would cause havoc with British and American forces. Felix and the others knew they had to get a warning to someone in Britain. The *Adolph Hitler* must never, under any circumstances, put to sea. The foursome discussed ways, but none were workable. The new generation engines on the fighters were very worrying, with no obvious way of propulsion, just a terrible whistling.

The routine of marching to work, then marching back to the camp, was telling on the slaves. More were dying as they were working, or marching to or from work. Winter was approaching, and the workers felt the feelings in the air, of the guards, and the civilians, then Felix started to see the German soldier again. Always in the same position, always next to Felix for a short distance, then turn off, down the same side street. But one morning, on the way to the dockyard, the German appeared suddenly by his side, and whispering urgently, told Felix to be prepared for the German to stumble against him, and knock Felix down, but no harm was to be meant, it just had to look realistic. Afterwards, when he was by himself, he would find a small pad of paper, two pencils and a penknife in his pocket. On the paper, the German wanted all measurements, engine power, number of boilers, and size of the hangar.

Felix and the others worried about the German, and the clandestine way in which Felix was contacted.

'I suggest that you ignore him Felix, he could be a plant. But why did he pick you out of all the hundreds of men he could've picked. Why? Did the Germans suspect him, and could this be a scheme to bring him to the surface, or, was the German a member of the little known German Resistance?' Otto muttered.

Felix was lost in worry.

'I'll write a note for him, telling him to leave me alone, or I'll report him,' Felix said one night, as he mused on the problem.

'There again, he could be the contact we need,' murmured Joseph, the eternal thinker. 'Ask him to prove he's honestly against the Nazis, Felix, he doesn't know anything about the hull we're working on, so when he contacts you, tell him to do something. Give us some news about the war, anything.'

Felix and the others, for the next few days, thought about the German, and the problem he was to them. Meanwhile, the progress on the ship continued to accelerate, being boosted by more and more slaves coming in to work. The quartet had to be careful, the Germans were always putting spies in the camp, and with the influx of men into the camp, it would be the perfect time to place a spy.

It happened unexpectedly, a weight fell on Felix as the labour force was going to work, knocking him over.

'Who are you? You surely don't expect anybody to trust you do you?' 'Felix said quickly, as the German helped him up, and brushed the dirt off Felix with his hands. 'I need proof before I do anything.'

'Listen, I am a German Jew, and some friends of mine want to do—Dummkopf, be careful you filth,' snarled the German, as a guard went past, looking at them. 'I'm so sorry,' as he walked off, down the turning he always used.

Arriving at the hull, looking more like an aircraft carrier every week, Felix discussed the incident with Otto, Carl and Joseph, eventually saying he was going to trust the German, but without saying anything about his three friends, which was too dangerous, for their own safety.

The next few days found Felix wandering around when he could manage it, taking measurements with his stride, and trying to keep his stride the same length, at the same time as carrying red hot rivets in a specially designed bucket. Guards were always present, forever ready with their whip, to punish severely anyone caught slacking.

Days were getting shorter and colder, but with the extra labour force, and quick replacements for the dead, work progressed on the hull. The food allowance had been increased slightly, a case of the donkey and the carrot, but Felix and the three compatriots were slowly introducing grit, sand and sometimes, when they found one, a nut and bolt, into engine sumps or oil tanks. Just a small bit at a time, but hopefully enough to eventually cause damage. The German was waiting at his usual place, and he slowly blended in with the long column of figures.

'Kom schweinhund, no idling here, you must walk faster, or you'll crawl to the shipyard,' then whispered, 'I'm sorry, but you can understand, there is a pistol in your pocket. No, don't feel for it! Tomorrow, I'll pick the book up. Throw it at my feet where I usually meet you. Good luck, next time I see you, will be the last, auf wiedersehen.'

He was gone by the time Felix casually looked, so putting his hand into his overcoat pocket, felt the small pistol in his hand. Walking in the long crocodile of bodies, he slowly removed his hand from his pocket, and looking at Joseph, nodded slightly, and pursed his lips for silence. The guard was catching him up for some reason, causing Felix panic. But it was a false alarm, he was hurrying to the next guard in front, to ask him for a light, and tell him about the young fraulein he had met last night, in the bier keller.

Felix was nervous all day, he had to carry the notebook, and somebody would surely find it in the hut that he called home. But the four worked on all day, distributing sand and gravel when they could, a little at a time.

The march back to the camp that night passed uneventfully, until just around the corner from the camp, a blast of machine pistol fire shocked them alert, during their trancelike walk. Felix later found out that five workers had tried to escape, by running down a lane, over some railway tracks, then along the canal bank, where the gunfire threw their bodies down on the ground, spilling out their lives

Chapter Thirty Five

Hans Knoepfler got to his safe hideout in the hills, just outside the city, sat down, and with his pal Reinhardt, studied the drawings and measurements Felix had supplied.

'I wonder how many Messerschmitt 262s it will operate?' wondered Hans, 'we haven't any measurements for the plane yet, but if the ship can only carry forty 262s, it'll be a formidable force for the Allies to face. Any Allied plane cannot catch the 262, it's an aeronautical revolution, and a man like Hitler is the driving force behind the plane, and the ship. Hitler has lost most of his capital ship fleet, through his own stupidity, but this new weapon is, well—'

Reinhardt agreed with Hans, knowing a lot of the German shipbuilding programme, before the war, but the ensuing witch-hunt threw up the fact that he was Jewish … He escaped from the SS clutches, half an hour before they smashed his door down, and when they didn't find him, they set his house on fire, burning it to the ground, after removing anything of value.

'We will send this information out tonight Hans, before the Germans complete their tests on these "jet" things, whatever they are called,' said Reinhardt, his eyes glittering at the damage to Hitler's propaganda machine, if the carrier was destroyed before the planes were ready.

Drinking some schnapps after the rabbit stew, the two men

waited in the darkness, their bodies running on pure adrenalin coursing through their veins. They were waiting for the allotted time for them to transmit their message. Hans and Reinhardt were getting jumpy now, as the clock devoured the time, so slowly and remorselessly, nerves jangling like wires in a telephone exchange. They had to infiltrate the German Army, and the dockyard, and cause as much trouble as the group could.

The Morse key started to chatter at the appointed time, stopping suddenly, as their acceptance code finished.

Reinhardt began the message tapping across the North Sea to London. The message was kept very brief, just enough to give the measurements and exact position in the dockyard. Reinhardt was automatically checking that particular day's code, before sending any of the information, and staying at his usual speed. Finally, the finished code was passed to London, who then sent a brief "Bluebell", Reinhardt's code name. Switching off the wireless, and turning around in his chair, the door burst open, and bullets tore the two men to pieces, dumping them against the wall, like so much rubbish that someone had got fed up looking at, so threw it away.

The echoes died as quickly as the two men had died, then a silence, a silence that you could feel, before a German officer entered the room, saw the refuse on the floor, and giving a self satisfied smile, walked out, and climbed into the wireless detection van sitting outside, its aerial, still for the time being. Now, some German troops would lie in wait, expecting to catch the rest of the resistance traitors, who were silly enough to return to the hideout. The only witness to the scene was the wireless lying on the floor, smashed to pieces, as Reinhardt died on his feet, knocking it off the table. As the van moved away, the German laughter went with it.

Chapter Thirty Six

Edith and Alec walked through the High Street in Glastonbury, on their way to Conduits, the popular little grocer's in the town. Baby Alec was snoozing in his pram, the sunlight showing flashes of gold in his hair, as he lay there. Getting to the convent school, Alec sat on the bench outside, the Conduits shop being too small to admit a pram, so Edith, blowing Alec a kiss, walked the short distance to the shop.

'Well son, you'll have to get used to waiting for females,' Alec murmured, his eyes twinkling, as young Alec stirred, and opened his blue eyes, then seeing his Dad, immediately gurgled, and held out his arms.

'Life without this war, would be so nice Alec,' said Dad, 'but one day soon, there will be peace, at least, I hope so, if only for you and people your age.'

But young Alec wasn't listening, he was back in the arms of Orpheus, and dreaming his dreams, whatever they were.

Edith returned shortly after the two Alecs had sorted out the world's problems, and with a crisp, 'Come on you two, we can't dawdle here all day, I've got things to do at home.' Her smiling eyes looked at her husband, saying with them, I love you, and in reply, her husband's eyes said, I love you too.

Returning home, they found a RN despatch rider waiting

for them, with a message recalling them to London now.

'Well it couldn't last long, could it?' said Edith, resigning herself to living in London again, after the leave that Alec had earned. Alec and Edith sadly packed away all their civilian clothes, and got into harness again, before getting into the staff car, and Edith assuming her role as confidante, and driver, wondering what they were going back into.

Alec sat in the rear of the car, brooding over the message the despatch rider had brought for him.

'You know Edith, I'm so pleased Mrs Howell is looking after your father and Alec, I didn't want Alec in London, it's too precarious,' said Alec, looking at Edith through her driving mirror.

'I presume we have a job on,' asked Edith, swinging the car through a military convoy.

'You're right you know, are you a witch?' joked Alec.

'I know all these things, for I am looking into the future,' said Edith in a monotone voice.

'But … I love you', and I think you're potty,' said Alec solemnly, 'thank you for that.'

Admiralty House turned up by the side of the car, after avoiding bomb damage, and glumly, the couple went up the familiar stairs, to the office. Alec's secretary was there, rearranging her diary, as her boss had returned from leave early.

'Is there a flap on sir, or did you get fed up with the peace and quiet?' she joked, as she gave them a cup of tea each. Alec smiled as he replied, 'No I don't think so, so it must be the flap option, nevertheless, I need a large map of Bremerhaven, with a perimeter of ten miles please.'

'Oh no, not that old chestnut,' groaned Edith, remembering all the bombing raids the RAF had put over there. Yet it still produced U-boats.

'Well Edith,' after the secretary left the room, 'Hitler has decided to build an aircraft carrier, capable of carrying the Messerschmitt 262. The Germans are more advanced than we are, with jet engine technology, although we have them, and we're experimenting with them. But Willi Messerschmitt has got them flying on a regular basis. Wonderful propaganda and a wonderful concept, if it's a reliable engine. But these aircraft can run rings around anything we put into the air, and flying them from a carrier, well, the idea doesn't bear thinking about.'

Edith saw the expression on Alec's face, and left him for half an hour, to study the map that his secretary had slid over a blackboard and easel. Phoning 'Tally Ho', Alec explained to him what he wanted, inviting him down for lunch tomorrow.

'Rather Navy, see you at noon tomorrow, and bring your darling wife, you lucky blighter,' replied 'Tally Ho', a laugh in his voice, as he replaced the phone.

'Edith, I've done a dreadful thing, without asking you. I've invited...er...uh...'Tally Ho' for lunch tomorrow, and he's accepted.'

Edith laughed and clapped her hands like a schoolgirl with a new skipping rope, as she heard the news, knowing that they both adored old 'Tally Ho'.

Being late in the day, they both decided to quit for the night. The new job, and the excitement of returning to the 'Smoke', had knocked the stuffing out of them. So sharing a cup of tea, and some toast, they cuddled up together, in front of the fire, with just the flickering flames to light the room, and their eyes.

Edith rested her head so nicely into Alec's shoulder, when

Alec gets up, muttering something about the office. Picking up his stick, he made his way downstairs, and went to the map of Bremerhaven. Aiming a high-powered desk light at the map, and picking up his magnifying glass from his desk, he sat down in front of the map, and started to study. Four hours later, Edith went down to the office, and there Alec was, asleep as he sat in front of the wretched map, and this wasn't Edith's plan, in any way.

'Alec, Alec, come to bed please Alec, oh I don't know,' she whispered in his ear.

Eventually Alec found himself being propelled up the stairs, and into his bed, where he fell asleep with his tin leg half off, leaving Edith to complete the job.

Chapter Thirty Seven

Waking up to the sound of the telephone ringing, Alec quickly answered it, finding Admiral Taylor on the other end.

'Have you read, and digested that message Alec? It sounds rather serious to me, that wretched little corporal, having such a sophisticated weapon like the 262, plus the carrier, it is becoming nasty,' he rattled.

Alec explained what he was going to do today, meeting up with Tally Ho, to discuss the Mosquitoes going on some photo reconnaissance flights, to discover, and identify the precise position of the German carrier, and any anti-aircraft guns installed around the dockyard. These guns were bound to be scattered around, like confetti at a wedding.

'This is an awful job,' said Alec to Edith, after replacing the phone. 'It's right in the heart of Germany, so the protection is going to be complete, this being the first carrier the Germans have ever attempted to build.'

Finding the list of ships that could be available, and the aircraft he might be able to beg, borrow or steal from Bomber Command, he quickly crossed out submarines and capital ships, the big lumbering gun platforms of the sea. Destroyers, or motor torpedo boats, would they measure up? Of course, using these, they would have to wait until the carrier was launched, before it was open to an attack from the sea, and the pressure of the timing was beginning to be felt by Alec and Edith. To use bombers would be, or could be, wasteful, the amount of anti-aircraft fire that could be on site. Once bombers were hit by enemy fire, they were virtually lost, the slowness of them being their own curse.

Tally Ho came into the office, with a shout of, 'Ha! The Navy wants some help again; still, it's the only time I eat properly. How are you my dear?' holding Edith's hand, and kissing it.

'Edith! You are blushing, and you better count your fingers as well,' laughed Alec, as he banged Tally Ho's back in welcome.

Tally Ho loved these two people, it was a shame that it took a war for them to meet. Sadness had shook Tally Ho's hand, the same as it had with Alec, but bouncability was his name.

As they went down to the dining room, the three chatted about the leaves they'd enjoyed. Young Alec was the main topic, how much like his father he was, and his sense of humour.

'Tally Ho,' echoed through the dining room as they entered, causing all the old duffers to jerk their heads up, at the unheard of noise. Looking at each other after they'd discovered the originator of the noise, they switched off, and carried on eating,

Edith and Alec were kept amused throughout the meal, with Tally Ho telling them all sorts of tales about the pilots at Waddington air base. Some of the stories were stretched a bit, but they were all funny. The lunch eaters in the immediate vicinity of the trio were laughing as much as Edith and Alec.

As always, life caught up with Edith Alec and Tally Ho,

and on returning to Alec's office, Tally Ho realised what was on Alec's mind: BREMERHAVEN. Bomber crews throughout Bomber Command hated Bremerhaven; it had claimed a lot of crew lives, either dead, or taken prisoner. The protective anti-aircraft gun emplacements, surrounding the city was something to be seen, especially from the air, when the tracer came up at you so lazily and slowly, and curving all the time, following you, until it hit you, and none of your controls answered, then you realised you were on fire.

Tally Ho thought he could get some useful photos, but not he personally, he'd been grounded because of his stump getting worse as he used it to get in and out of the cockpits, it was worrying the RAF doctor. He protested of course, but to no avail, he stayed grounded.

'I promise Navy, I'll send a good pilot, he's worked for you before, and knows what' you want. You look after yourself, and that popsy of a wife of yours. Tally Ho then you two, we're off!' Tally Ho finished, stumping off to his staff car, for his return to Waddington.

'Coo, he's hard work Edith, and that's no mistake,' smiled Alec, his eyes having seen the hidden despair and pain in the RAF officer's face, 'But what a good chap he is.'

'I'm glad he's on our side, and not the Germans,' replied Edith, colouring slightly as she recalled how Tally Ho talked about her, then remembered his sad history at Waddington.

With a deep sigh, Alec returned his thoughts to the map, and methods. A sea strike would be the most realistic; anti-aircraft guns couldn't be trained to aim at ships. There weren't any bigger calibre guns that would be effective against a sea strike. All these calibre guns were on the two fronts that German forces were fighting, much to the regret of the civilians, in the major German cities. The only suitable weapons were on German destroyers, of which there wasn't many left, and the U-boats were still in the Atlantic, filtering through to the Mediterranean, because of the Allies attack on Italy. "Photos would tell the story in the finish," Alec thought, hoping for good weather in the morning, so that the Mosquitoes could do their job, but the strain was telling on him as it always did; it was the waiting, he spent half his life, waiting.

Edith brought in some tea and biscuits, then sitting down, she told him, 'Alec, I realise this waiting rips you apart every time, but please darling, don't let it, you have me, and baby Alec. We both love you so much. Please don't punish yourself anymore, for our sake,' her voice breaking as she finished, and hiding her face in Alec's arms.

Alec stroked her tear-streaked face, and kissed her hair, before kissing her tender lips so lovingly, it made her gasp, her face red and hot. Smiling at Alec, Edith untangled herself from Alec's arms, sat down, and cooled herself off with a sheet of paper she waved in front of her face,

'Later Alec, later,' she whispered in his ear, then poured the tea, and put some biscuits on a plate smiling a secret smile that only women could do. Alec stood up, and walked to the map, frowning at it, and willing it to tell him its many secrets, but like the Thames, it said nothing, so after a few minutes, both Edith and Alec turned the lights off, kissed, and went upstairs, to be alone.

There, they undressed, got into bed, and made love to each other slowly, and lovingly.

Chapter Thirty Eight

The day started with a nice warm sun beaming down on a grateful London, making the people feel better both mentally and physically. Alec opened the door of his office early, and sat down at his desk, reading his paper, but he was joined shortly afterwards, with his breakfast, and his wife.

'Edith, please stop smiling at me like the Mona Lisa, you make me feel as though we're being naughty,' Alec said between each mouthful...

Edith smiled wider, and carried on eating, like she knew something, but kept it from Alec. She knew the torment he was going through, waiting again for the Bremerhaven photos, simply because he needed to decide the method of attack. The method most on his mind at present was the use of destroyers, but they could not be used until the carrier was launched. If it were launched, the Germans would take extra special care of it, being the last hope of the Third Reich, unless the threat of bigger rockets than the doodlebugs wasn't empty. The 262 jet planes were frightening too, a few Spitfire pilots having seen them, though unarmed. The 262 went past the Spitfires, as though they were stopped. They were incredibly fast, with that infernal whistle, terrifying in itself. Frank Whittle had recently got a jet plane flying, and the RAF were putting it through a series of strenuous tests. Tally Ho thought they were absolutely wonderful, but Alec secretly thought they were mainly for propaganda purposes.

The thoughts rushed around in Alec's head; bombers would be best at this moment, the hull was on the slipway, but the anti-aircraft fire would be fearsome, he thought. Roll on Tally Ho; let's have some good news, trust a man like Hitler to spoil his and Edith's leave! Alec jumped as the despatch rider pulled up outside Admiralty House, at fifteen hundred hours, and then ran up the stairs.

'Cor strike a bleeding' light sah, let me get in, the ride from Waddington isn't a stroll in the bleeding park you know, stone me', he protested then allowed a nice little Wren officer to give him a cup of tea.

"Typical innit, she's tied up," he thought, as he supped his tea.

Alec got to his desk in record time, grabbing his magnifying glass on the way. Tea was already sitting on his desk, with Edith hovering, waiting to help. Two hours later, Alec put the last of the photos down. Drinking his cold tea, he looked at Edith, a smile on his face as he touched her hand.

'Tally Ho will have to come down Edith, I've got a serious decision to make, and I need the RAF point of view. I know the Navy's view, and it's not good. Would you give him a tinkle? I wonder if the Yanks would have any ideas, they're new to the war, so…, they may have some new ideas,' finished Alec, looking at a particular photo.

'I think Tally Ho is the best bet,' Alec mumbled, leaving Edith nodding and smiling vigorously in the background.

The photos were soon aligned around the map, giving a slightly different view of the area. But better photos were needed, as soon as they could be taken. The phone message to Tally Ho pleased Alec, when Tally Ho said he'd have the two Mosquitoes out again tomorrow.

'So Navy, you'll have to wait old man, but in the meantime. Tally Ho!' the latter thundering down the phone, opening Alec's eyes wide.

Alec went to the map again, wondering how the Germans were progressing with the huge shipbuilding programme they had embarked on, considering they were embroiled in a very nasty war, but the Germans were using slave labour, so the German forces could still fill the ever growing gaps in their lines.

As it was the first aircraft carrier the Germans had ever built, Alec was sure they would meet all sorts of problems, the same as the RN had. The RN had learnt to their cost, that carriers were public enemy number one, and being so big, they had to have a lot of protection from destroyers and cruisers.

As the phone rang, Alec snatched it up hoping it would be someone with an answer to the problem.

'Hello Navy, yours truly again, now Alec, I've studied these photos, and I don't think you have a choice. As you rightly say, the bloody things not floating yet, so I'm afraid it'll have to be the bombers. From the photos, there is a hell of a lot of work to be done yet, so in the time it takes to launch the thing, the Germans could get this new jet fighter perfected. Alec, I can assure you, I don't want our old crates flying against that beast. I'll be there, at Admiralty House, in the morning, and we will put our heads together. I might bring a squadron leader bomber pilot with me, he can be a lot of help to us. I'll see you tomorrow. Tally Ho!' he finished, and put the phone down.

Alec thought about having the pilot down, knowing that Tally Ho would never have suggested it, if he hadn't a trick up his sleeve. The pilot might be the clue, perhaps he knew the area of Bremerhaven from experience, and the dangers of the anti-aircraft fire there. But Alec would have to wait and as Edith watched him looking at the map, she smiled as he put an index finger over his pursed lips, his forehead wrinkled, studying the docks, and the slipway.

'Come on then funny face,' said Alec, 'Let's call it a day, we can't do anything until tomorrow, then Tally Ho will surely entertain us.'

Edith looked at Alec, a smile all over her face, then switching off the lights, and making sure the blackout curtain was doing its job, they strolled out, and went upstairs to their flat, far above London town.

Chapter Thirty Nine

Edith and Alec were woken up at seven o'clock, by somebody calling, 'Tally Ho Navy, up and at 'em.' They looked at each other, a look of amazement on their faces blossoming slowly like a flower.

'He doesn't sleep, I know he doesn't, and he forgets that everybody else does,' growled Alec, getting his tin leg on, and dressing gown. 'What's going on? Do you know what time it is Nigel? You're more than welcome here, but at a reasonable time, you must have driven all night,' Alec finished.

'I was flown here, and arrived at Croydon an hour ago,' said Tally Ho. 'The reason for such an early start, apart from there being a war on, is because I've scraped up seventy Lancasters at short notice. Dick Chapman, the Lancaster pilot, is downstairs having a coffee. He flew me here.'

Tally Ho was warming up to the subject now, and Alec was intrigued. Edith brought in the eternal tea and biscuits, looking very smart in her uniform, smiling first at Alec, then pulling a face at Tally Ho for calling so early, then grinning at him gave him a cup of tea. Sitting at Alec's desk, Alec and Edith prepared to listen to Tally Ho's news.

'The moon this month is perfect for bombers, and I've put this plan to Downing Street, after all, if Winston accepts it, no more questions, just get on with it. He will phone you here later on today. Now, I believe that if the Lancasters fly low, at five thousand feet, to carry out a carpet-bombing attack on Adolph's toy, there is every possibility that we could either destroy it, or virtually render it impossible to repair, or damage it so much, it wouldn't be economical to do so. Is that any good? The anti-aircraft gunners will be sleepy, and from the photos we have already taken, some guns appear to have been moved elsewhere, perhaps on the Eastern Front.'

Tally Ho yawned after his explanation, and drank his tea, looking at Alec while doing so then continued talking to the couple.

'I realise I've carried out this without first seeing you, but Navy, it's the only course open to us. If we can destroy it, it'll mean a slipway out of action for a while. What do you think now?'

Alec looked at Tally Ho, an amused expression on his face, while holding his teacup loosely in the saucer. Glancing at Edith quickly, Alec said, 'Listen Tally Ho, it's so simple it's perfect. But do the bomber crews know their target?'

'In a word, no, but they will have the chance to drop out, as they do on any of these high risk missions, but they do know the risks, as well as anybody else, so don't worry,' replied Tally Ho, looking earnestly at Alec. 'The Yanks won't do any night bombing, so they offered to do it in the daytime, and they would hit it big time with the heavies they've got. They'd lose too many in those circumstances, the American public would be enraged, if their boys helped us and got killed. I think our idea is best,' ended Tally Ho, picking up his fresh cup of tea to drink it.

Going downstairs to have breakfast, they met Dick Chapman talking to a pretty Wren, who was welcoming the handsome RAF officer into her life.

'Come on Dicky, the Navy's buying our breakfast, so put the young lady down, we mustn't pinch all the Navy assets, I don't know though, it might be interesting to—'. Tally Ho was abruptly halted by Edith asking him, 'Will you be a gentleman Tally Ho? Our pure young Wrens don't want the attention that you RAF types pay.'

Tally Ho looked at her in surprise, saw her smiling, and quickly replied, 'Yes we know don't we Dick,' then Tally Ho and Dick grinned.

Tally Ho and Tricky Dicky made the breakfast a raucous occasion, finally causing lots of groans all round the otherwise quiet, wood-panelled dining room, with the walls decorated with paintings of heroes of the Navy, and paintings mixed with photos of ships of yesteryear. The most recent photos were of the *Hood, Warspite* and the *Prince of Wales,* all lying in the cold grip of the sea.

Returning to the office afterwards, Alec, Edith, Tally Ho and Dicky, stood around in a semi-circle, looking at the photos, and map of Bremerhaven.

Dicky stood up in front of the map and explained what a pilot would see as he approached Bremerhaven, with Hamburg lit up, not very far away.

Using a ruler as a pointer, he said, 'This range of hills to the west of the city is the danger. On a low altitude attack, obviously we have to climb over the hills, and drop down again, to go over the target. The problem is, there's a lot of flak guns at the base of the hills, on the city side. Consequently, as we lose altitude from the hills, those guns can shoot at our exhausts, which quite obviously glow white at night. So I think the best direction of attack is from over the estuary. I realise that it is from the north, but if we follow the river for a while, then head north, running a dummy if you like, there aren't as many guns in that sector.'

They all looked at each other, starting to appreciate the plan, when the telephone burst into life, making them all jump. Alec grabbed it, and before he could say who he was, a voice on the phone said, ''It's on, as soon as you like'', then the phone clicked dead, leaving Alec looking at it with a blank look on his face.

'Well, the man says it's on you lot, as soon as you like indeed,' repeated Alec, passing on the message to the others, all looking at him, with their mouths open.

'Come on Dick, we've got to get back to Waddington as fast as you like. Thank you Navy,' and looking at Edith, Tally Ho said to her, 'If you ever get fed up with the Navy, come up and see me some time,' the last words being said like a popular film actress of the time. Then with his sticks in one hand, and his other hand on his hip, he slowly made for the door, with Edith, Alec and Dick, crying with laughter.

Waving them off from the main doors at Admiralty House, Edith and Alec recovered enough to walk into the wardroom, and had a cup of coffee. Alec felt relieved now that a plan of action had been put into force, and was looking forward to a successful deployment of the Lancasters, and the crews, a very valuable asset to Bomber Command. But the losses that might occur were frightening Alec, and Edith knew it, as she reached over, and squeezed his arm.

'Let's go to the cinema tonight Alec, we haven't been for a long time, and it might do us good to get out,' suggested Edith, surprising Alec, by echoing his own thoughts.

Chapter Forty

The thunder of two hundred and eighty Rolls Royce Merlin aero engines shattered the quiet of the Lincolnshire countryside, as the Lancasters, moving sluggishly to the runway, had their engines given a last check, before taking off into the night, the fuselages full to the brim with bombs and napalm. Pilots checked instruments, pressures and hydraulics, then giving a thumbs up to the ground crew, taxied in line, a line of leviathans, all waiting. Waiting for the signal to go, ever creeping nearer, while crews fingered lucky charms, photos of family, or girl friend, or just touching a crucifix, while praying, eyes closed.

The green flare whistled up suddenly, and the dark, relieved by the exhaust manifolds, was pierced by a huge machine, trying to lift its own weight off the ground, slowly increasing speed, and bouncing slightly on the undulating airfield. The tail wheel came up slowly as the Lancaster increased its speed, until suddenly, the drumming sound of the main wheels stopped, as they lost contact with the earth, and the aircraft was in the air, increasing both its speed, and altitude. Circling around the airfield in an anti-clockwise direction, all the bombers eventually made it into their circuit and altitude, the seven squadron leaders all agreeing everything was A1, and turned off into the direction of the North Sea.

Slowly, the air armada moved over the sea, rendezvousing with the twenty-five Spitfires that would be their air cover for the outgoing flight. Pilots gave the air gunners permission to test their Browning machine guns, which they did with great gusto, because coffee would be passed around after the check, the drink being greatly appreciated, as the Lancasters didn't have any heating. The engines settled to the distinctive Merlin drone, a sleep-inducing sound if it wasn't for the coffee, which was laced with anti-sleep pills, to prevent any accidents.

Dick Chapman recorded three aircraft returning to base, all with engine trouble, one of the things that a pilot could do without. As the three turned, every other pilot wondered if it would happen to them, and touched a rabbit's foot, or a china elephant, or rubbed a cup or something, just for luck.

Droning on course, the squadrons turned north at the correct time, slashing into the German airspace. The Spitfires could stay with them for another fifteen minutes, then would be homeward bound, running on their under-wing tanks that gave them the extra range.

The minutes passed, all crews, with adrenalin flowing through their veins, were alert, the gunners never stopping from swinging their guns from left to right, their fingers on the triggers, white with tension, and cold as it was, all sweating with anticipation of squeezing the triggers that final fraction, before a German did the same thing.

The moment came for the bombers to turn to starboard, heading south, towards the river, and the target. Everybody hoped the pathfinder Mosquitoes, who would drop incendiaries on the target, would make it. At this point, taking off from Waddington, were two all black Mosquitoes, armed with cameras, four cannons and six machine guns. It was a machine that a German pilot would not like to bump into.

Tally Ho was flying the leading plane, safe in the knowledge that nobody knew he was flying. He was joyous, as he followed far behind the bombers, he was in his element again, and he was doing something useful. The Lancasters neared the target, the fuselages trembling with the engines, with the nerves of the crews, like over-tight violin strings, stretched to the limit. Suddenly appearing on the horizon, flares went up, and then fell slowly on parachutes, guiding the bombers directly on to their goal. Anti-aircraft fire began arcing up to the Mosquitoes, after the searchlights had discovered the aircraft hurtling away over the target, all of them escaping the scything fire.

While the first ten Lancasters flew straight; on towards the flare-lit target, the remainder of the bombers peeled off, to circle until it was their turn. The anti-aircraft fire began curling slowly up, then zipping past their targets, like angry hornets, some hitting the underbellies of the bombers. A flash appeared *in* the front or the ten, and where there was a Lancaster was nothing. Another started its final spiral to earth, the pilot shouting over his radio. 'I'm hit. I'm hit, I'm—' then erupting in a flash, followed by a boom.

The remaining Lancasters kept on course, opening their bomb doors, the bomb aimer at his window at the nose of the aircraft, with his release button in his hand.

'Left, left, steady, right steady, steady, bombs gone,' the bomb-aimer shouted, his thumb squeezing the release button hard. As always, the aircraft shot up twelve feet, as it released its load of man-made hell back to earth, where they started, and where they finished.

The raid continued, the guns taking their toll of the bomber fleet, the stricken of which, either exploded in the air, or twisted into the ground, flames and smoke destroying the crews, before they hit the ground. Pressing on, Dick steadied the bomber on the directions of his bomb aimer, and felt the aircraft lift, as the bombs fell away. Climbing out of the area, he suddenly heard, and felt shells hitting the plane, then a flash as the fuel tanks blew up, then nothing. Dick, and a lot of others had' gained the peace they fought for, but they couldn't enjoy it.

The raid was over as quickly as it started. Complete silence ruled again, but the target was no more, its shattered shell, lying on its side, a load of scrap metal. The hull would never kiss the ocean, a great achievement, at such a tragic loss, Forty Lancasters returned to Waddington, some damaged, some as good as new, but the crews had aged, developing a cavalier attitude, that would hopefully bring them through.

After sending the other Mosquito back to Waddington, Tally Ho reached the target-areas, the flames reaching like fingers, into the morning sky. The whole shipyard was devastated, and Tally Ho smiled, his cameras clicking, and taking home the evidence, unless Tally Ho got hit. But Tally Ho, being the sort of man he was, didn't think of that, his Mosquito had the edge on anything the Luftwaffe had, except the deadly 262, and that was an exceptional aircraft. If Adolph had been given the 262 at the beginning of the war, Tally Ho knew it would be different now, but Frank Whittle had nearly finished his experiments.

He watched a stream of cannon shells passing his port wing. Instantly, Tally Ho climbed, thumbing the safety catch off his weapons at the same time. The Mosquito trembled with the power Tally Ho was feeding it. Levelling off, he saw the culprit; a Messerschmitt 109G had bounced him. Tally Ho was very cross, as he weaved a crazy pattern of vapour trails high above the earth. But the 109G stayed there, firing at Tally ho as often as he could.

Tally Ho suddenly shut his two Merlins down, and pushing the stick forward, the Mosquito dropped like a stone. The German overshot him, but trying the same move, found himself with his belly exposed to Tally Ho's guns.

Gunter watched his wing leaving the fuselage as he went into a spin.

'Must get out, get out,' Gunter screamed, but his legs were smashed under the column, so he couldn't move. He saw the RAF roundels on the Mosquito as it headed back to England, the 109G flattened out, then he died. Civilians came rushing out, threatening the retreating Mosquito with their fists, but to no avail, it flew on, the pilot wondering what he was going to say to Alec, when he found out he'd flown the mission.

'We'll cross that bridge when we come to it. Tally Ho!' he shouted, and headed for Waddington, landing ninety minutes later, his Mosquito bouncing on the uneven apron, then finally cutting the Merlins in his allotted space.

A sergeant ran forward, to empty the cameras of their films, develop them, and send them to some RN brass in London, probably never having to leave his desk.

"Well, it takes all sorts dun' it," the sergeant thought, as he made his way to the development room, knowing he'd be the first to see the damage done to the Germans by the Lancasters.

Two hours later, Tally Ho got on the phone to Alec.

'An absolute disaster Navy, we destroyed not only the carrier hull, but the whole shipyard as well! No more U-boats, or anything, not even a rowing boat can be produced there. The truth is I flew the recce, I just felt I had to— so the *next* meal is on me, ' said Tally Ho, sounding ashamed.

'Listen Alec, it wasn't cheap. It cost a lot of men, including Tricky Dicky. Twenty-three Lancasters and crews lost. But Alec, they knew the risks; it wasn't their first mission, so it's a job well done. Good bye Navy, Tally Ho!' The phone clicked dead.

When Edith came in, she found Alec, with the phone still in his hand, and looking at the map of Bremerhaven. His face was white, whilst he was repeating to him, 'I'm sorry, I'm so sorry, please, I'm sorry. Please forgive me.'

Edith stroked his dry, gray cold face as he looked at the map although his eyes were not focused. She held him, not knowing what happened, but willing to comfort him, so that she could share his heartache, whatever it was, and then she could ask him. But he stayed where he was, in his own world, so badly damaged, so full of pain.

Edith phoned Tally Ho, and he told her the losses sustained by the raid. Speaking calmly, she told Tally Ho what had happened to Alec. Tally Ho was shocked, and told Edith he would be in London, at Admiralty House, in two hours, by plane.

Promptly, in two hours, a very subdued Tally Ho arrived at Admiralty House, met by Edith at the main door.

'He's in the sick bay at the moment, he's sleeping, but he wouldn't let go of the phone, since you phoned. He was holding it as though his very life depended on it. Oh Nigel, poor darling Alec, he's known such pain the same as you, losing *Hecla* hurt him, but losing his family like that, how cruel,' sobbed Edith, with Nigel giving her the comfort of his arm around her shoulders.

'Mrs Hamilton. I say, Mrs Hamilton, he's awake,' shouted a RN doctor from the open door.

Edith and Nigel got in as fast as Nigel could, to find Alec sitting up in bed, and drinking tea... 'What are you doing here Tally Ho? Do you know Edith, this man flew a recce mission, when he was told not to,' he greeted Edith and Nigel. Drawing them close, Alec whispered, 'Thank you, I didn't know them, but we all owe them so much'.

So the war will grind on, destroying lives, destroying families and countries, but we will win, we've got to, to make any sense of this world, we must win.